The Silver Candelabra & Other Stories

A Century of
Jewish Argentine Literature

The Silver Candelabra
& Other Stories

❖═◉═❖

A Century of
Jewish Argentine Literature

Edited and Translated by
Rita Gardiol

Latin American Literary Review Press
Series: Discoveries
1997

The Latin American Literary Review Press publishes Latin American creative writing under the series title Discoveries, and critical works under the series title Explorations.

Library of Congress Cataloging-in-Publication Data

The silver candelabra and other stories : a century of Jewish
    Argentine literature / edited and translated by Rita Gardiol ;
    [Alberto Gerchunoff...et al.].
            p. cm.
    Includes bibliographical references.
    ISBN 0-935480-88-9
    1. Short stories, Argentine--Jewish authors--Translations into
English. 2. Argentine fiction--20th century--Translations into
English. 3. Jews--Argentina--Fiction. I. Gardiol, Rita Mazzetti.
II. Gerchunoff, Alberto, 1883-1950.
    PQ7776.2.J49S5 1997
    863'.01088924'--dc21
                                                    97-15868
                                                    CIP

Cover art courtesy of Lunwerg publishers.

The paper used in this publication meets the minimum requirements of the American National Standard for Permanence of Paper for Printed Library Materials Z39.48-1984.∞

Latin American Literary Review Press
121 Edgewood Avenue
Pittsburgh, PA 15218

Editor/Translator's Acknowledgments

The editor/translator wishes to express her gratitude to Ezie and Sara Lipkin of New York whose sterling qualities first started her thinking about the Jewish contribution to Argentine literature. Because work on this manuscript was done in two stages, she wishes to thank the administrators at Ball State University in Muncie, Indiana for the sabbatical that made her initial research possible, and Veva McCoskey and her dedicated library staff at Ball State for their tireless efforts in finding obscure materials.

Enrique Walfish and Ricardo Feierstein of Buenos Aires both provided invaluable assistance—the former, with continuing encouragement, helpful suggestions about Argentine history and assistance in obtaining authorizations; the latter, with encouragement and untiring assistance in tracking down publishers and heirs for authorization to publish.

At the University of South Carolina, the editor wishes to thank Professor Isaac Levy for his generous assistance in translating from Hebrew and Yiddish; Warren Slesinger for the encouragement to pursue publication of the manuscript; history Professor Michael Scardaville for his careful review of the section on Argentine history; Nayda Rivera and Mary Lou Sonefeld, staff members of the Department of Spanish, Italian and Portuguese for their helpful suggestions on the first reading of the translations; Olga Rodriguez who patiently typed and retyped them, Professor Ashley Brown of the English Department who spent endless hours painstakingly editing the manuscript, and Dean Lester Lefton who provided moral and financial support.

The editor/translator is also indebted to the following for their kind permission to use the material reproduced: Editorial Paidos for the story by Samuel Eichelbaum; Ediciones de la Flor for the selections by Cecilia Absatz; Centro Editor de América Latina for the stories by German Rosenmacher; Eduardo Payró Gerchunoff for the stories by Gerchunoff; Horacio Verbitsky for the stories by Bernardo Verbitsky; Bernardo Kordon, Eugenia Calny, Silvia Plager, Alicia Steimberg and Ricardo Feierstein for their own stories and Carmen Balcells for the stories by Isidoro Blaisten. The stories by Enrique Espinosa, now in the area of public domain, did not require permissions.

The editor/translator would also like to thank Yvette Miller, Editor and Connie Mathews, Assistant to the Editor for their careful reading of the manuscript and their patience in bringing this book to successful completion.

Without the help of all these people this book would forever have remained merely a work in progress. They deserve recognition for their part in bringing the work of these twelve worthy authors to the attention of an English-speaking public.

Contents

Preface

It is not difficult to imagine that this volume of short stories will occasion a certain degree of astonishment from the average reader, both academic and nonacademic alike. The advent of the so-called "boom" in Latin American literature during the 1960s led Latin American writers—admittedly a select group—to the forefront of global readership. The postboom generation of writers have likewise enjoyed relative success among readers outside their respective countries and in particular in English translation. Recently there has been an overwhelming surge in Latin American women's writing with the appearance of numerous translations and anthologies which now seek to bring attention to this vast corpus of works which was largely overlooked during the boom period. Likewise, other marginalized literary voices, such as gay and lesbian, Afro-Hispanic, and indigenous writing, have begun to enjoy a certain privileged position as postmodern and postcolonial cultural studies have begun to focus on the margins of Latin American societies.

Latin American Jewish writing as a socioliterary phenomenon is one of the most recent of these marginal groups to gain recognition as a viable sociocultural voice. The average reader is likely to be astounded to learn of the large Jewish communities of Latin America which have made significant contributions to the cultural and artistic production in their respective countries, and will also be amazed to know that Argentina is home to the world's fifth-largest Jewish population. Subsequently, there are more Jewish writers from Argentina than from any other Spanish or Portuguese-speaking nation of Latin America.

Certainly, literature written by Jewish authors in Argentina is not a new literary trend. Indeed, it has formed a significant part of the national literary scene for most of the twentieth century. Historically, however, it has also suffered significant marginalization. Two recent bibliographic publications illustrate the enormity of the Jewish Argentine literary community: David William Foster and Naomi Lindstrom's primary bibliography of works by over 300 writers, "Jewish Argentine Authors: A Registry," and the two-volume bio-bibliographical source book, *Escritores judeo-argentinos: bibliografía*

1900-1987 (Jewish Argentine Writers: A Bibliography 1900-1987; 1994), compiled by Ana E. Weinstein and Miryam E. Gover de Nasatsky, which lists over 200 authors.[1] Neither listing, it should be mentioned, is all-inclusive. Only a minimal number of these authors ever appear in anthologies, dictionaries, encyclopedias, or histories of Argentine literature to be considered as part of the national literary canon. This is not to say that this body of literature has gone completely unread or unstudied. Nevertheless, it has only been within the past ten to fifteen years that any serious critical consideration has been afforded to Jewish Argentine writing as a socioliterary phenomenon. Such critics as Leonardo Senkman, Saúl Sosnowski, Naomi Lindstrom, and David William Foster have been instrumental in informing the critical consciousness of Jewish writing in Argentina and delineating the course of investigation.[2]

Similarly, Latin American Jewish studies has only recently begun to evolve into a fully-developed academic discipline. This has been achieved by the formation of such ground-breaking organizations as the Latin American Jewish Studies Association (LAJSA), which has attracted a large worldwide membership and has been instrumental in providing a forum and a network for the advancement and dissemination of research in all areas of concern to the history and culture of the Jewish communities of Latin America. Specific to literary studies, the Asociación Internacional de Escritores Judíos en Lengua Hispana y Portuguesa (International Association of Jewish Writers in Spanish and Portuguese), which publishes the literary journal *Noaj* from its headquarters in Jerusalem, has been invaluable for its efforts to promote Jewish literature in Spanish and

---

[1] Foster, David William, and Naomi Lindstrom. "Jewish Argentine Authors: A Registry," parts 1 and 2, *Revista interamericana de bibliografía/Inter-American Review of Bibliography* 41.3 (1991): 478-503; 41.4 (1991): 655-82; Weinstein, Ana E., and Miryam Gover de Nasatsky, comps. *Escritores judeo-argentinos: bibliografía 1900-1987.* 2 vols. Buenos Aires: Milá, 1994.

[2] See Senkman's *La identidad judía en la literatura argentina* (Buenos Aires: Pardés, 1983), Sosnowski's *La orilla inminente: escritores judíos argentinos* (Buenos Aires: Legasa, 1987), Lindstrom's *Jewish Issues in Argentine Literature: From Gerchunoff to Szichman* (Columbia: University of Missouri Press, 1989), and Foster's "Argentine Jewish Dramatists: Aspects of a National Consciousness" in his *Cultural Diversity in Latin American Literature* (Albuquerque: University of New Mexico Press, 1994. 95-150).

Portuguese. University curricula have also begun to reflect the growing interest in this area, as courses in Latin American Jewish literature and history are now being offered, though primarily as special topics courses.

The present volume provides an ample and well-balanced representation of this body of writing as it has evolved throughout successive generations of writers: beginning with Alberto Gerchunoff, the cornerstone of Jewish Argentine—and indeed of all Latin American—literature, and ending with stories by contemporary writers. The stories contained in this collection reflect the dual cultural and ethnic heritage of the writers who rely upon at least two distinct cultural traditions for the creation of their texts. Jewish writers in Argentina, as elsewhere, by no means form a homogeneous group. Each writes the Jewish Argentine experience from a unique perspective, shaped by the historical and political circumstances in which they live. Literary texts by Jewish authors in Argentina are most readily characterized by the way in which they seek to examine specifically Jewish concerns. Immigration, assimilation, Zionism, antisemitism, Jewish culture, and the Holocaust are themes common to many texts. Often, however, issues of Jewish identity are secondary to the more compelling immediacy of Latin American realities such as political unrest, economic woes, and military repression.

As a vehicle for a culturally-specific discourse, though not necessarily a homogeneous one, Jewish Argentine writing constitutes a socioliterary phenomenon that exercises and contributes to the creation of cultural identity. Also, as a social text marked by its decentered marginal status as a minority discourse, Jewish writing serves an important function as a countervoice to official discourse. Jewish writing in Argentina, like other minority literatures, endures as a contestatory response to the hegemonic telling of social history. Jewish writers offer a different version of events and challenge the facticity and authority of the established canon as the authentic voice of Argentina. This does not imply that they seek to demarcate a new set of truths, but rather to question the process by which accepted truths have been established as such.

Argentine literature has a history of wide readership in English including Jorge Luis Borges, Julio Cortázar, and Luisa Valenzuela, to name only a few. *The Silver Candelabra and Other Stories*, is among the first to present the singular and seldom recognized body of Jewish Argentine literature to an English-reading audience. The twelve authors included here represent the vast scope of this literature and provide a unique lens through which to read Argentina.

Darrell B. Lockhart

A Brief Overview of Argentine History
Relative to Its Jewish Population

The authors presented in this anthology represent a sampling of the Jewish Argentine literature written throughout this century. Arranged chronologically, they reflect the events in Argentine history that directly or indirectly affected their lives and work. This brief historical overview is provided to chronicle those events so that the reader can situate the stories in their respective contexts for a more insightful reading.

While Argentina is known as South America's "melting pot" of predominantly Spanish, Italian, German and English immigrants, it also has a lesser known, but significant representation of immigrant Jews who started arriving on the continent fleeing pogroms in Russia, Poland and the Balkans during the 1880s. Due to Argentina's "new" constitution instituted in 1853 containing assurances of religious freedom and tolerance, many victims of persecution were attracted to the country.

Having finally settled the long conflict between the federalists and centralists with the Compromise of 1862, the Argentine government turned its attention to economic development and immigration initiatives. Convinced that if the country was to prosper it would have to settle the pampas, officials actively courted European emigrés believing that they would have the skills necessary to establish settlements more rapidly and effectively than would the area's scattered gauchos and Indians. This appeal for immigrants was conducted on a large scale especially during the administration of Bartolomé Mitre (1862-1868) and that of his successor, Domingo Faustino Sarmiento (1868-1874).

Rather than distribute public lands directly to immigrants for farming as the United States had done in its homestead plans for the west, the Argentine government sold property in the pampas to politicians, military officers, and foreign capitalists with the understanding that they would develop settlements there. It was one of these foreign capitalists, Bavarian-born Baron Maurice de Hirsch (1831-1896), who realized that Argentina's need to settle and populate the pampas could provide Eastern European Jews with refuge from the threat of escalating pogroms abroad. Envisioning Argentina as a possible site for a new Jewish homeland, Hirsch purchased large tracts of land and founded the Jewish Colonization Association to distribute that land and provide assistance to Jewish immigrants. Under his plan, colonists were allowed twenty years to pay off what was essentially a low-interest loan from "The Jewish," as his association came to be called. They were given the option to pay off their loans after twelve years to obtain clear title to the land. The first colony developed by Hirsch's association was established in Entre Ríos in 1889. It was named Moisesville.

Because these Eastern European Jewish immigrants shared a common language, religion, and cultural background, they soon developed a strong community life. Given the rich tradition of Yiddish literature, especially in short story and drama, they began to perform plays for community entertainment. Later, groups and associations like the Asociación Mutual Israelita Argentina (Mutual Israelite Argentine Association) and the Federación Israelita Argentina (Argentine Israelite Federation) were founded to coordinate the growing number of cultural activities. To keep abreast of news and happenings in both the Old World and the New, they soon established their own Yiddish newspapers and journals.

Since most colonists were artisans and tradesmen from villages and larger cities, rather than farmers, many of them endured the harsh life of the pampas only until they could pay off their mortgages. Beset by drought and plague, without the appropriate tools and adequate skills required, and disillusioned with the inadequacies of the limited schooling they were able to provide their children, many sold their land as soon as they earned title to it. They then moved to the cities where their children had better educational opportunities, and they themselves could once again earn a living at their former skilled trades and businesses.

Although a number of foreign agricultural colonies had been established in Santa Fe and Entre Ríos provinces during the 1870s and 1880s, high property values and declining wheat prices in the 1890s undermined most of them, forcing the remaining settlers either to become tenant farmers or to leave the countryside and move to Buenos Aires. This was the beginning of a large-scale migration of

Jewish settlers to the cities that started in the last decade of the century and continued into the 1900s.

When these relocating settlers and new immigrants moved to the cities, they lived first in *conventillos* (tenement houses) and tended to group together in ghetto-like enclaves. In Buenos Aires, Italian immigrants congregated in an area called La Boca (near the mouth of the Río Plata), while Jewish immigrants settled in the Barrio Once and Villa Crespo areas. Although at first these Jewish arrivals worked as itinerant peddlers and day-laborers, they soon became shopkeepers, tradesmen and artisans.

This generation of Jews were the parents of some of the authors represented here, who generally entered Argentina as children, arriving with their parents to either the agricultural communities or the city's tenement houses. If they did not grow up in the city, they soon moved there. A few received a formal education, but most were self-educated and strove diligently to adapt to their new environment, speak Spanish, and gain access to the mainstream community.

When in later life they wrote of their experiences in adapting to the different culture of the New World, these early authors tended to avoid starkly realistic descriptions. Rather than appear critical of their new country, they preferred to stress the gratitude they felt for the freedom and opportunities it offered them, and to emphasize the willingness they and their fellow immigrants felt toward adapting to Argentine ways.

Among these early authors were Alberto Gerchunoff (1884-1950) and Samuel Glusberg (1898-1987, who wrote under the pseudonym Enrique Espinosa). They were the first Jewish immigrants to achieve national prominence as journalists and authors–Gerchunoff for his newspaper writing in *El País* and *La Nación* and popular episodic novel *Los gauchos judíos;* Espinosa, for his short stories and work as editor of the prestigious literary reviews *América* and *Babel*. They were followed by César Tiempo (1906-1980) who had entered Argentina at the age of three and later achieved renown throughout Latin America as a literary critic and poet of extraordinary talent evidenced in the volumes he composed on Sabbath themes. Later, José Rabinovich (1903-1978) who arrived from Russia as an adult, wrote his first poems and short stories in Yiddish. They were later translated into Spanish when they had proven popular. As he became more fluent, Rabinovich began to write directly in Spanish using a candid, straightforward style that ably conveyed his proletarian leanings.

Aided by well-established literary friends who recognized their talent (Gerchunoff by Leopoldo Lugones, Glusberg by Horacio Quiroga, Tiempo in turn by Gerchunoff and Glusberg), they rose to positions of prominence as journalists and authors. Glusberg became the first secretary of the Argentine Writers Association, while Gerchunoff was chosen to write a commemorative piece for the two hundred year anniversary of Argentine independence. Tiempo captured the popular imagination in poetry, essay, theater, radio and even television. These immigrant authors were trailblazers, pioneers who over the course of their lifetimes successfully bridged the gap from marginal recognition as minority writers to mainstream recognition as authors of outstanding literary talent.

Their children, first generation Argentines who grew up in the city and received university educations, were able to go on to professional careers in business and government. Overall, by the early 1900s, Argentina's Jewish immigrants were settling comfortably into the mainstream of Argentine life.

After the Saenz-Peña Law established universal male suffrage in 1912, the newly-empowered immigrants (now looked upon as active and responsible members of the community–whether they were laborers or from the middle class) found themselves suddenly courted by bourgeois radicals. President Hipólito Yrigoyen (1916-1922) found it good policy to incorporate Jews and other immigrants into his administration. Unfortunately, the economic problems of the time caused his alliances with labor groups to fail. As labor strikes grew both more frequent and more violent between 1916 and 1919, government spokesmen began to blame them on "socialist" and "anarchist" immigrants from Russia. Because the great majority of Jewish immigrants had originally come from Russia (the Spanish word "*ruso*," "Russian," had already become a household word used to refer to the immigrants), it was not long before all Jews were perceived as activists and socialists responsible for the strikes.

Fueled by economic unrest, these generally accepted perceptions grew, bringing about sudden and violent retaliation against all Jews. From January 7 to January 12, 1919, Jews were physically attacked in the streets and Jewish owned businesses were vandalized or burned in attacks led by the Argentine Patriotic League, an organization made up of middle and upper class reactionaries. Instead of denouncing this violence, Yrigoyen's radical government encouraged party members to join the vigilantes, allowing the antilabor movement to degenerate into an outright persecution of "communist" Jews. In what came to be called "Semana Trágica" (Tragic Week), these unexpected happenings destroyed forever the illusion of acceptance that Argentine Jews had thus far cherished. Although this racist violence was publicly condemned by numerous prominent non-Jewish intellectuals and civic leaders, their support did little to assuage Jewish anxieties.

In the decade following, under the presidency of Marcelo T. de Alvear (1922-1928) social unrest eased, although underlying economic problems continued. During this period, a number of first generation Jewish Argentine intellectuals gained prominence as writers, editors and publishers. Argentina's first Jewish publications in Spanish appeared: *Vida nuestra*, a cultural journal, and *Mundo israelita,* a daily newspaper. They were quickly followed by others. Editorial houses were opened by Jewish authors who were also on staff at some of the country's major newspapers and journals. The Sociedad Hebráica Argentina (Argentine Hebrew Society) was founded in 1926 and soon developed into a cultural center featuring leading Argentine and world renowned artists, writers, and lecturers. The "Hebráica" established a Jewish library which it named for Alberto Gerchunoff, one of its founders, who had already gained recognition as one of the foremost authors of the day.

Many first generation Jewish Argentine authors achieved widespread recognition: Natalio Budasoff (1903-1981), who perhaps because he was not a new immigrant eager to please mainstream society, wrote more candidly than his predecessors about the harsh realities of the agricultural communities in novels like *Lluvias salvajes* (*Brutal Storms,* 1962); Samuel Eichelbaum (1894-1967), who, despite a collection of short stories called *El viajero inmóvil y otros cuentos* (*The Stationary Traveler and Other Stories,* 1933), was better known as a playwright addressing racial and ethnic problems that Argentines had, until then, preferred to ignore; Lázaro Liacho (1896-1969), a poet, novelist and short story writer who dealt with themes ranging from the persecution in the Old World to experiences in

Buenos Aires and in the newly established state of Israel (*Sobre el filo de la vida/On Life's Cutting Edge*, 1968) and whose poetry (*Pan de Buenos Aires /Bread of Buenos Aires*, 1940) praises his adopted land; Bernardo Verbitsky (1907-1979), who centered his work so concretely in Buenos Aires that he became known as the virtual chronicler of the city, savoring its characters, dialects, sights, sounds and smells in his novels and short stories, and whose autobiographical novel *Hermana y sombra* (*Sister and Shadow*), chronicled much of his family's and his own personal story of adaptation and integration into Buenos Aires culture. These Argentine authors of immigrant parents, most of whom were born around the turn of the century, experienced a lifetime of change: the experimentalist and social movements of the 1920s; the chaotic global economic problems of the 1930s; the Peronist upheavals and Second World War of the 1940s; the relative prosperity of the 1950s; the political instability of the 1960s; the social unrest and spiraling inflation of the 1970s, and the anarchism and repression of the 1980s.

It was during the 1920s that Argentina began to experience the political and economic problems that continued for the next sixty years. Between 1922 and 1928 labor and political unrest grew under the presidency of Hipólito Yrigoyen. The troubles of this decade are articulated in the work of Bernardo Kordon (1915-), who wrote of the struggle for human rights and dignity, social strife and the violence that occurred during these rapidly changing times.

Following this era, Argentina experienced an uneasy period of conservatism and military intervention under General José Felix Uriburu (1930-1932). This conservativism grew more threatening during the next presidency: Shortly after General Agustín P. Justo (1932-1938) was sworn into office, he began removing most Jews from public office and tightening immigration regulations and requirements for naturalization—all actions indicating that Europe's growing antisemitism had now made its way to Argentina.

Concerned by increasing incidents of anti-Semitism under Uriburu's and Justus's administrations, Jewish leaders organized the Comité Contra el Antisemitismo y el Racismo (Committee Against Anti-Semitism and Racism) to work against racist activity. In 1936 a number of small Jewish organizations united to form an umbrella organization called DAIA (Delegación de Asociaciónes Israelis de

Argentina/Delegation of Argentine Israelite Associations) to lobby for Jewish causes, interact with government officials and defend Jewish interests.

In the 1930s and 1940s political change in the country became increasingly frequent and chaotic. The ailing Roberto Ortiz followed Justo as president in 1938. Unable to perform his duties, he turned the government over to his arch-conservative Vice President Ramón Castillo just two years later. When he died in 1942, Castillo officially succeeded him but was overthrown by the army in June of 1943. From then until the 1946 elections, three generals heading a military junta successively ruled Argentina.

Meanwhile, in the world arena, World War II was taking place. The war found Argentina officially neutral, but idealistically pro-Axis, indirectly supporting the Italian government with which it had long had close ties, and the German government on which it was dependent economically. Because of this pro-Axis sympathy, Jews who tried to flee the Nazis during the 1930s and 1940s were deliberately discouraged from immigrating to Argentina by strategically enacted laws that created demands that refugees could not possibly meet. As a consequence, very few immigrated to Argentina in the first few years after the Holocaust (1945-1949).

The long period of political turmoil and the subsequent military game of musical chairs finally ended when the charismatic General Juan Perón was swept into power in 1946.

Perón's administration (1946-1955), although popular with laborers and the lower classes, had disastrous effects on the country's economy and quality of life. As president, Perón's erratic policies proved disastrous. His program of paying inflationary wages to workers almost bankrupted the business sector, his farm policies destroyed the argricultural industry, and his "educational reforms" decimated the national university systems. Although he opened government and party positions to Jews and spoke against anti-Semitism, Perón deliberately retained known Fascists in government, implemented immigration policies that effectively impeded the admission of Jewish refugees, and facilitated the entrance of wealthy Germans fleeing postwar retribution. A general "pardon" for all illegal immigrants in 1949 was intended to benefit German and Nazi refugees rather than Jewish ones: Perón literally made

Argentina, home of Latin America's largest Jewish population, a haven for fleeing Nazis.

By changing the constitutional decree that limited the presidency to one term, Perón managed to be reelected. He then solidified his power by founding the Peronist party. As his excesses grew, the Catholic Church, which had at first supported him became increasingly critical. Unable to tolerate dissent, Perón retaliated, flaunting the church, becoming increasingly anticlerical, calling for divorce and even ordering a number of churches to be burned. Outraged, the conservative arm of the military, the church hierarchy and the traditional bureaucracy all united to overthrow him. When they succeeded in September of 1955, Perón went into exile in Franco's Spain. He was replaced briefly by General Eduardo Leonardi who in was turn overthrown by the army in November of 1955, and then replaced by General Pedro Aramburu.

Aramburu's provisional government (1955-1958) was marked by inflation, labor unrest, efforts to discredit the Peronists, political polarization, the harassment of Jewish cultural activities and anti-Jewish attacks by the press. Aramburu's major achievement was returning the country to democracy by calling for presidential elections in 1958.

The radical Arturo Frondizi (1958-1962) who followed Arumburu, successfully restored some measure of liberal and democratic rule to Argentina, going so far as to nominate several Jews for prominent positions in his government. This goodwill was short-lived however, for Frondizi's attempts to seek a rapprochement with labor were soon undermined by a combination of economic turmoil and lack of political consensus. When Israeli agents seized Nazi refugee Adolf Eichmann from Buenos Aires in a commando-like raid in May 1960 and extradited him to Israel, the Frondizi government was outraged and public opinion against Jews was reignited. Random assaults against them occurred throughout 1961 and 1962, and Tacuara, the anti-Semitic organization which had been founded in the 1940s by a Jesuit priest, reemerged. Terrorist activity increased, Jewish social and religious centers were attacked and bombed and Frondizi's government, unable to control the country's mounting economic problems and its escalating general violence, was driven to proclaim a state of emergency. Military leaders tried to intervene and eventually, after thirty-five coup attempts, succeeded in ousting Frondizi in 1962.

The interim regime of José María Guido which followed was marked by an increase in anti-Jewish activities by Tacuara, the Arab League of Latin America, and other groups. Arturo Illia's government (1963-1966) which followed, was well meaning but unable to stop the escalating anti-Semitic activity and violence.

To restore order, the military once again intervened. General Juan Carlos Onganía deposed Illia in a military coup in 1966 and immediately set about purging liberal elements from the government. He suspended all democratic policies, imposed authoritarian controls, and replaced all Jews in government with Catholic appointees. During July 1966, the Onganía administration raided Jewish businesses and neighborhoods, initiated controls calculated to harass small Jewish businesses, and allowed Tacuara and other right-wing groups to continue their terrorist activities unrestrained. When the government went so far as to attack numerous university students and professors, labelling them communists, many faculty members resigned in protest. Not until the United States government threatened to withhold recognition of his government did Onganía stop harassing Jews and liberals and attempt to control terrorist groups like the Tacuara.

In 1967 when Israel's Six Day War occurred, it raised serious questions about the support of a Jewish homeland in Palestine and caused many in Argentina to question yet again whether it was possible to be both a Jew and a loyal Argentine. In turn, this generally increasing suspicion and distrust of Jews and Jewish activity caused many young Jews, especially university students, to distance themselves from both the Israeli cause and their own cultural identity. This tendency was facilitated by the fact that assimilation had become increasingly commonplace as more and more first and second generation Argentine Jews entered the professional and business classes, earned higher incomes and moved out of their enclave in Barrrio Once to more affluent residential areas like Belgrano and the suburbs of Barrio Norte, Martínez, and Olivos.

By 1969, however, other concerns took center stage in Argentina. Onganía proved unable to control student and labor unrest and terrorist activities increased. An extreme left-wing group known as the Montoneros began terrorizing the nation, bombing selected targets, kidnapping wealthy industrialists, raiding police stations, and carrying out daring robberies and assassinations.

Over the next few years terrorism reached such unprecedented levels that the military, casting about for a strong leader who could stave off further social disintegration, saw no alternative but to recall the still-popular Perón. The fraudulent elections of March 1973 resulted in the election of Juan Perón as president and his second wife, María Estela (called "Isabel"), as vice president. Unfortunately however, when the triumphant and victorious Perón returned to Argentina he was in poor health and died less than a year later in July 1974. He was succeeded by his widow. Isabel ruled in name only under the control of the Welfare Minister at the time, José Lopez Rega, until she was deposed by the inevitable military coup in March 1976. Although intellectual repression eased during her presidency, violence by guerrilla militias and paramilitary groups increased, social disintegration accelerated and the continuing economic crisis worsened. Escalating terrorism caused the government to declare a state of national emergency and carry out increasingly repressive measures until, eventually, a state of undeclared civil war existed. The government committed so many ruthless acts of violence in the course of this antiterrorist campaign that its activities during this period came to be known as the "dirty war."

Once again, because of the association in the public mind linking liberal dissent and socialism with the Jewish community, suspicions grew. University students and young adults were especially targeted. Young Jews made up the majority of the suspected "subversives" who were arrested, imprisoned, and who later disappeared. Perhaps the best known example of such arbitrary arrests is the case of author/publisher Jacobo Timmerman whose public denunciations of the military government led to the closing of his press, his imprisonment and torture. After universal public outcry brought about his release, Timmerman chronicled his experiences in the book *Prisoner without a Name, Cell without a Number*, bringing world attention to the government's flagrant violations of human rights, the anti-Semitism of the ruling junta and the fact that a significant number of people in Argentina were "disappearing." Fearing they would be similarly targeted, nearly one million liberals, including many Jewish intellectuals, emigrated to Mexico, the United States, Spain, France and other countries during this period. Fortunately, the testimonial writing of the authors among them subsequently made a remarkable contribution to Argentine and Jewish literature–a contribution that at this point was possible only for authors who resided and published outside Argentina.

By 1980 the government had completely "won" the "dirty war," and while the military was split over the issue of state-sponsored violence (between the "duros," the hard-liners and the "blandos," the moderates), criticism of its excessively repressive measures was increasing within the country as well as around the world. By 1982 human rights problems and a growing lack of public confidence had seriously eroded the military government's authority; government policies exacerbated the country's economic problems; wages had declined drastically and inflation was increasing exponentially. The military, in an effort to distract the Argentines from their worsening situation and unite them in a "common cause," decided to resurrect an old wound to Argentine pride. They started a territorial conflict with England over the control of the Malvinas, or Falkland Islands. They expected little resistance and an easy victory that would bring about the restoration of national pride and confidence. When the British unexpectedly retaliated with massive force, causing Argentina to declare defeat after just ten weeks, the country's military leaders were so thoroughly discredited that they were forced to resign and implement the democratic elections that the public had been demanding.

Argentina's long period of military rule finally came to an end in December 1983 when Radical leader Raúl Alfonsín was elected president. His open and nondiscriminatory policies helped the country effect a difficult, but peaceful transition back to democracy. His civilian government called for full legal prosecution of all military leaders accused of crimes committed during the "dirty war." Under his government, a number of Jews were named to high-level public offices (the author Marcos Aguinis, for example, was named Secretary of Culture, 1983-1989). Despite Alfonsín's well-meaning intentions, his economic initiatives proved ineffective in controlling the country's outrageous inflation. Disillusioned, the public turned yet again to the Peronist party for leadership and elected the party leader Saúl Menem to succeed Alfonsín in 1989.

Taking tough measures that only a staunchly supported Peronist leader would dare attempt, Menem privatized railroads, airlines and the telephone system, and renegotiated foreign loans to reduce government debt and encourage industry and development. A strong advocate of free trade, he sought the liberalization of trade between Argentina and the United States through the 1990 Enterprise of the Americas Initiative and the 1994 NAFTA agreement. His success in reducing inflation from 120% to 13% in just one six–year term facilitated his reelection to a second (current) term in which inflation continues to decrease, the economy continues to grow and the ever recurring threat of military intervention finally seems to have been laid to rest. It is encouraging that Menem, of Syrian origin, has named several Jews to cabinet positions.

Throughout the oppressive era of military rule, some authors had been too inhibited to write. Others, like Cecilia Absatz, had been banned or censored, while still others had chosen self-exile. Encouraged by the new climate of democracy that began after the junta stepped down in 1983, many of the country's exiles returned home. Together, the newly returned community of Jews along with the one that had kept a low profile during the "dirty war" years now began to reassess and reaffirm their Jewish heritage. Realizing the importance of being more proactive, they began to voice their dissent and speak out in support of their beliefs.

Today, the country's estimated 200,000 Jews increasingly tend to associate with organizations like the Sociedad Hebráica (Hebrew Society) and the AMIA (Asociación Mutual Israelita Argentina/ Mutual Israelite Association of Argentina), which serve as centers of Jewish intellectual and social activity. AMIA provides a variety of classes and scholarships, a library, economic assistance to orphans and the elderly, and even burial services. Despite the fact that the AMIA building was destroyed by a terrorist bombing in 1995, the association continues to provide services from improvised quarters and is actively planning to rebuild on its previous site.

In recent years these organizations and other smaller, more specifically focused ones like the United States-founded Latin American Jewish Studies Association, have encouraged frank discussion of Jewish concerns by sponsoring conferences on topics such as Jewish Argentine literature, culture and society. Under the aegis of these organizations, worldwide attention has been drawn to the need for change in Argentina's long record of anti-Semitism.

This new activism has awakened Argentine Jews to a greater appreciation of their cultural identity. In recent years, associations, groups and individuals have worked at gathering personal stories and official documentation in order to record a specifically Jewish Argentine history. The result, throughout the 1980s and 1990s, has been the publication of a surprising number of books dealing with Jewish immigration, Jewish Argentine culture, and Jewish contributions to Argentine life. Today, Argentina's Jewish authors are freer than ever before not only to reflect on issues and attitudes derived from their own Jewish heritage, but broader political and social issues as well.

Inevitably, perhaps, Jewish values that had held firm under tacit or overt opposition tended to relax during peaceful periods of acceptance. At such times, assimilation and secularization occurred, accepted by many and decried by others. Early in the century, Gerchunoff wrote of a Jewish girl running off to marry a gaucho goy. A generation later, Verbitsky wrote a story of an observant Jewish grandmother whose visit surprised her daughter's family while in the middle of nonkosher culinary preparations. Ricardo Feierstein, a contemporary author, satirizes this increasing secularization in "A Plateful of Latkes," depicting the ignorance or confusion of today's young Jewish families regarding the traditional food and customs of specific religious holidays, their willingness to ignore kosher precepts, and their unquestioning acceptance of current social fads whether it be the psychotherapy of the 1970s or the currently popular yoga and physical training.

Other contemporary Jewish Argentine authors deal more often with social problems. Isidoro Blaisten and the late Germán Rosenmacher, for example, tend to present society's marginal types and the struggling lower classes. Women authors, from the more traditional Eugenia Calny and Alicia Steimberg to the more liberated Cecilia Absatz and Silvia Plager have achieved prominence in their novels and stories by chronicling the changing perceptions of commonly accepted female stereotypes and roles.

Today, both men and women Jewish Argentine writers seem comfortable and at ease with their identity as Jews and reveal a greater freedom than ever before to reflect their Jewish heritage in their works or even simply to ignore the issue of cultural differences in favor of expressing their own individual personalities and perspectives.

The experiences that Jewish Argentine authors have had as they made their way, despite intermittent repression, from the margins of Argentine society to its mainstream have been challenging and eventually rewarding. Today, their work, personal yet universal, Jewish, yet indubitably Argentine, is attracting growing recognition and acclaim both in and outside Argentina. Latin American scholars no longer consider their writing marginal but recognize it as an integral component of Latin American literature.

It is my aim, in this book, to bring some of these authors to the attention of an English-speaking public by introducing them and translating their stories. The twelve representative writers whose works I have translated here have all made noteworthy contributions to Argentine and Jewish letters and deserve to be brought to the attention of a wider public.

Alberto Gerchunoff (1883-1950)

Born in Russia, Gerchunoff immigrated with his family to Moisesville, one of Baron Moise Hirsch's agricultural communities, when he was eight years old. His father was killed by a drunken gaucho a year later and his widowed mother moved the family to Buenos Aires when he was twelve. To help provide for his family, the young Gerchunoff worked as a street vendor and factory worker by day while studying by night. As a university student he met the wealthy Enrique Dickman, who was so impressed with his ability and promise that he introduced him to prominent literary figures such as Leopoldo Lugones, Manuel Gálvez and Roberto J. Payró. The latter helped him join the staff of *La Nación*, Argentina's most widely-read newspaper.

In 1910, when Lugones organized cultural activities for the hundred-year anniversary of Argentine independence, he asked Gerchunoff, who had already published anecdotes on the Jewish immigration and colonial experience in *La Nación*, to write a novel on the topic. By collecting and adding to his articles, Gerchunoff produced *Los Gauchos Judíos* (*The Jewish Gauchos*), a novel with twenty-six vignette-like chapters idealizing the immigrants' experiences and stressing their appreciation for their adopted land. Gerchunoff described the colonists' hopes, despairs, challenges and problems of adaptation so lyrically that even stories of plague and death are narrated with the sensitivity and embellishment of the modernist period in which they were written. Nevertheless, Gerchunoff's writing is undeniably original and this novel, idealistic and romantic though it may be, depicts a unique aspect and period of Argentine and Jewish social history. As the first such work written in Spanish rather than Yiddish, *Los Gauchos Judíos*, considered the cornerstone of Jewish Argentine literature, has earned Gerchunoff an enduring place in Argentine letters.

The first Jewish author to gain entree to Argentina's elite literary circles, Gerchunoff at first encouraged accommodation to mainstream culture but later became active in the Jewish community. He helped found the Sociedad Hebráica Argentina (Argentine Hebrew Society) in 1926 and used his influence to bring prominent writers, philosophers, and cultural leaders to the SHA, making it a center of intellectual life in Buenos Aires. In his honor, the SHA named its 40,000 volume Jewish library the Biblioteca Alberto Gerchunoff (The Alberto Gerchunoff Library). Gerchunoff's published books include *Entre Ríos mi país* (*Entre Ríos, My Land*, 1950), a biographic collection of essays, *Cuentos de ayer* (*Stories From Yesterday*, 1919) and several other collections of stories, essays and biographies.

The Silver Candelabra

by Alberto Gerchunoff

The ranch was enveloped in that intense brightness, that placid brightness the sun has on autumn mornings. Through the open window in the thick, rough adobe wall, one could see the countryside extending off into the distance, beyond that, the hill where yellowing thistles waved their nervous branches at the lonely sky. Not so far off, the cow with a length of rope around her neck, licked the rump of her calf. It was the Sabbath. The colony was quiet and now and then one could hear a neighbor's voice singing softly.

When his wife came in, Guedali had already donned the white tunic and, absorbed in his opening prayers, scarcely noticed her presence. He gestured to her, pursing his mouth and moving his head back, so that she wouldn't interrupt him. The woman looked in from the doorway and left without a sound. Guedali heard what she said to her daughter on the other side of the door: "I can't ask him now because he's started his prayers."

Guedali was very religious. He wasn't considered among the most learned in the colony, nor did he speak out during the arguments they always started at meetings in the synagogue about difficult commentaries and obscure points of the texts. He was a good humored man with a deep, sad voice. A sweet timid look burned like a weak flame in his deep eyes, darkened by ashy, bushy brows. With his face turned toward the east, his tall thin body seemed elongated beneath the tunic, which fell in even folds to the ground.

Suddenly, he felt that someone was creeping around near the window. Without ceasing to pray, he turned his head slowly to see what was there, thinking it must be the neighbor who had served in the military and always made fun of his devotion. It wasn't the neighbor, but a stranger who slid his hand in to reach for the silver candelabra, the silver candelabra, the noble family heirloom that in his rustic immigrant's home made plain his origins; it rose majestically and shiningly, with its seven arched arms, in whose clear rosettes the light shone as if the wicks of large ritual candles were burning.

Guedali didn't interrupt his prayers: he looked severely at the stranger and broke the sacred words with this warning, "No...it's the Sabbath, it's the Sabbath..." That was as much as he could say without blasphemy. The stranger took the candelabra and Guedali continued praying, his breast moving with the rhythmic phrases of the verses. He recited the blessings, murmuring in a melancholy tone until he concluded the last prayer. Then he breathed deeply. The clear light bathed his emaciated face, his wrinkled forehead, his long, thin, graying beard.

He carefully folded his tunic and put it away in a drawer of the dresser. When his wife entered, Guedali announced tranquilly: "They've stolen the candelabra..." He took a piece of bread from the table and started to eat, as he usually did after praying. His wife let out a shout of indignation: "Weren't you here, you piece of...?" Calmly, as if he hoped to persuade her that he'd done his duty, he answered: "I told him that it was the Sabbath..."

The Divorce

by Alberto Gerchunoff

"Let Rabbi Jonas speak to the case…"

"I cede to Rabbi Abraham, who, as *matarife*,[1] understands justice and the laws."

The *matarife* counseled: "It would be better to let the elders speak their words first."

The scene took place in Israel Kelner's home. The oldest neighbors had met there to intervene as judges in the matter of a divorce, which, because it was doubtless the first in the colony, had aroused quite a bit of curiosity. None of the venerable greybeards was absent, and near the window the angular figure of don Moisés de Abinoim, the Moroccan Jew, stood out amongst them. He happened to be in the village visiting his son, a teacher in their colonial school, and therefore, as a man learned in sacred scripture, he was invited to take part in their deliberations. He spoke classic Hebrew and a kind of old-fashioned language in which he expressed himself slowly.

Rabbi Israel bowed toward him and said: "Let our guest express his opinion." And don Moisés Urquijo de Abinoim, fingering his heavy beard, asked to be informed about the situation. Then they seated themselves around the table whose cracked wood was covered with the tablecloth of the Sabbath, and the explanation began while the servant served *mate*,[2] and the woman of the house received elegiac praises for her tea and pastries.

"We have here the representatives of each spouse," said Kelner. "They are Rabbi Malaquías, on behalf of the husband, and Rabbi Joel, on behalf of the wife. The couple, married for three years, lives near San Antonio and are honorable people."

[1]matarife: the ritual slaughterer
[2]mate: a popular herbal green tea in Argentina

Rabbi Malaquías spoke up: "Rabbi Simon is not asking for divorce."

Rabbi Joel intervened: "Let us follow the law in writing down the statements to be made by the *matarife*. We and the witnesses will sign it later." Then he added, "The woman insists on getting a divorce."

Don Moisés Urquijo de Abinoim, a man who adhered to the minute details of the holy books, asked permission to question the representatives, and having obtained it after a profound bow, asked: "Tell us very honestly, Rabbi Malaquías, if in the name of Rabbi Simon, you accuse this woman of anything before the judges."

"I do not," he responded.

"And you, Rabbi Joel, do you accuse the husband of anything, in her name?"

"I do not."

Don Moisés arose, and delivered this speech: "We see, respected gentlemen (and for that we would do well to thank God), that sin is not the reason for this process. Let us praise the Highest for His great goodness for not bringing us Hebrews, His good children to ruin. This, wise gentlemen, is a case which requires meditation. I hope that Rabbi Abraham will enlighten us in that respect and tell us what the law says. Those who are getting divorced are honorable. Therefore, it is not because of adultery, which the holy book condemns. It is because of what the Hillel (blessed be its memory) calls in its first sentences, 'small details of everyday life.' And I say that we should not separate them."

Rabbi Israel Kelner spoke up: "I won't give my vote."

"I will not sign the declarations," the *matarife* added.

"Let's not grant the separation," several exclaimed.

Then don Moisés, assuming a solemn demeanor, invited the representatives to express their thoughts. Rabbi Joel, a man versed in theology, leaned back in his chair, and after the usual drink of water, expressed himself slowly: "The woman is virtuous. She knows how to respect her husband and tend to her home. But she doesn't like her husband. She married, one might say, in obedience to her parents, and now finds, in a case such as the sacred books foresaw, that such a problem is serious and makes married life difficult. Not to like one's husband is to live condemned to profound suffering without having any pleasure at all. Remember, therefore, the precepts of the treatise on matrimony in the Talmud, whose counsels are admired by the wisest Rabbis. The Talmud says in the book of Nuschim, 'If the woman, for whatever cause, ceases to love her husband, she should separate from him and not receive his caresses, for the child who would be born of them will suffer the consequences of a loveless union.' Gentlemen judges who hear me, in name of the Holy Law, I beg you to grant the divorce."

"Rabbi Joel," don Moisés said, "we have heard you with satisfaction. You are eloquent, but let us permit Rabbi Malaquías to speak."

"I have nothing to say," the latter said. "Rabbi Simon loves his wife and considers her exemplary. Nevertheless, he is disposed to consent to the divorce, for the poor man knows that she can't stand him. He doesn't wish to afflict her further. Moreover, his life is upset by endless disillusionment. How can he live under the same roof with a woman who does not respect him? Understanding this, I join Rabbi Joel in requesting the divorce. Be just."

The *matarife* asked them to deliberate on the topic. While the elders gravely, solemnly gathered in a Sanhedrin in the countryside of Entre Rios and discussed Talmudic clauses, the servant came and went with *mate* which they preferred to tea. Unfamiliar with the laws of Argentina, they applied the laws of the kingdom of Israel, and in this way the wisdom and jurisprudence of Hillel, of Gamaliel, and of Ghedalia, lived again in the colonies of Baron Hirsch. Nor was their lacking at the meeting a descendent of the Talmudists of the Spanish Golden Age. There he was, courteous and gentlemanly, don Moisés Urquijo de Abinoim, with his eloquence and his sensible reflections of mind that had matured in the praiseworthy work of the spirit. Pompous and subtle, he renewed, within the walls of that little mud-walled home, the medieval disquisitions of Toledo and of Cordoba, leading his audience with florid and profound Jewish thought which, under the laws of Castile, maintained the tradition of the sages of Jerusalem.

On the parchment brought by the *matarife*, shining and dense Hebrew characters had been drawn. Kelner invited don Moisés to pass his judgement.

"The law," he said, "obliges the judges to work towards the reconciliation of the spouses, to return peace to their home. I insist then on prudent judges and good representatives."

Rabbi Joel and Rabbi Malaquías repeated their arguments. The

Talmud and jurisprudence, the Bible and the best known dictates and most authoritative comments were brought forth in support of their theses.

Finally, the *matarife* advised granting the divorce and endorsed the papers.

"Such is the will of God," affirmed don Moisés. "We, by order of the law, have first denied the divorce; but seeing that the representatives discuss with clear reason in favor of the separation; seeing that the spouses cannot live together for there is no love between them, we declare that it is by force of the same law that we grant the divorce, so that there may be no Hebrew home where discord reins, and so return to each his peace of heart. Thus we swear and sign, conceding the right to a new marriage to the divorced persons, who are honest and worthy of our respect."

And each of the judges put his signature in Hebrew on the parchment, using his paternal family name. Upon signing his name, don Moisés Urquijo de Abinoim congratulated himself that Jews can always find justice in their law which espouses men's happiness through liberty. And he concluded, moved by his importance as a high judge, with the phrase: "Let us celebrate with wine the sentence in which your discretion and wisdom shines, and let us praise the Lord for having inspired us in the duties of His justice."

"Let us praise the Lord!" all the elders exclaimed.

The wine was brought and glasses clinked. Outside, the sky grew pale and the stars looked out on the still light earth.

"It is prayer time, and there are enough of us to fill a synagogue," Rabbi Malaquías said.

"Let our illustrious guest take the dais," said the *matarife*.

"It is a great honor and I thank you."

"Let us pray, then."

And don Moisés Urquijo de Abinoim extended his arms toward the East and began praising God:

"Baruj Atha Adonai…"

Samuel Glusberg
(Enrique Espinosa, 1898-1988)

Samuel Glusberg was seven when he arrived in Argentina with his family from Russia. Like Gerchunoff, he labored, studied, and had the good fortune to make influential friends. The prominent author Horacio Quiroga became his mentor and helped him into the elite literary and intellectual circles of Buenos Aires.

Glusberg, who wrote under the pseudonym Enrique Espinosa, is best known for his work as a journalist and short story writer. His stories, many of which are either autobiographical or drawn from real life, are spare and unaffected. Unlike Gerchunoff, who idealized the immigrant experience and romanticized the colonists' struggles to retain their own customs while adapting to their new environment, Glusberg's descriptions are realistic. His protagonists are generally Jewish immigrants imbued with Jewish consciousness and presented in situations which are sometimes wryly humorous and at other times ironic, poignant, sad, or even tragic. In a simple, almost conversational style, sometimes pausing to address a brief aside directly to the reader, he describes the immigrants struggle to cope with the varying problems of adaptation, assimilation and acceptance that inevitably arose as they strove to adapt to their new life in the colonies or in Buenos Aires.

In addition to his work as a journalist and author, Glusberg edited A*merica* and several other literary journals, founded a literary journal titled *Babel* and later, his own editorial house, Biblioteca Argentina de Buenas Ediciones Literarias, (BABEL/Argentine Library of Fine Literary Editions), both of which published avant-garde works by most of the leading authors of the day. As an editor he was active in organizing literary contests to encourage the young writers of his time, and also helped organize the Argentine Writers Association, becoming its first secretary.

His best known collection of short stories are *La levita gris* (*The Gray Frock Coat*, 1924) and *Ruth and Noemi* (*Ruth and Naomi*, 1934). He has also written several collections of essays and a number of biographical works on figures as disparate as the South American hero José de San Martín, the German author, Heinrich Heine, and the Dutch philosopher, Baruch Spinoza.

Betsy's Death

by Samuel Glusberg

The village of Villa Mauricio, with half a dozen Jewish families in wooden ranch houses isolated in a distant corner of Lanus, is asleep in the darkness of the autumn night. Only in the house of Kopel Bender, the widower, does a kerosene lamp reflect a few rays of light on the window. And that is because Betsy, his oldest daughter, who until, exactly one week ago Thursday, had taken care of her little brother Yánquele, is seriously ill. So seriously ill that, in the afternoon the doctor gave up hope for her. In spite of this, her poor father still hopes for a miracle. Arched like a question mark over his daughter's bed, he holds her languid head and wipes her sweat-soaked forehead with a towel.

In his usual way, he thinks: "Doesn't everything depend on God anyway?" And in the depths of his devout Jewish faith he is sure that nothing will be taken from him without the will of the Almighty.

Beneath the blankets, the little one's body curls into another question mark. At times, her voice husky with fever, she cries: "Water, Daddy, water!"

And her breathing becomes more labored with each request.

Her father, knowing that water has been forbidden, consoles her with honeyed words.

"My dear little girl," he says, "you will soon be well and then we'll have some liqueur. Do you remember the liqueur we made with wild cherries? How good it was! And how much Yánquele liked it! As soon as you get well, we'll buy wild cherries again and we'll make liqueur again, all right? But we can't do it now."

The child looks at him with a feverish stare that ages her little thirteen-year-old face. Then she stammers again: "Water, Daddy, water!"

Her father, with that tenderness that men are capable of only during poignant moments, prolongs his words of comfort: "My little one, my darling little one! Tomorrow you'll be better, and I'll give you water. Now you can't have anything at all."

The man's voice becomes increasingly tender and husky. He raises his eyes to the ceiling to hold back his tears.

Six nights in a row beside the specter of galloping pneumonia exhausted him. But a father's heart finds unsuspected strength in such cases. That's what helps Kopel Bender stay on his feet. Certainly, his deep faith helps him, the faith of a man who is sure of his God, the God that saved Moses from the waters…But his paternal concern is no different from any father's. Because, after all, what difference does it make if relief comes to us from heaven or by chance?

In Betsy's case, thanks to some deity or other, something happens at dawn. Seeing her somewhat better, the poor man prepares to say a prayer of thanks. But this fatal improvement, is soon followed by death, and his prayer of thanks turns into a funeral lament.

Rigid, beneath the covers, the little girl's body is now a great question mark, a sign of the surprise her open eyes express there under the lamplight.

Beside her bed, the anguished man studies her, but sheds no tears…Then, according to ritual, he begins to murmur the proper prayer: "Baruj daien emes…Blessed art Thou, the Truthful Judge…"

❧⋅❦

At the querulous echo of the prayer, Yánquele awakens in the next room. He is an eleven-year-old child, a bit sickly, with mousy eyes, which always seem surprised.

"Papa! Papa!" he calls from his bed, "How is Betsy?"

His father doesn't answer. And when the child, still half-dressed, attempts to enter the room, he mercifully closes the door on him. But, in a house where children have once seen the specter of death, it is difficult to deceive them. So Yánquele throws himself on the floor weeping, sure that his sister is dead.

❧⋅❦

A few minutes later, doña Deborah, a tall, heavy neighbor who usually looks after the widower's children, enters the house.

"Damn mud!" she complains as she enters the hall, "you can scarcely even walk now!"

And when she discovers Yánquele sobbing on the floor, in typical Jewish fashion she screams: "*Oi vei is mir*!...Woe is me...What misfortune!"

At the woman's cries, the poor widower looks up, and putting his finger to his lips, makes a barely perceptible sign for silence. But doña Deborah, as if she didn't see it, throws herself on the little one's death bed, wailing and weeping. Yánquele also enters the room, and shaken by the woman's cries, wails with wrenching sobs. Seeing them overcome by so much grief, the poor widower tries to get them out of the room. As a good Jew, he is sure that he has done everything he could have before death came. Therefore, he now says resignedly: "There's nothing to do now, nothing! God's will has been done."

With great difficulty, doña Deborah leaves followed by the boy.

Half an hour later, the six Jewish families of Villa Mauricio learn of the misfortune. The men, all laborers, go to work as usual. All the women, without exception, come to the little house.

Once inside, they form a strange chorus of lamentations. They clamor: "Yesterday the mother and today the daughter! First the queen and then the princess! After the branch, the flower...My God, where is Your mercy? Aren't You all powerful, after all? How can You leave this poor father in such a situation? What will become of his poor boy?"

And the laments and meaningless questions continue because the women speak heedlessly while weeping.

With all this, and after finishing his morning prayers, Kopel Bender leaves to get his buggy.

Just as when his wife died, he knows that he has to go in person to obtain the many papers necessary to procure a place in the Jewish cemetery in Buenos Aires.

So it is that, once the buggy is hitched up, he begs the woman to look after the dead girl, and after telling Yánquele not to cry, he leaves in the cold, sunless morning.

➤-◄

From Villa Mauricio to the station of Lanus is a distance of five or six kilometers, that in good weather, can be covered in an hour. But after a rain, it can't be done in less than two hours. That is, if the vehicles' wheels only get stuck once during the trip, which depends on the driver. And in this respect, Kopel Bender's spirit is not one to punish anyone, much less an animal.

In the driver's seat of the buggy, the man lets the horse lead the way. With downcast eyes, and his gray beard folded over his chest, he mentally organizes the tasks he has to carry out.

First, he has to see the doctor for the death certificate. Then, go to City Hall on Avellaneda street for the permit to transport the body to the capital. Then he has to arrange to have the cemetery administration assign a grave. Finally, he has to buy a coffin and return to Lanus. All this before nightfall, because it is the vigil of the Sabbath. He cannot for anything in the world violate this sacred law.

When he arrives at the station, it's almost eleven. According to his plan, he stops at the doctor's house and requests the certificate. Fortunately, he doesn't have to wait and shortly continues his trip to Avellaneda. Over the stones of Pavon street, he quickens the horse's pace. As he nears don Ramiro's feed store, he stops again. He has forgotten the horse's feed, the horse in whose company he has to do so many things. So he gets down for a moment, loads some alfalfa onto the buggy, and after exchanging a few words with the shopkeeper, takes up the reins again as he gets into the vehicle.

But don Ramiro, having learned of the poor "Russian's" misfortune, can't let him leave without asking why he doesn't bury the child in Lanus.

"Anyway," he says, "isn't it all the same? I can give you a hand. I know the administrator of the cemetery."

And the Jew has to explain from his cart: "The thing is, Israelites can't be buried alongside Christians. That's why we have our own cemetery in Liniers."

Don Ramiro doesn't seem convinced and insists that as far as the child is concerned, Lanus is the same as Liniers.

Only when the widower adds the reason that there, in Liniers, Betsy will sleep beside her mother, the shopkeeper seems to be moved. He's not entirely convinced that this has any importance, but he concludes: "God help you! Be it as you wish!"

With a gesture that seems to express, "you don't know what burial means to an Israelite," Kopel Bender sets off down Pavon street.

In Avellaneda he gets the permit easily. Now he has the two certificates and all he needs is for them to give him a poor man's plot in the cemetery.

After an hour he's there. He explains his case: a poor widower whose only daughter has just died. Then he presents his papers and says that he himself will see to bringing the girl in on Sunday morning.

It's useless. They can't give him the authorization.

They reason thus: "Less than a year ago we did you a favor; so now it's impossible…Only the president or the secretary can do it. Go and find them."

And the poor widower spends all afternoon going from the president's house to the secretary's house, until he manages to get them to help him again…

Finally, at four-thirty in the afternoon, after buying a small coffin, he can begin his return home with all the papers in order.

"Blessed be the Most High!" he thanks God in his heart, while he hurries his horse because it is late. He has to arrive back at Villa Mauricio before the first stars appear.

❧

It's an uneasy trip. The street traffic is heavy and he loses time. The fear of arriving late causes him anguish. In all his thirty-seven years, this is the first time he finds himself in peril of not being at home on Friday at sundown.

He continues hurrying his horse, who trots as fast as he can along the road to Lanus. When he arrives at Pavon street an hour later, it is beginning to get dark. A quarter of an hour later, as the first lights come on, the man stops at don Ramiro's feed store.

What to do? A devout man cannot continue the trip. The Sabbath has begun.

Kopel Bender finds no other option but to leave his buggy in the stable at the feed store and continue on foot to Villa Mauricio. This had occurred to him in town when he was trying to move through traffic. But now, unfortunately, he can't do this because don Ramiro is away and his wife doesn't know anything about all this.

Finding no other way out, he waits for two hours. He uses the time to mumble the prayers of the Sabbath vigil. Finally, convinced by a servant, who has just come in from the storehouse, that don Ramiro won't return soon, he begs him to go ask permission for him to leave the buggy there until Sunday.

The servant shows surprise at the "Russian's" proposal; and incapable of understanding that it is because of religious reasons that the Jew can't return in his vehicle, he kindly offers to take him.

He wastes no words to convince him of the importance of the Sabbath, a day of absolute rest, when an Israelite can't even light a match, or tear a piece of paper.

Although hardly convinced, the servant leaves and returns immediately with the news that don Ramiro doesn't mind if he leaves his buggy in the stable, "if that's what he wants to do."

And Kopel Bender, after thanking him, starts out on foot toward Villa Mauricio. But now at the station at Lanus, he remembers the coffin he'd left at the house of the goy and goes back for it. To carry a coffin, he reasoned again—is not work. God couldn't see anything wrong with that.

Alone at night on the muddy road, the poor widower with the coffin on his back looks like a crazy musician fleeing the world with his violin.

→·←

Meanwhile at home, surprised by his delay, doña Deborah awaits his return. During the whole afternoon, the woman has been busy arranging the rooms. With the help of the other women she has the furniture taken from the bedroom, and the dead girl placed on the floor, and sheets put over the dresser mirror in the dining room, according to Jewish custom.

Yánquele caused her some trouble, for all day long he refused to eat even a mouthful. That is exactly what doña Deborah is thinking about now, satisfied that the boy is finally sleeping. But the truth is that Yánquele fooled her. After pretending to be asleep, he got up to sit at the table where he is now writing a letter to heaven.

In his eleven-year-old child's imagination, the idea that Betsy, who was so good, can deliver it to his mother seems perfectly logical.

He writes with that candor that is possible only for a child who knows the Bible well:

"My dear Mama: Betsy, who was as good as you, died last night. Through her, without Daddy knowing it, I plan to send you this letter. I pray that God will unite us all in heaven. Far from you and Betsy, I don't know how Daddy and I can live. It's possible that he's already dead, because it's nine o'clock on Friday night and he still hasn't returned. So if he doesn't come, I'm going to poison myself with matches, because…"

But, precisely at these words, sleep and fear overcome him. And with the matches in his pocket, he falls asleep with his head resting on the letter and the pencil in his hand.

That's how doña Deborah found him an hour and a half later, just as his father arrived, covered with mud and worn out by the grueling walk.

Anticipating who knows what disaster, the woman cannot restrain a shout of anguish: "*Oi vei is mir!* A disaster! My heart warned me!"

At that greeting, the man cannot overcome his astonishment.

"What? What's going on?" he exclaims, overcome.

"Nothing…Yánquele…"

"Yánquele?"

And the poor man, beside himself, runs toward the child.

"Yánquele! Yánquele!"

But seeing that he is asleep seated at the table with a letter and an overturned ink well, he suddenly has a horrible feeling. "Another misfortune?" he asks himself. And he tries to remove the letter without awakening Yánquele.

He can't manage it because the boy's elbow is resting on a corner of the paper. Then, making an effort, he manages to read over his head. When he gets to the last lines, he can no longer restrain a shout of pain:

"*Gott!!!*"

Yánquele awakens, startled: "Papa!"

And on realizing he's been found out, breaks into tears

Doña Deborah, a fatalistic Jew who hasn't stopped moaning for even a moment, between sobs repeats her refrain of "*Oi vei is mir!* Oh woe is me! What misfortune! I knew it in my heart!"

And the poor widower, amidst so many tears, not knowing what to ask the boy who has thrown himself at his feet to beg forgiveness, responds with a biblical quote that comes to his lips. Lifting him up, because he's fainted in his arms he again feels uneasily suspicious: "Did Yánquele have time to poison himself?"

Desperate with grief he puts the child to bed, begging doña Deborah to massage his eyes and temples so that he'll revive. Meanwhile, he looks for some sign on the table. When he doesn't find anything but the letter, he turns toward the woman with it: "The matches? Where are the matches?"

Doña Deborah raises her arms in a sign of ignorance.

"I left them on the table," she says with a husky voice. "Yánquele…"

At that moment, Yánquele comes to: "Water! Some water!"

And while doña Deborah goes for water, the poor widower overcome by grief, nervously crushes the letter until he reduces it to a small ball, and finishes by burning it in the lamp…now completely forgetful of the Sabbath and the heroic sacrifice he made to keep it even in the face of Betsy's death.

The Cross

by Samuel Glusberg

"Sonia!…Sonia!…Where the devil have you gone, child? Sonia!"

A Jewish woman calls her little girl in from the patio of her apartment.

It's five in the afternoon, and as it's midwinter, night is falling.

The woman—Sara is her name—has just finished blessing the Friday evening candles and she and the household are already entering the Sabbath.

"Sonia…Sonia…" Sara continues calling.

No one answers.

Finally irritated, tired of the cold, she enters the room.

"Have you seen your little sister? What a shameless girl!" she says in Spanish to Ruben—a nine-year-old who'd arrived a bit earlier from Hebrew school and was just having tea with his sailor cap pulled down to his ears.

And she adds in Yiddish: "It seems the devil's taken her; that child is always wandering around."

Ruben, busy having tea, doesn't answer her. But finally, when he finishes with a loud and noisy slurp, he raises his head—the name "General Belgrano" on his cap in gold letters. Then he answers:

"Sonia's probably with the Castro girls." And he shakes some crumbs off of his windbreaker.

"No, what a thought! She'd have heard me. I've been calling her for half an hour!"

But Ruben, realizing that his mother is exaggerating, opens the door and goes out in search of Sonia.

➤-◄

The boy returns after five minutes.

"I have gone," he says, "to all six apartments and haven't found her anywhere." Then he adds: "Doña Teresa told me she thought she'd seen her going off to school with her daughters."

"What!" Sara exclaims, surprised, "in school at this hour? Washing the seats with lemon oil again! That can't be!"

"Do you want me to go look for her, Mama?" Ruben proposes.

"No, I'll go," the woman says, and asks, "Where's my shawl?"

"Ah, in the other room," she answers herself, and goes to look for it.

She's back in an instant, covering her head and shoulders with a thick, checkered shawl, like the ones Jewish women bring from Russia.

"Take care of the baby, he's sleeping," she tells Ruben before going out. And at the door, she turns back to remind him to be careful with the candles.

⇥·⇤

A few minutes after doña Sara's exit, Reb Sujer, her husband, enters the house. He is small with a pointy chickpea-colored beard, black cap, blue overcoat and a bill collector's satchel under his arm.

"Good afternoon, Papa," Ruben greets him as he hides his pen knife and takes off his cap.

"Good Sabbath, son," the man answers as he enters and asks, "Where's mama?"

"She went to look for Sonia; she'll be right back."

In fact, Sara arrives shortly dragging Sonia behind her, a little eight-year-old redhead who is pouting and rubbing her eyes with her free hand.

"*Oi, vei is mir! Vei is mir!* A misfortune has befallen us; a disgrace!" doña Sara clamors, seating her round body in a chair and taking off her shawl.

"What's wrong, woman?" Reb Sujer turns to her frightened while Ruben opens his big eyes in surprise.

"*Oi Vei is mir! Vei is mir!*" clamors doña Sara even louder. "They've made us lose our child—my God what a misfortune!"

Because of her yelling, the baby in the next room wakes up and begins to cry.

"Ruben," his mother says, twisting her fingers and sighing, "go check on the baby."

Ruben obeys.

"*Oi vei is mir!* What a misfortune!" the woman wails again.

"But what is it, Sara, what is it?" Reb Sujer asks impatiently.

"They have converted our Sonia...*Vei is mir!* What a misfortune! My God, if you only knew!"

And while Sara loudly explains, without her husband understanding a word about the misfortune that has happened, the baby continues crying and wailing in the next room.

Finally, in answer to Ruben's insistent calls, the woman goes in to the next room.

"Straighten things out with your daughter," she says to her husband before leaving the room. "Teach her about becoming Christian with a good beating!"

Sonia, who was leaning on the edge of her seat, starts sobbing even more at this threat. Reb Sujer, a bit angry, his gray eyes moist and shining, looks at the menorah with its ritual candles and thinks about the sacred calm of the Sabbath. This thought makes him turn gently to his daughter.

"Where were you, little Sonia? What happened? Tell me about it," he says tenderly, drawing her to him.

Calmed by her father's voice, the child answers:

"Nothing, Daddy, nothing," still weeping.

"But where were you, little one? Where did Mama find you?"

"In school, Daddy. I went with Magda and Angelica, to religion class, and Mama came to get me out."

Having said this, Sonia breaks into tears again.

"Come now, that's enough tears. Tell me, what class? Where?"

"In school, Daddy, when the afternoon session is over, a priest comes to teach us catechism. All the girls go and I do too."

Reb Sujer buries his face in his hands.

"But don't you know," he shouts, "that a child of Israel cannot have anything to do with priests or the church? Who gave you permission to go?"

At this sudden change in her father, the little girl again bursts into tears. Then overcome by this paternal anger, she pleads in a tremulous little voice:

"Forgive me, Daddy, forgive me…I won't ever go again."

"The thing is you never should have gone! This is all we need! Your father is an Israelite, your mother is an Israelite, you and your brother are Israelites, all the family are Israelites…and you are going to be a Catholic! Whoever heard of such a thing?"

"I'm sorry," Sonia says, "I won't ever go again; but I get so bored at home. Doña Teresa's girls go there and leave me all alone. Doña Teresa lets them go…"

"Of course, because she's Catholic! But you have nothing to do with Jesus. Do you hear? I forbid you to go and that's the end of it…"

Because the little girl continues to cry, Reb Sujer softens his voice and promises to let her learn to play the piano so that she won't get bored.

At that, Sonia's little face lights up.

"And you'll send me to the conservatory, Daddy?"

"Yes, little one."

"To Saint Cecilia's?"

"Yes, my child."

"How wonderful, Daddy! How wonderful! I swear, I'll never go to religion class again!"

And to confirm her oath, Sonia pulls a small chain out from under her blouse and kisses the cross hanging there.

"Oh woe is me! Woe is me!"

Samuel Eichelbaum (1907-1967)

The son of immigrant Russian colonists, Samuel Eichelbaum was born in Dominguez in Entre Ríos and lived there until he left for Buenos Aires at the age of twenty-one. There, the young man who had never even completed elementary school educated himself by reading avidly and by frequenting literary conferences and *tertulias* (circles) where he met writers like Alberto Gerchunoff, who encouraged his literary inclinations and became a lifelong friend.

A translator and critic as well as an author, Eichelbaum published two collections of short stories: *Tormenta de Dios* (*Tempest from God*) and *El viajero inmóvil* (*The Unchanging Traveler*) but is best known for his work as a playwright.

Eichelbaum, who had no formal training in psychology, was fascinated by the complexities of human nature, man's capacity for good and evil, and the interactions of the human mind and heart. In his works he gently mocks the *porteño* (a person from the port city–i.e. Buenos Aires) attitude of superiority, and other human foibles like obsessiveness, hypocrisy, egoism, pride or arrogance. Rather than the action, it is the motivation behind the action that interests him and gives a universal quality to his work even when it is essentially Argentine in theme.

One of the few Argentine writers to treat ethnic and racial issues openly, Eichelbaum dealt with the problems of Jewish, Italian, and African heritage and identity in a number of his plays: *El judío Aarón* (*Aaron the Jew*), and *Nadie la conoció nunca* (*No One Ever Knew Her*) deal with Jewish protagonists; *El guapo de 90* (*The Brawler of the '90s*) and *Pájaro de Barro* (*Mud Bird*) with Italian immigrants, and *Dos Brasas* (*Two Embers*) presents a black protagonist.

"A Good Harvest," the story which follows is believed to be based on a real life incident. Some say it is the story of Eichelbaum's father, an unhappy immigrant farmer driven to desperate measures to relocate his family in the city.

A Good Harvest

by Samuel Eichelbaum

For four years now he had been working the two hundred acres of farm land they had given him when he arrived in Argentina from Russia. The Roschpina colony of Entre Ríos was the most cheerful one in the area, but this fact didn't affect his aversion to rural tasks. When he'd sailed for these lands, he'd agreed to accept the farm solely with the goal of getting to America and then later being able to dedicate himself to his trade. Never for a moment had he resigned himself to the idea of working the land. He didn't feel competent enough to do it, nor did he think the countryside was a suitable ambiance for his spirit. On the trip, because of unforeseen events he had to renounce, for the time being, his desire to settle in the city and dedicate his energies to mechanics, which was the trade that he loved as one loves his chosen work. It had been a trip so full of tragedy that it had totally exhausted him. Upon reaching port in Buenos Aires he no longer had any hopes, plans or desires. He never disagreed with his wife's suggestions, and she never dared to disagree with her mother.

So it was that Bernardo Drugova, to his mother-in-law's great and understandable surprise, without realizing it, turned into a bland and submissive son-in-law. When he didn't oppose his wife's desires, he indirectly obeyed his mother-in-law, since she always exercised total control over her daughter. He took possession of his farm with an indifference that was in visible contrast to the joy felt by other colonizers who had immigrated with him. Farm chores were completely alien to him, but because he had an extraordinary gift for learning manual labor, he very quickly became one of the most expert farmers in the area. Nevertheless, Drugova hated the land. When his wife gave him his first son, it reawakened in him more intensely than ever, his desire to live in the city. He expressed this to his wife and mother-in-law a number of times, and each time, he met with aggressive hostility from the old lady. Although his wife wasn't opposed exactly, neither did she share her husband's desires. Her attitude was one of indifference more from fear of her mother's anger, than from a desire to preserve the well-being she might enjoy where she happened to be. Drugova didn't pursue it. He didn't want to cause his mother-in-law's suffering, because of her age on the one hand, and her grumbling disposition on the other. He didn't believe that the stress that the move to Buenos Aires might cause the old woman would be a major and decisive factor in her health, as they wanted him to believe. Nevertheless, he sometimes thought, since both of them said this, it was better not to be too suspicious. Thus, Drugova rationalized and kept quiet. For the rest, the old woman knew how to argue skillfully when it came to upsetting her son-in-law's plans:

"Here you have bread and a roof," she would say, "nobly earned bread and an honorable roof. You have no reason whatsoever to reject the destiny you accepted when you started out."

"What would you do in the city? Work in your trade? Every city has a thousand men more competent than you in the same trade."

"It's important to think about the child," he would dare to argue. "We ought to give him a good education. I don't want him to be a laborer like me, ignorant like me."

"Educate him in what is good and honorable, which are the only things that matter. Let him learn to plow and sow the land and he will be good and honorable. Do you think, by chance, that he might become a rabbi? It would be a sin of vanity to aspire to that; a sin as great as if you aspired to make a scholar of him. Aspiring to grandeur is a sin unbecoming to poor people. My love as a grandmother is as great as your love as a father, but mine is sensible and humble. It doesn't need anything grandiose to nourish it. I don't demand anything from my grandson in order to love him."

The discussion would invariably come to an end, thanks to the discreet silence observed by Bernardo, who, although he felt violent sometimes, always managed to control himself.

For a long time, maybe a year, Drugova stopped talking about moving to Buenos Aires. To his wife and mother-in-law it seemed evident that he had abandoned the idea, a supposition doubly pleasing to them: because of the renunciation it implied in itself and the triumph it implied for them. Bernardo worked with such effort that they thought he had completely adapted to his situation. Moreover, the harvest promised to be bountiful enough to complete the well-being which reigned on Drugova's farm, where three enormous stacks, two of wheat and one of oats, stood like hills of gold. The little one, meanwhile, had grown strong and beautiful. The color in his eyes had finally settled and whether it was so or not, the fact was that he seemed to look at the fields with utter indifference, as if his progenitor had transmitted to him his hatred of the land.

In Roschpina, the neighbors had already closed deals for the sale of their harvest. Drugova hadn't done so yet. His wife, on several occasions, suggested that he get on with the threshing, fearing that prices would suddenly suffer a strong drop as sometimes happened.

"I'm not saying you should be in a hurry to sell it, but I do think you should ready the harvest. You might get a really good offer on condition of immediate delivery, and you would be obliged to refuse it, hurting yourself."

Bernardo, a man of few words, answered such exemplary and sensible observations with silence, communicating the sense of having heeded the advice they always carried.

One morning, long before daybreak, Drugova awakened. He looked around, probably in search of some filter of light that would help him guess the time. He found everything dark and decided to get up. First he checked on his wife, who was in her usual deep sleep, her dark and muscular arms outstretched, her thick dark hair undone. Two minutes later, from the door of his tool shed, he pensively observed a tenuous and whitish-blue sky announcing good weather. A full moon, pure, limpid and transparent, adorned everything. Slowly he walked toward the fields. The farm dogs saw their master and followed him, although he tried in vain to stop them. Drugova reached the first shock of wheat, magnificent, unmovable like a house on strong and deep foundations, passed his rough hand over some stalks, as if he wanted to caress them, and felt the soft, pleasant moisture of the dew. Then, almost as if without thinking, he extracted a box of matches from one of his pockets, lit one and put it as far as he could under the stack which seemed to shudder at the threat from the insignificant little flame. When the man was sure that his intentions were being carried out, he directed his steps toward the next one, scarcely fifty meters from the first, and repeated the operation. When this was done, he noticed that the first stack of wheat was giving off a thick blackish smoke that thinned out disappearing entirely at a few meters.

Bernardo started back in haste. Carefully, he undressed and got back into bed. About half an hour had passed when he heard the dogs barking furiously and immediately heard some knocking on one of the window shutters. It was Rogelio, a native servant from the neighboring farm, who had seen the smoke and then came at a gallop to give the warning.

"Don Bernardo, your wheat is on fire! They have set your wheat on fire!"

Drugova's wife woke with a start: "Bernardo, someone has set fire to our wheat."

"I heard," he replied in a dry tone of controlled violence, and started to get dressed while his wife jumped out of bed after thanking Rogelio.

When they went out to the patio, everything was already burned. Both stacks had turned into flames—unattractive because the dawn, which was just now breaking, took away any beauty that might have come from the fire. The woman observed the voracity of the flames; her eyes flooded with tears. As soon as Bernardo appeared, she said in a scarcely audible tone:

"By the time you get there with water, there won't even be a grain left!"

Beside the barn gate to the left, the squalid figure of the servant stood out.

"It seems to have been burning for a while. I rode bareback and came at a gallop as soon as I saw it." And after a silence he added, "How could it have happened, I wonder?"

In his fractured language, Drugova managed to say that this could not be an accident but rather an intentional act. Rogelio commented:

"Can there be Christians so mean spirited?"

A month later, with what he got from the oats (it was the only stack spared from the disaster), Drugova, his wife, his mother-in-law, and his little son, all moved to Buenos Aires.

Bernardo Verbitsky (1907-1979)

Born in Buenos Aires, the son of Russian immigrants, Verbitsky described his family's struggles to establish their new life in an autobiographical novel entitled *Hermana y sombra* (*Sister and Shadow*), 1977. Although he earned a degree in medicine, the young man soon embarked on a career as an author. As a writer, he was greatly influenced by the realism of Russian authors like Gorki, Dostoyevsky and Tolstoy (whom he read in the original Russian), and by the social and political consciousness of the "Boedo group" of Argentine authors with whom he associated. His themes and characters often reflect his personal experiences and Jewish consciousness. With insight, moral intensity, and a keen eye for significant detail, Verbitsky writes more about character types than about events in novels like *Villa Miseria también es América* (*A Slum is America Too, 1957*), or *Enamorado de Joan Báez* (*In Love with Joan Baez*, 1979). He makes no attempt to solve the social or moral problems he describes, but simply presents them in a direct, journalistic style that allows the readers to make their own judgments. Considered the "chronicler of life in the port city," he infused the city into his works by frequently referring to specific streets and places and making frequent allusions to actual political events and people, current stars in cinema, tango, and radio, popular movies and music, radio news, and headlines of the day. This artful construction of milieu helps the reader better understand his characters' problems whether they are immigrants, young professionals, or adolescents.

In the story that follows, "The Flaw," from *A Pesar de todo* (*In Spite of Everything*, 1979), a parody of Hitler's persecution of the Jews, he abandons his usually direct style and uses long, convoluted sentences to describe how the discovery of a minor physical "imperfection" led to the branding, isolation, and eventual extermination of those who had it by an authority called "El Absoluto" ("The Absolute Being"). Frequently alternating between simple narration in past tense and vivid description in the present, Verbitsky achieves an effect of escalating horror. "The Visit" from a much earlier work, *Café de los angelitos y otros cuentos porteños* (*Little Angels' Café and Other Porteño Stories*, 1949) is one of his few humorous tales.

By the end of his career, Verbitsky had written fourteen novels, several collections of short stories, and a collection of poems. He had also served for many years as editor of *Davar*, a Jewish journal published by the Sociedad Hebráica Argentina (Argentine Hebrew Society).

The Flaw

by Bernardo Verbitsky

For Carlos Rojas

$\mathcal{A}$ scientist who has not been identified, but who belonged to the inner circle of *El Absoluto*'s[1] consultants, had been informed by one of his teams, the anatomicopathological one, that in two autopsies, when dissecting a foot, a fusion of the first two metatarsal bones had been discovered. This worried the scholar, who, faced with further verification of new cases, informed *El Absoluto* of the novelty and of the concern it caused him. This anomaly wasn't revealed by any exterior symptom, nor did it cause any difficulty in walking, but in his opinion, was verified by a series of secret experiments which produced apparently irrefutable conclusions. *El Absoluto* proposed to the scholar a theory that dealt with a process of morphological involution, a process to which it was, of course, necessary to pay attention. The initial manifestation was small, and didn't cause the affected individual any discomfort, but one of the goals of *El Absoluto* was the attainment of total physical perfection by all individuals—a perfection measured precisely by norms the scientist had determined as a result of his studies on the aboriginal Kanta race (the country's ancient population), to which he had dedicated a good part of his life. All this confirmed intuitions that had once been considered obscure and enigmatic by *El Absoluto*. As his ideologues explained, it wasn't a matter of returning to that primitive civilization, but rather of finding in its aesthetic norms the initial energy that would help shorten the steps necessary to attain and exceed the present human condition and form a new prototype capable of fulfilling the potential envisioned by

[1] El Absoluto: The Absolute Being.

El Absoluto. Although the deformity discovered was minor, it was nonetheless significant since it could possibly compromise the attainment of his established goals by getting passed on to a greater number of persons as was shown by complicated and precise forecasting calculations. For some time, the topic didn't go beyond a few closed scientific circles, but as the significance of the malformation created problems in projecting the regime's philosophy, and had an even more direct tie to the reality of sociological structures that might need readjusting, it wasn't long before references to it filtered out to less exclusive sectors. This in turn gave way to rather confused conjectures, since the unconfirmed news was extended to groups with less scientific preparation, so that assumptions were confused with rumors. The commoners had very little idea about what was happening with their metatarsals, and the first mention of them awakened a certain curiosity about anatomy which suddenly became a discipline whose outlines were unclear, but that began to take on some importance in conversation. Doctors began to be consulted and had to have special meetings to determine what course to follow. Since the strange defect couldn't be distinguished by mere sight, or even by a superficial examination of the foot or by feeling it externally, it was necessary to turn to radiology, which implied exhausting state-owned x-ray services. Fundamentally, the cause for this public curiosity and the reasons for satisfying it were unknown. When this concern reached a degree of uneasiness increased by strange stories, and the physicians consulted the authorities, they received the order to calm the population by denying any reason for the kind of uneasiness that was spreading. The doctors' response seemed to calm the people, but in another way, it helped keep interest alive in the two little bones whose existence hadn't mattered to anyone until then. Despite the fact that no one knew of any official notice of the significance of the mysterious fusion, rather than calming spirits, this seemed to excite them subtly. And we say *subtly*, since a change in attitude had occurred in the people so that, if at first they spoke of the matter, later they preferred to omit it from their conversation, which obviously caused an increase in internal tension—since it was now necessary to call it that—creating even greater malaise because it was hidden and imprecise.

It so happened that an indeterminate number of people, by surreptitious means, through friends, or relatives, managed to get X rays of their metatarsals and took them to doctors who were friends or members of the nuclear family, and, according to the accounts circulating, one percent of those examined showed that kind of calcification. According to certain accounts leaked by the exclusive circles where all this was carefully studied, the fusion implied a biological inferiority, whose significance no one knew how to evaluate for the moment. Nevertheless, a contradictory interpretation soon spread with unexpected impetus, converting those with this characteristic into privileged persons, as if they were select and chosen by destiny, whose designs no one dared interpret, since such speculations were the prerogatives of *El Absoluto*, and his alone. It was also he who decided if the public should or shouldn't be uneasy, but in this case, at least, his control could not be total, since of course, even though people knew that it exceeded their rights, they began to hide their feelings of fear. The time had already passed when people jokingly told one another that they had five metatarsal bones, giving the statement the character of an amusing bit of news and an oddity at the same time. Now people began to look at their own feet and those of their neighbors' with a feeling of distrust, as if an obscure danger emanated from them that might affect themselves or someone else. There was a time when tension diminished and the causes of it seemed to be forgotten, since other worries concerned the nation according to the calculated gyrations to which it was permanently subjected, but suddenly everyone received a peremptory order to have an X ray of his feet, or rather, it was communicated to everyone that in his place of work—in factories and offices for laborers and employees, in schools and universities for students, teachers and professors, in barracks and bases for soldiers and officers—x-ray equipment would be installed that would take care of this universal foot catastrophe. Women would have to go to their husbands' or fathers' workplace if they themselves were not employed. Not even old people or children of any age were exempt from the X rays (it was established later that this examination would take place in the hours immediately following birth); indications were given in the instructions everyone received as to how this demand (that certainly couldn't be said to take anyone by surprise) was to be fulfilled. In the inaccessible circles where the country's highest decisions were made, the preliminary studies (conducted conscientiously and slowly without haste to avoid any margin of error) had been considered concluded. These conclusions were to be announced in the form of a radiographic census, which was to begin without delay within twenty-four hours. It was the usual state procedure: a detailed study in the silence of scientific offices, an analysis of their conclusions, and then the abrupt applications of the measures decided upon without possibility of appeal or revision.

Fifteen days later every person in the country, tagged according to the dictum of the X rays, received a card on which the results were noted: yellow for those who had the fusion and green for the rest. For the time being the cards were to be presented at every occasion, even those for which documents weren't normally needed. Then, almost immediately, another decree was handed down. *El Absoluto,* to maintain the spiritual cohesion of his people, subjected them to carefully incremented steps that acted like galvanizing charges of electricity effectively attaining flexible and unanimous responses from the national body. Thus he decreed military mobilization, and in a lightning swift attack without even a battle, his troops achieved the annexation of a small neighbor united to us by ties of origin, race, and language. The majority of the nation scarcely noticed that yellow cardholders were excluded from this mobilization, scarcely noticed because they were a minority, less than one percent, but naturally, those who were part of this minority took note of the circumstance. I can testify as to the state of their feelings because I myself—I might as well say it—had also received the yellow rectangle. Personally I preferred it, because I totally lacked any warlike spirit, but I could not avoid the disappointment one feels when being left out of something that others participate in, a feeling that was accentuated, when, even though there was nothing to stop me, I could not even share spiritually in the great festivities celebrating the annexation to which I had not contributed, aside from my reservations on the question. Many people—friends with green cards—had shown the same reticence as I, but later let themselves be dragged along sincerely by the reigning climate of euphoria, a happening that surely aggravated my feeling of isolation.

This began to create new relationships among those of us having yellow cards, producing unforeseen closeness among those who had not had any previous contact because of differences in life-styles, status and tastes. A vague indeterminate compulsion created bonds of uneasiness and expectation too, since until then, this sense of being grouped together hadn't been felt, although it now developed naturally. It's a fact that many of those who had received the yellow card even walked with greater difficulty as a result of observing their feet so much. Their depression and irritation caused by feelings of being observed by everyone else who, one shouldn't forget, comprised the immense majority, contributed to our withdrawal so that our relationships with them began to shift imperceptibly until they changed completely. We felt ourselves excluded from those calls and exhortations to a great future that were part of the daily dialogue between *El Absoluto* and his disciplined nation. Until this moment it has been difficult to guess, despite the pessimism of some, what importance or influence the simple (otherwise unbelievable) fact that two of our metatarsal bones were fused through a caprice of nature, unknown until then, could have on our immediate role in the society we belonged to, and to which we had given, until then, our best efforts and deliberately or otherwise, enriched with our activity. Moreover, as a distinguished scientist respected until then by the entire nation, but now in my group, suggested the recently discovered characteristic had probably always existed and the fact that no one had ever noticed that it caused any differences, proved that it lacked importance. This thesis was not at all echoed officially, and sure enough, once the cards were in use the idea of a difference began to take hold here and there. An indefinable tension was born between the two groups and began to have consequences, since many of us became increasingly less natural even in our simplest of acts.

A recent military exploit of *El Absoluto's* suddenly worsened our situation, confirming our fears, since it was simultaneously ordered that the possessors of yellow cards were to be separated from their families. This was accomplished in just one night, a night in which the songs of those departing for the war certain of victory contrasted with the sinister silence amidst which we were all dragged half-asleep from our homes. Although we and our families showed the same discipline in controlling our emotions as those who carried out those implacable orders, this didn't keep our suffocated emotions from weighing doubly upon us. It was evident that a new era was beginning, one in which, because of something totally inexplicable we were set apart from the community we had belonged to until then. We feared for our families as much as they feared for us. The farewells were heart-rending, but kept to ourselves for we were all trying not to increase our mutual pain.

When they took us away there were a few words of explanation, or rather an insinuation that new studies and new experiments would be undertaken to isolate this incomprehensible fusion with the apparently obvious intention of remedying the flaw in our favor. This attributed a dangerousness to it that I was just beginning to see, although not fully comprehend. We found out then that *El Absoluto* had had a brilliant inspiration: in the conquered territories he ordered investigations into the existence of the anomaly, which, in fact, was shown to exist there in even larger proportions, thus testifying to his notable foresight. What happened to us in our confinement is known and there's no need to repeat it. Our families had been left pretty much alone meanwhile, except for the distrust that encircled them because of their ties to those of us who were different. But when military stagnation occurred on some of the fronts, and continued longer than anticipated, and when there were difficulties in advancing, *El Absoluto* fell into that trancelike state in which he revised his great decisions; then he understood that the families of those who were confined exercised a malignant influence from which it was necessary to protect the community. As usual, his analysis culminated in brilliant synthesis. This time the families had to be jointly segregated with those who possessed these cards. This would suffice, he told his people (who were obviously disconcerted by the increasing resistance coming from recently attacked countries), to retake the road to victory and its great objectives. In the capital of one of the occupied nations the order was given to enclose one of its neighborhoods with a raised wall and all those singled out by their X rays were taken there. With the same efficiency with which his orders were always carried out, we were quickly isolated. When those who belonged to our group—the invisible fusion had generated a category that was nonexistent before—began to flow in from other places, our living conditions worsened a great deal, although a short time ago we had thought that this was impossible. Through conversations with our new brothers in misfortune—how ordinary things recover their value in the most serious of situations!—we understood that *El Absoluto* had foreseen that the X rays would be powerful allies in subjecting the invaded countries to his rule, because despite losing their national liberty, those who didn't have yellow cards would feel secure. Thus, he broke their spirit of resistance, since they somehow came to terms with these new rulers who seemed to reserve the severest of restrictions for those in the other sector. While not entirely clear, this provided a glimpse into something. Out into the darkness in which we lived concerning the reasons for our sentence which in and of itself undoubtedly implied suffering the mysterious modification of the metatarsals, our minds reached for any sign whatsoever that could orient us, but this was also forgotten as the conditions of our lives became increasingly intolerable. The union with our families had been terrible because of the condition we all found ourselves in after the various medical and surgical experiments we had to endure. We were subjected to feeding and fasting, to various tests in which they measured our reactions, to various atmospheric pressure with minute diminutions in percentages of oxygen and nitrogen; even our resistance to various substances injected into the blood stream was tested. (At one time we speculated that they were trying to find out if the fusion, far from signifying an inferiority, might not represent some unexpected biological progress.) We preferred not to talk about what happened to us during this time, and a kind of shame distanced us, although our physical appearance made all pretense useless and impossible. But always worse than our privation, punishment, and desperation, was our sorrow for our children. We had brought them into a world of horror and we didn't have any answers to all the innumerable *whys* reflected in their eyes, although actually, they never asked questions nor held us responsible for our common fate. Looking at them, our impotence became pure desperation. After developing a quick friendship with Professor Balko, a native of the country where we were confined, I learned some details about what had happened to them once the bombs of *El Absoluto*'s planes completely wiped out all military resistance. There was a period in which total chaos reigned. The conquerors did not hurry to impose order. The previous infrastructure was totally destroyed and nothing, absolutely nothing, from any kind of governing to basic services (including running water and electricity) was functioning. It was necessary to eat, but delivery trucks couldn't get to the capital, since most of them were destroyed, or lacked the fuel to make them run. The streets were rivers of blood strewn with the bodies of military men, civilians and horses whose guts were split open. In the frightful chaos where mothers searched for their children and infants sought out their mothers, the worst thing of all was, nevertheless, hunger. The country was conquered, and became broken, disjointed, before abandoning itself to its fate. The soldiers to whom a few days before the people had entrusted the defense of their lives and the nation, returned from the front in small groups, mud-smeared, wounded, with red-stained bandages, but their spiritual state was even more disastrous than their appearance. Civilians besieged them with anxious questions for general or specific explanations and news about their relatives. They didn't understand or know anything, they had scattered out from under a hurricane of fire and steel, and an idiotic look was the only response they could give. The people, impelled by hunger, cut pieces of meat off of the dead horses.

The victors' first manifesto was read in proclamations providing information about a registration in which everyone should enroll, stating that a foot X ray would be one of the elements to be included henceforth among the documents necessary to obtain a card assuring a daily food ration. They proceeded as they had in other conquered territories. The anxiety everyone felt in submitting to the examination was matched by that of the invaders as they set up the necessary x-ray stations. Meanwhile, the more enterprising and daring persons managed to bring some potatoes in from the country and distributed them, but since there was no fire or water to cook with, they were eaten raw. The majority of people received a green card, while a minority found with some amazement that they were marked for yellow ones. Through an assistant at the x-ray examination, I was able to find out what the difference meant, but the explanation rather than clarifying anything, only increased my confusion. He didn't spend much time trying to give me an answer, because just then the soldiers started installing stoves in the streets, which was rather fortunate given the unexpected cold of an early autumn. Long lines formed for soup and bread. Some patriots dared to ask people not to lose their dignity and not to accept anything from the enemy, who—it was evident—was expelling yellow card holders from the hungry lines. This was one of the first indications of the disadvantage of the card. Those who had green cards instead of waiting for the call, fearful that there wouldn't be enough food, began to clean out the lines on their own initiative, anticipating the presence of the new military. Note that as long as the soup bowls were being filled, the victors were filming the scene, but we soon learned that when the filming ended, the kitchens disappeared. For some days, this evened out our situation, regardless of the color of our cards.

This was in the days immediately following the defeat, but let us return to the period following our confinement behind the high wall. Not everyone there fears or resigns himself to the invaders' control. A girl of sixteen slips out into the evening and rips an official notice from the wall. Then a soldier kills her with a bullet to the head. The young girl's body remains lying there. The insecurity of the people increases minute by minute. Suddenly a cordon of armed military encircles the area, arrests all the men, loads them on to trucks, and transports them back to the conquering country for labor. They break into houses at night and do whatever they want, sadistic behavior that goes on senselessly against both men and women. A woman commits suicide with her seventeen-year-old daughter whom they had violated in her presence. And alongside the terror, hunger spreads. The people, deranged, think and dream about food, one only hears about bread, meat, chocolate. The hungry are delirious, they seem to feed on memories.

A new order decrees that the yellow cards must always be exhibited: no one—it is warned—should hide them. (The wife of a doctor who didn't wear this distinguishing card visibly was jailed and forbidden to use the bathroom for three days. They returned her to her home with peritonitis.) We estimated that we numbered half a million concentrated there. The fact that this mass of people had been made equal because of their yellow cards did not preclude all kinds of differences among those who comprised it, and one of the things that intrigued me was how naturally this new bond came about, because until then only a spiritual affinity could unite or separate me from others. Now the treatment we received from the invader made us equal, hunger made us equal, and this distinguished us definitively from the possessors of the green cards who, as we soon learned, rebuilt the normalcy of their lives outside the wall helped by accommodations from the conqueror who, despite causing them such harm, permitted them to bury their dead and go on living, working, procuring food. Each hour that passed taught us that *we* could expect nothing more. Scarcely were they imprisoned, than the most energetic men organized workshops where artisans, shoemakers, carpenters and tailors could work for themselves and engage in the frequent barter that helped them live. Others dedicated themselves to creating a flow of contraband with the other side of the wall. Thus, they managed to bring in some food clandestinely, although many paid for this with their lives. But the alternative was to die of hunger. Great efforts were made to maintain the appearances of normal life. The musicians formed a band. Poetry and song recitals were organized. There were some people with real talent like a very promising eighteen-year-old soprano and a violinist of twenty. This kept morale up and distracted us from the hunger which was possible to stave off a bit but not forget. Certainly if people hadn't been dying of starvation in the streets the place would have exploded from congestion, since new arrivals with yellow cards came from all over as *El Absoluto's* conquests continued. They arrived in herds like cattle. Those who came from a place where the invasion had met greater resistance arrived ragged and skeletal. They told how on the road a doctor had invited the most exhausted people to get on board a cart that brought up the rear of the column. Women, old people and children were the ones let on. Then the cart fell behind, shots were heard, and later the empty vehicle caught up to them. But those who were lost along the route this way were far fewer than those who survived and made it.

We knew that when the influx of new arrivals was interrupted it was because things weren't going so well for *El Absoluto*. But things weren't improving for us either. The smallest children cry from hunger and there is nothing to give them but rotten potatoes. People wander through the streets where there is always a meeting of specters who suddenly disappear as if scattered by magic, but some remain behind, confused. From the roofs an assassin whom everyone nicknamed Frankenstein, accompanied by a number of armed buddies, takes aim and shoots everyone in sight. These are some of the experiences that followed the medical tests. They aren't the only ones. The military officers burst into the midst of families milling about the streets, striking tremendous blows with the butts of their rifles. Those who back away or try to avoid the blows, are shot. At other times they fire from automobiles roaring by at full speed, gunning down those who don't get out of the way in time. "They're getting bad news," we would say, but this didn't mean that we had any cause for hope. There weren't enough funeral cars to pick up all the bodies that blocked traffic. Those who live near the jail hear shots all night and in the morning see the blood reaching the street. In this slaughterhouse there was initially a novelty that caused some confusion. Trucks would arrive with food and transform various empty spots into grocery stores and they obliged us to act as if we were buying the things that were there, and then removed them as soon as the filming focused on others who would repeat the same farce. Everyone hid in their houses to avoid participating in such a spectacle, but they were pulled out by force and half-conscious they still had to comply with orders, mocking our very suffering and the hunger of our children who were dying in front of this luxurious exhibition of breads, cold cuts, and all kinds of nourishment. Under threat of death we had to compose ourselves. After being expelled from these transitory grocery stores we fought over scraps with the dogs whose growling seemed to say: "we have more rights." A man arrives, hesitates before the shrinking pile that others are examining. He decides to gather some potato peels, wraps them in paper and turns away, but almost immediately stops and devours them. Faced with starvation, the suicides and the daily assassinations committed by brutal jailers (who suddenly break into our homes, beating and killing anyone who looks out) lose their importance. What was death, and what was life? Balko told me: "Only one thing comforts me, that I don't have anyone else in the world, no wife, no child; I'm not sorry for those who die but for those who see them die."

The children were heroic. Gangs in which no one was more than twelve years old, climbed walls, dug under walls, hid under large trucks to get to the living side. Because on the other side of the wall was the side of life for those with green cards, who didn't know about us. The children who managed to get out put potatoes or whatever they could find in the lining of their burlap rags. If they were discovered, they were killed, but there was nothing to eat at home and they risked their lives to save the lives of their parents, who had lost their fighting spirit. One six-year-old child would sing a happy song, dance and wave his little hands in order to get a crust of bread for himself and his parents. Across from us, near the wall, the jailers discovered four kilos of potatoes in the house. They arrested the evildoers responsible—

four children (the oldest was eleven)—and even though there were still people incredulous enough to doubt they'd go to such extremes, they condemned them to death. They erected four gallows in the center of the plaza and at a set hour, before the frightened crowd, strung the rope around the neck of each one. But the public official who'd pronounced the sentence hadn't arrived yet and he had to be present for this exemplary punishment to be carried out. They had to wait an hour, time in which the parents experienced mixed hope and despair, still hoping for a pardon while looking at their children from afar. Finally they were hung when he arrived. The next day the same official, upon learning what had happened during the delay, ordered the detention of some hundred people to whom he had delivered a speech in the same place where they had gathered. He announced that they were condemned to death for their bad behavior the previous day: they had wept at seeing the execution of the four children. Their immediate slaughter with machine guns confirmed the belief of those few who foresaw a plan of total extermination underway. But the people were slow to realize this, even though the hunting continued in the streets, and they loaded everyone into trucks later, and it was never known if anyone ever came back.

After a rather long period of time, new arrivals came. Subjected to the usual reception, they were relieved of the few things they were carrying, but were given receipts for all of them. These new arrivals believe that they'll be able to wait here for the end of the war and the nightmare. A few nights later jailers break into the places assigned to them and hitting them, beating them with rifle butts, take them away, almost naked. Some time earlier the artisans and clandestine merchants had disappeared and it was thought that they had gone to work in large shops whose creation had been announced, but we were upset by the news that they were taken to the East, where they could find work. Very shortly afterwards, nevertheless, tailor shops, projectile factories and shoe stores were set up where those who could still practice some trades were taken. These were considered the privileged ones. They were happy with their work cards because they were assured that they would stay there. The same guarantee was extended to their wives and children, as was the crust of bread which was their only pay. But, what of those who had not been employed? They waited uneasily when powerful automobiles burst into the streets revving their motors crushing or scattering like dummies everyone they found in their way. A bad premonition for the unemployed. Now they are talking about transferring fifty thousand to the East. And even before they were expected, large trucks did in fact arrive to be loaded, always for trips to that unknown place in the East; five thousand people a day, after having first been persecuted and hunted down arbitrarily. They leave only those who have work cards, but even their condition worsens suddenly since it is established that only those who are less than thirty-five can work in those shops and they—necessary as a work force to meet production plans—are the only ones sheltered by any guarantee. Meanwhile there is a noticeable increase in the ferocious struggle to get rid of the rest. Their relatives lose all privileges, their families are constantly torn apart by separations, assassinations and kidnappings that give variety to the tithe of grayish and routine hunger that continues filling the streets with dead, the majority of the garbage. It was commonplace to discover a loved one or a friend on a pile of trash covered with paper. We recognized them with no emotion. It was a time in which the living envied the dead. Anyone who did not have a work card knew that the end could come at any minute. Mothers could only contemplate helplessly the way they assassinated the children before their very eyes. They tried not to separate themselves from the smallest ones. They hid them in their clothing when they went into the workshops, where they had to manage to hide them again under the vigilance of the jailers. Older children even hid themselves in funeral cars where they spent the day until their mothers gathered them up at night, despite the fact that in doing so they were in more danger than among the cadavers. The killings occurred at any time. People without work cards have to hide in cellars, niches, attics. Where scarcely five fit, fifteen crowd in. Walled up alive, they are asphyxiated. When the persecutors discover these refugees, they shoot to kill everyone inside. They search furiously. Many children are thrown from upper storey windows. The children lie dead in pools of blood. I have seen with my own eyes how a man in uniform picked up one of these children who was still alive, broke his spinal column over his knees and tossed him as far as he could. Seeing these things, I went on saving my own life. But in what a world. I would hide myself in the corner of a high-rise building at the end of a very narrow corridor where it seemed impossible that anyone could squeeze in. The rooms were full of debris, ripped mattresses, battered and broken furniture, tattered clothing, braids of hair, letters and photographs scattered about. On the porches were bed-springs, rusty buckets and dented pans. There is no electricity or water, all the drainage sewers are broken. The only available way to build a fire is by breaking up the furniture. Splashes and pools of coagulated blood are everywhere, the same with human excrement, since all sanitary services have been cut off since the day when a frightful massive bombardment marked the beginning of the invasion. And flies. Swarms of flies everywhere, buzzing tirelessly and aggressively, entering your nose and mouth. There is no way to get rid of them, they seem to be the true owners of the place sharing even every piece of bread, if we happen to find one.

In the workshops work goes on, but it's as if some of the foremen do not have orders about how long the labor force has to last. The boss of one of the workshops, Wuga, beats the sewing women with the whip he always carries until they bleed. Underfed and exhausted, it wasn't at all unusual for one of them to fall asleep while working. I have seen Wuga come up and beat a woman's head against her work table until she passed out, and then, to make her revive—laughing at his own procedure—drag her by her hair along the floor until she opened her eyes and came to. Often he forced the women to work naked in order to assure—he would say—that they were not hiding any pieces of cloth under their clothing. He undressed the women on any pretext. In order to disinfect them, for example. Once he sprinkled them with some chemical substances and later kept them naked the whole night, standing and sleepless. At dawn they were taken to the bath, but before letting them enter they were kept outdoors, exposed to the raw weather waiting for who knew what. It began to rain and they stayed there hours in the rain. Half died of pneumonia, some had more luck and died sooner. A group of women was to arrive the next day, and as there wasn't room for all of them, they had decided to make room that way. The women were em-ployed in all kinds of tasks. Some had to sort the clothing, overcoats and shoes of those who had been taken to the East. They didn't come back but their clothing did. Among the smaller garments, some mothers recognized those of their own children from whom they had been separated. One of them found her little girl's handkerchief and swallowed it in order to make something that had belonged to her little girl a part of herself.

Suddenly the rumor spread that new medical experiments would be starting, since *El Absoluto*, in one of those feverish dreams with which he faced his difficulties, intuited that the people with fused metatarsals might have greater resistance in carrying out certain warlike missions, he issued an order to test this. This made us suddenly remember the whole process that had brought us to this situation. We were there because we had been given yellow cards. We had been given yellow cards because of the peculiar calcification of our feet. We had all completely forgotten that. Of course remembering it at this point did not add anything to our insensibility. One of the experiments consisted of putting twenty-five men into a train car in which the atmospheric pressure could be increased or decreased. The object was to observe the effect produced as the air began to thin as it does in greater heights, since they were trying to find out the maximum height from which a parachutist could be launched. The suffocation, asphyxiation, oppression and palpitation, converted the closed coach into a coffin where they were buried alive. Many died in the experiment because of pulmonary and cerebral hemorrhages. Those who survived all spit blood, turned purple, and were slow in recovering their speech. They also analyzed the effects of immersion in frozen water until the subjects became unconscious. They measured their temperatures and each time it went down a degree they extracted blood from their throats where it was still fluid and tested its makeup. The lowest temperature that a live body would reach was 19°C, but the majority died at 26° or 25°. When they removed them from the frozen water they tried to revive them using different sources of heat: ultraviolet rays, hot water, electrotherapy, or animal heat. Animal heat was provided by the women of the Pleasure Division at the service of *El Absoluto*'s soldiers and it is said that he came to see how the body of a frozen man was placed between two of these women who surely from the beginning were selected from among those with yellow cards. I was a friend of one of those who provided animal heat. She died three days later, but I had the opportunity to talk with her for a few minutes and she confided to me something of the horror, which in spite of her pity, she felt alongside that icy cadaver. The end of three human beings, even with fused metatarsals: the final destiny of two women torn from whatever part of the continent, and converted into prostitutes, and an unknown man who ended up going to his death in a tub of frozen water, unable to be resuscitated between two bodies grounded in horror.

Meanwhile, as had been announced, five thousand people went to the East in trucks daily. One afternoon, I found myself among the thousands gathered in the plaza near the station, waiting to be loaded into wagons. I had been able to postpone that moment but finally fell into the raid in which they broke my left shoulder with one blow from the butt of a gun. We've been there for two days waiting our turn—there's a scarcity of trains—and I feel weakness from the wound more than pain, and the rest of my body is cramped, numb. It's almost impossible to fall down there because of the crowding, but it's also impossible to move. Everyone there is hungry, of course, but now only thirst is torturing them, but if my feverish neighbor on the right becomes confused and thinks that we're waiting for them to serve us food and drink, I know that's not so and I'm planning to bend over to somehow scoop up and drink the dirty water running along the ground. But the problem is that if anyone bends over he's shot. At any rate, the jailers beat those closest to them, when they note the least movement in that crowd of specters in the darkness of this cold afternoon, they shoot randomly without taking aim. I am immobile, stiff. Standing in my own excretions running down my legs and drenching my skin horribly, and reaching from the ground, to my ankles, I can't even try to move. Yesterday the stench made me ill. Today I don't smell anything. The stench is part of what keeps me standing. Perhaps I myself am the stench. I seem to see Balko nearby, but I know that it is not him, Balko died a few weeks ago. I recognize Reson a few meters to my right and when I turn my face away, since it displeases me to see him, I catch Lafe's glance, but I don't turn away from him and even send him a greeting, or think I do. I seem to note an imperceptible response. It's curious that I can be so near them consigned to the same shipment, although this is less certain, since the capacity of the wagons could separate us. Nothing surprised me so much at the beginning, or rather, nothing angered me so much as this equalization based on the metatarsals. Reson always struck me as a gross minded, petty little politician whose ambition to be in on everything I had always considered unjustified and in Lafe I had never seen anything but a proclivity toward the stupidest word games which, by their nature, appeared ingenious to him. I think that they didn't like me either, perhaps because I never hid my opinions. But the fusion of the two little bones in my left foot had linked me to them, more than any other element capable of bringing human beings together. I admit that literally I have disdained them, something I don't regret, since it couldn't have been otherwise (just as Balko was inevitably meant to be my friend). Now I don't respect them any more than before, but I know what they have suffered and I feel sorry for them; they on their part, perhaps just think that adversity has made me less proud. It's all the same. If anything matters now, it isn't even knowing how long they'll keep us here, but rather this twisting that stirs my bowels. But why think about this twisting? Why oppose it? What I remember now is that some years ago I wanted to write a short, fantasy novel starting out in a realistic style about a group of people who work in a medical laboratory; it would have permitted me to assemble a group of men and women, technicians, chemists, bacteriologists, pharmacists, doctors, and pathologists when they are about to begin their day's work on the morning the administration is to decide about their raises and promotions. Through references to each one of the characters a sketch is made of their rivalries, jealousies, professional and other more intimate envies, arising from episodes of living and working together in the institution. N is annoyed by the simple prospect of finding himself in the laboratory with F whom he doesn't like or respect, but whom, he already knows, is going to be his boss in the next reorganization. R is furious, because after having vacillated a lot about making C his lover, he realizes when he finally makes up his mind, that the same person who took away his former co-worker, also got her first. He thinks he has no recourse but to ask for a transfer, where he'll have to put up with some other mediocre person and place himself in line with those striving for merit, but it's all the same to him, and moreover it seems fair: he doesn't consider himself better than others and he despises and hates himself as much as he does them. In his anger, he keeps in mind a constant: there were three of them and two were always united against the third. And he thought that in the millions of offices and work places around the city this pattern was repeated. When a woman entered into it, it caused a different kind of tension. R and F meet by chance in the subway and try to get some information out of him about the raises and promotions waiting for them. In the doorway, one of them, R, reflects that his interest in the work that once made him so happy is disappearing in this whirlwind of confusion. In the elevator he meets the young C which increases his discomfort. He is uncertain what attitude to adopt and when he finally attempts a smile of greeting, a terrible light blinds everyone and a terrible shaking and cracking bewilders them. At this moment there is the blast of an explosive that is being used on the city for the first time and for a fraction of a second it illuminates the abyss of R's repugnance and resentment, which he confuses with the notion that this is the apocalypse, the end of the world. It is a definitive weapon and does not leave a single survivor. Those who love one another, those who hate one another, those who despise one another, are all dead ten seconds later.

Why didn't I ever write it? I ask myself as a formidable shove moves the heap of partially hardened excrement which held me to the ground. They are taking us to the train. Shouted orders, shoves, shots, were moving this filthy and compact mass of absent beings. When they had to move, some fell never to rise again. We were not a herd of animals but a thick mass of worms, and so we climbed up into the wagons. I slept from exhaustion but I awakened immediately. I had a great dream, it turned out that on going to look at my card I had discovered that it was not yellow but green, it had all been an incredible error, and now, happily…The wagon is full and still they keep entering. We are encrusted one onto another. A child licks the cold sweat from his mother's face, since there's no other liquid for his thirst. At my side, someone gasps desperately because of lack of air. A woman who had the fortune to be able to save a jar has the child in her arms urinate so that she can give him something to drink. Now I don't see anyone around me. Someone whispers a word in my ear, whose meaning I don't know, something like Tr…bln…k…

The Visit

by Bernardo Verbitsky

*I*n the kitchen his sister was already preparing the *mate* and when Roberto asked her if she knew what time their grandmother, whom they expected that morning, was coming, he saw the chicken eating bread crumbs. It was a first-rate chicken, with red feathers like freckles all over its body.

"Are they still letting this one live? You know, he's just like Spur!"

"Isn't he?" said Rosa, who hadn't expected her brother to notice the resemblance. Years ago when they were small, they had become attached to a chicken bought to celebrate some holiday or other and their mother had accepted their plea for clemency when they begged her. It had turned into a beautiful rooster they named Spur, and they kept him at home for a long time.

Roberto got closer to observe it better, calling it with a snap of his finger as if it were a puppy.

"The maid just called," their mother said entering the kitchen, "to tell me that today of all days one of her little brothers decided to get sick. So I'll even have to take care of this little pest this morning."

"You're going to kill it?" Roberto asked.

"Yes, of course."

"Better let dad kill it," Rosa suggested.

"It's all the same."

"So he's awaiting execution. He already looks a little like chicken salad," said Roberto.

"But this guy," Rosa continued, "is not going to be anything more than chicken soup. Isn't it true, mama, that he looks like Spur?"

"Don't talk about Spur, because then we won't be able to eat him. No one can eat his childhood recollections," Roberto said.

"All right, but we have to hurry. If Grandmother finds him here…"

"Are you going to kill him?" Roberto's little twelve-year-old brother, Leoncito, asked him.

"God forbid. The most I can do for you is give you a good demonstration of a dissector. I'm an ace at cutting one up."

"Let me kill it," the child said to his mother. And at her negative response, he added, turning to Roberto, "Ha! You kill it. I can take care of this one myself with one good twist of the neck," he said, approaching the chicken.

"No!" his mother shouted. "Are you crazy?"

"Just look at this butcher," Roberto said, drawing him aside. "Don't you realize that Grandmother's coming? How could you wring his neck? Would you really be up to doing it?" he asked the boy.

"And why not?"

"Well, what's going on here?" their father asked, entering. "Who's going to give me some *mate*? And Leoncito, why are you drinking *mate* instead of milk and coffee?"

"It seems to me," Roberto said to Rosa, "that if I had the courage to kill a chicken then I could kill a person too. But this sounds like a court-martial. We should listen to the one who's condemned. I say, why isn't it kosher to roast a chicken on the spit?"

"Let's see if we can prepare everything in time. Rosa, do the bedrooms. I'll take care of the rest."

Grandmother's visit demands certain preparations, an adaptation of daily life and customs. Tablespoons mustn't be placed with the rest of the silverware; butter shouldn't be spread on bread with the same knife used to cut meat, and so, in Grandmother's presence, they'd use a small knife with a black handle exclusively for this job. Also, they had to be careful not to use soap in the kitchen to wash the cups and glasses they'd drunk milk from, all because of the tenet not to mix milk products with anything that was a meat product.

Mother warned Leoncito: "And don't show up in front of your grandmother eating a sandwich."

"But what if it's a cheese one?"

"Don't get smart. If it's cheese, then it doesn't matter. Let's see, bring me some of the change I left on the dresser. I want you to go to the pharmacy and get me some moth balls."

"Let Rosa go."

He refused to go and his mother got impatient.

"Keep it up, cutie, so that when you're grown up you'll send your mother to the asylum, huh? Don't forget," she said, giving all of them an inkling of her concern.

At this turn in the conversation, their father intervened and his serious voice lost its calm.

"Leoncito!"

"Go on, little Benjamin. Don't start, please," Roberto interceded.

The point was that Grandmother's visit awakened a dormant family bitterness they all tried to defend themselves against, but which the child had nevertheless brought up. The visit caused some tension because of everything it made them remember, apart from the preparations and modifications they weren't accustomed to and which they had a hard time remembering. Grandmother had left the house to go to the retirement home for several reasons and food was one of them. She was seeking a place where all the customs she'd observed into her old age would be respected. She always said that she was not prepared in her final years of life to waste the lifelong devotions she had always carried out with conviction. For some years she had lived through stormy interludes with them, cooking her ritually pure kosher dishes herself. One fine day she got tired, and egged on by another old lady, went to the home, carrying out an old threat which had always seemed absurd. They saw each other periodically. They visited her and she in turn, spent several days at her daughter's home. And it was she who seemed the saddest upon her arrival. It was by now a familiar, lamentable and painful family situation. For the mother, it was like opening an old wound. It made Roberto and his sister uneasy as they watched with fear and incredulity the transformation of their family ties. They looked at one another and grew closer as if to deny that this would ever happen to them.

"Is there any alcohol to make the pot kosher?" Rosa asked.

At that moment, the doorbell rang.

"Let's see who it is. It must be the potato vendor I'm waiting for," said Mother. And she went to the door. From the hall she saw who it was.

"But it's Grandmother!"

They went to meet her, uneasy, because she had arrived earlier than expected. They filled the little entryway around her. Father arrived after all the others, putting on his woolen slippers. And between questions and greetings the hall seemed to get smaller.

"I don't even want to see this goy," grandmother said, pinching Leoncito's cheek, smiling at him, nonetheless, asking if he had already had his breakfast and his *mate*. The child barely understood her Yiddish, and, wanting to be useful, asked his sister, "Should I get her some *mate*, Rosa?"

Grandmother seemed large because she was wearing a lot of clothes and an overcoat on top of that. When she removed it all, she appeared small and neat. She said she was warm; a great walker, she had walked the twenty-four blocks on foot. She arrived before she was expected because she'd left earlier, impatient to come. She asked questions, she was interested in their news, and even in Roberto's and Rosa's friends. While they talked, it seemed impossible that they could start arguing or quarrelling, that anything could distance them…They were standing and talking animatedly. Then they were about to walk through the patio and to one of the bedrooms. Suddenly mother remembered: "The chicken, my God, I forgot about him. You all talk for a while, I…"

"Let me mama," Rosa said, and she went out before anyone could answer her.

It was important that Grandmother not understand. A feeling of catastrophe fell over everyone, and they almost felt afraid when they remembered. And Rosa had gone, as upset as her mother, to carry out her difficult job. Grandmother knew that something was happening, but thought that maybe there was some spilled milk or something like that in the kitchen. She didn't pay attention at first. She asked about Rosa's work in the attorney's office. The rest waited. It was that kind of family. A bit childish. In such circumstances the chicken seemed to them the center of a terrible problem. They tried to please their grandmother. They could not shape their lives to the old woman's demands, but the authority vested in her weighed on them. It was for them the embodiment of a law whose rules they didn't follow. How then had they been able to send her away? It wasn't easy to explain. It seemed, for example, simple for the family to adjust itself to a kosher kitchen but at this point in time it wasn't possible. And that wasn't the only thing they had to keep in mind.

Father went out after Rosa, prepared to help her, sure that she'd need it. The nervous girl was clumsy and on picking up the chicken, couldn't stop the beating of its loud wings and cackling. The job was beyond her ability. She had to quietly carry out the task of an experienced *matarife*. A delicate cut so that the grandmother wouldn't realize that the bird hadn't been sacrificed by the hand of a *schoijet*.[1] The father, seeing her difficulties, tried to help her control the chicken that was opposing his fate. It was urgent to finish quickly and without thinking too much about it, he efficiently applied the popular and sure way of doing it advocated by Leoncito. He stopped to think how his wife would find a way to hide its final, unexpected and inconvenient end. But feathers had flown around the kitchen, the cackling had been heard. Grandmother understood everything even before she looked into the kitchen and what she saw when she did, confirmed her suspicions.

She stood before them, facing them with her characteristic decisiveness. "What have you done to me?" their mother asked, hopelessly. Contempt, pity, and even pardon, could be seen in the bitter smile with which the grandmother took in the scene. At first she seemed disposed to be magnanimous with the little people caught red-handed this way, and who continued to be upset, unable to calm themselves.

"Well, it's all over now," Roberto managed to say.

For the moment they had to think about another lunch without the chicken. There it was occupying the kitchen sink.

"When, when are you all going to learn?"

But her forgiving mood quickly passed, and she added, "Yes, you really have to have the heart of an assassin. But what can you expect of someone who…"

From then on, her tone got more violent. What education, what example, were they giving their children? And she pointed out to them the urgency of returning to the path of God, in whose name she evidently seemed to speak and with whose help she was made strong. She used her words like bolts of destruction. Was this the reception they had prepared for her?

It was perfectly clear that all this had been methodically calcu-

[1]schoijet: the Yiddish term for a ritual slaughterer

lated to make her stop visiting, so that she wouldn't come back. They were anguished, listening to her. And she went on: they shouldn't think that they were always going to be young.

Roberto looked surprised at everything she was saying, although it wasn't new to him. He tried to sidetrack her, but she went on, violent and cruel, all but announcing the destruction of the world as punishment for "what they had done to her." Roberto's protests went unheard and didn't succeed in making her understand that it was a great injustice to interpret what had happened as premeditated.

"How could you think such a thing?" he repeated without making himself heard.

Their father, not saying not a word, opted for withdrawal. More pressing than all this, was finding a practical solution. The mother, when this happened, fell into a depression that at first completely drained her of all willpower.

"At least you could have had him killed at the goy's place," Grandmother said. She didn't know whether there was one near, but never doubted that they would find someone there who would be willing to kill a chicken.

She ended by saying that she was inclined to leave immediately. They knew, nevertheless, that she wouldn't do it for fear that if she returned too soon, the other women at the home would say that her daughter or her son-in-law had thrown her out because she was difficult. They knew her very well and understood that the brunt of her anger had already passed and that now the reconciliation could begin with goodwill. Their mother tried to turn the conversation in another direction, and asked Roberto and Rosa for help in dissipating her anger. It was necessary to work at convincing her not to leave, she would give in if they found the way. That was all she wanted.

The mother explained that all this had happened because the maid, who was supposed to take the chicken to the house of the s*choijet*, who lived far away, hadn't been able to come that day. They'd now forget about the chicken and eat whatever she wanted. Some herring, for example, and some potatoes boiled in a pot with their skins to avoid the proximity of the pots in which they usually cooked meat, even though, having burned alcohol inside them, they were already purified.

Grandmother, still serious, begged them not to even mention food. Didn't they know that a cup of tea and a bit of bread were enough for her to live on?

"A cup of tea?" The mother considered it a good time to offer her one. "Roberto, stay with her a while."

"Roberto," the grandmother repeated, seeking a motive to continue her rage, "What kind of name is Roberto?"

"Who would think to name a child that when there are so many traditional names?" She accepted the tea and proceeded to drink it, calmer now.

Then together they went into Rosa's room, where there was a big trunk of her things, which she checked through periodically. She took the cretonne cover off the trunk and after using the key which she took out of her deep pocket, raised the lid. Rosa, behind them with her brother, watched this task with interest; a task they had already seen so many times before. Grandmother had slow but sure movements, and carefully took out the various fabrics which she protected with her load of moth balls.

"And what are you going to do with the chicken?" she asked, interested.

"We're going to give it to the maid," Rosa said.

"And you're going to give it up as lost? What a shame! It's a beautiful chicken, quite a rooster. And what are you all going to have for lunch?"

"The same thing as you, Grandmother," Roberto said in Spanish. "Papa went to buy something at the market on Corrientes."

"I don't need anything," Grandmother, who didn't want them to have any expense on her account, said hurriedly. She preferred to eat the same thing as everyone else. Really, she scarcely ate.

"When you're old, you'll remember your grandmother and then you'll understand better. I talk and I complain. A heavy heart has to speak out. You think I come from paradise? And what happens? I barely get here, and see there's no place in this house for me and I should leave. What does the chicken matter to me? When are you all going to behave the way people should? Being careful to keep a kosher kitchen isn't just religious. It's healthy. Very intelligent men, those of ancient times, established it that way and they had their reasons. But you have to do everything backwards."

According to Grandmother, the whole world ate kosher except them.

And she went on: "And moreover, aside from everything else, you have to have some heart! Aside from everything else, the *schoijet* knows how to do it, and when he kills, the animal doesn't suffer. It's a living, breathing thing, and you twist its neck until it dies suffocating the life inside. How could you?"

They listened to her, calm now; at least on this they understood each other.

"Once I killed a duckling without meaning to when I fed it. They are very delicate. How long ago was that? Thirty, thirty-five years, perhaps, and I can still see it before my eyes and feel it as if it were yesterday."

Continuing, she told them a story about her hometown far away, that centered on a very old man who had a huge family, one hundred fifty grandchildren and great-grandchildren, and who left his son's house because he had seen his daughter-in-law kill a hen herself.

"And your grandfather, would he have stayed? If your grandfather had seen his son-in-law kill an animal this way, he wouldn't have hesitated one moment to leave. But it's better not to speak up."

Nevertheless, after a pause, she blurted out sarcastically: "But what can you expect from a man who didn't even have his younger son circumcised?"

With that she came to the worst of the charges, and one of the irremediable problems between them. She would not pardon her son-in-law for it, and in whatever settling of accounts that were inevitably repeated, this was always included in the score.

"Nevertheless, I still have hope that when he's grown up and understands, the boy himself will take care of it."

Grandmother trusted that Leoncito through his own will would establish the tie which ought to link every Jew to Abraham, the Father. She affirmed that it was simple, and that it's never too late, and she wasn't lacking for stories of documented precedents. Professors asserted that it was healthier.

"Aren't you ever going to forget that?" Roberto asked.

Grandmother looked at him as if forgiving him the question.

"And how can I forget? Even in the next world they would remind us of it. It's something to be ashamed of forever."

She went on taking garments from the trunk and laying them over the bed. A strong smell of mothballs filled the room. Rosa examined everything curiously: an embroidered bedspread, a black coat with braided decorations, a shawl of heavy but delicate black wool lace. A black opaque cape with a silky shimmer. All this was more than forty years old and the fabric remained the same. Rosa, enthused, tried on the cape.

"But this is lovely!"

She ran out to show it to her mother. Roberto looked at the shawl admiringly and it seemed to him he was beginning to understand something new. Grandmother praised the styles of bygone days. Then she added, as if it were some sort of a corollary: "But I can't get anything out of any of you. Not even a name. Roberto. What kind of a name is Roberto?"

She would have preferred that they had named him Jaim Hersch, after her own father, and in a way, considered that his real name. Roberto whispered to himself this name that sounded weak to him. He looked at the clothing. And without thinking about it, he began to whistle.

"That," said the grandmother "is exactly what the radio plays every afternoon."

Roberto realized that he was whistling a tune that a radio program dedicated to Jews used as its theme song.

"How *nign*,"[2] said the grandmother. "How they danced in our city! I remember someone called "Motel the Carpenter." What moves! You couldn't even see peoples' feet!"

She smiled, and her clear blue eyes lit up.

"In the old days, people knew how to enjoy themselves. That dancer Motel makes me remember something. Near our house there were some neighbors who had several sons. One of them played the violin and many of us would get together to listen to him. I went too, several times, I liked his playing a lot, but my father found out and forbade me to go back. What times those were! I must have been about fourteen. What was wrong with going there? But who would have thought then, not just of arguing against an order but even to think of disobeying it?" It seemed to be a very pleasant memory for the grandmother, the young people going to listen to the town violinist.

[2] nign: nice

— 57 —

"Your mother's been wrong not to teach you any Yiddish. It doesn't matter that you're from this country, you should know it anyway. It's above everything else. I cannot forgive her for converting you into *goim*. And what is more beautiful than being Jewish? But you don't know what world you live in and its all the same to you."

It irritated Roberto to hear her speak this way, describing him as ignorant of all ritual and formality, and disinterested in Jewish life. He reacted vehemently to this injustice which wounded him for what it implied. Great though his own lack of understanding was toward his grandmother, hers toward him was equivalent at the very least and more fundamental. It wounded him more, because the closeness established in their chat made him feel better toward her and even made him want to talk to her to find an answer to many of the questions he had accumulated in the past few months. Innocently, he felt that perhaps she could help, but the answers he had so often heard referred to an orthodox Judaism, to her native town, and were not easily adaptable to his recent problems, augmented lately with concrete situations in his first year at college. He would really have liked to confess this and explain it to her sincerely, more than with anyone else in the family. But her admonition that he go with his father to buy *alies*[3] on holidays, or her advice on eating kosher was a likely and hardly helpful answer. He relieved his disappointment by imagining himself comically eating ritually prepared meat. He didn't even like meat. But how to explain to her that he was not as wrong as she thought? How to explain anything to her? Grandmother did not appreciate subtleties. Hadn't they shared that physical horror of the animal's death? That was already a step toward understanding one another. He was overcoming his reaction against the old lady.

Grandmother had reached the bottom of the trunk and now held a package which she was trying to undo. With her fingers she tried to untie the string. Helping her, Roberto noticed the old lady's hands and once more recognized his own hands in them. They were the same in size, shape of nails and identical above all at the index fingers. Thin, bony, they turned in, slimming at the point. Roberto

[3]alies (*aliyah*): an offering for the reading of the Torah or a blessing

was aware of this likeness, but it never had caused him the uneasiness and emotion that it did now. He felt that his grandmother was a link in a chain whose end was his own life.

"My shroud," Grandmother said, "it must already be moth eaten. You'll see it later," she said, putting it down.

But this didn't frighten Roberto now. He wanted to see it. Grandmother carefully put away her last dress. *Tajrijim,*[4] she called it. Had she made it herself? It lay between the two of them, peaceful, the impersonal and pale phantasm which *theù sudarioú* had evoked. There it was—her shroud—a simple gown for her wedding night with death. Roberto savored this approximation to death, he enjoyed it in silence. How to explain this feeling to his grandmother? This was perhaps the whole point of being close to her. Rosa entered wearing the cape.

"What's the hurry with that cape? It's going to be yours all the same. Everything in this trunk, except for just one thing is going to be yours."

Rosa didn't pay attention to those words and said: "Come eat. Papa brought an enormous package. At least today we won't eat *reef!*"[5] There were olives, pastrami, white cheese, peppers, dark bread and even *jalva.*[6]

"But hey," Roberto said, alarmed, "they aren't going to bring the smoked meats and the dairy things to the table…"

"No, son. And will this be peace or just a truce?"

"With a good glass of tea," Grandmother said, "it will be a better meal than with chicken."

As she descended the stairs, she was humming the melody heard earlier. Then, she said to herself: "So even the song came to America. Who would have told me we would ever meet in Buenos Aires. But it's better off than I am, it's as happy as it ever was."

[4]tajrijim: garment for a special occasion
[5]reef: probably from "trefah" meaning non-koshered meat
[6]jalva: candy made of sesame seeds

Bernardo Kordon (1915-)

Kordon, the son of Russian immigrants was born in Buenos Aires. His father, an ardent socialist, arrived in Buenos Aires with a printing press, prepared to earn his living and predisposed to political action. The author credits that press with encouraging his interest in writing and credits the frequent movies he viewed as a child with influencing his cinematic descriptive techniques. Self-educated, Kordon claims that his universities were first the city streets in and near his barrio and later, the streets in Buenos Aires, Chile, Europe and even China. He describes himself as an inveterate wanderer who, in collections like *Manía ambulatoria* (*Wanderlust*, 1978) simply describes the people, places and things he met and saw in his many travels on foot, by taxi, bus, rail or air.

As a radical young author Kordon found it politically expedient to move to Chile for some years. His leftist writings consistently championed the underprivileged poor and marginal types he met in his journey through life: a deaf mute, a maid, an Indian peasant woman, a Jewish boxer, a truck or taxi driver, a mistress or prostitute, a beggar, a traveling salesman, a teacher. He presents each of them in context, in stark vignettes compassionately portraying their quiet desperation, stoicism, and essential human dignity.

"Hotel Commerce," illustrates Kordon's ability to incorporate unexpected elements of fantasy, the mysterious or the preternatural into apparently realistic stories, while "Beat It, Paraguayan!" expresses Kordon's political views by deliberately shocking the reader with a masterful juxtaposition of scenes from two different court trials: one describing how the outraged public champions the rights of an Argentine woman whose real life story was popularized in the media in 1972; the other showing how public ignorance of explicit acts of government violence, torture and repression during the "dirty war" allowed the simultaneous, secret trial of an innocent woman, arrested and tortured on suspicion of political activity, to take place.

Kordon's collections of short stories include: *La vuelta de Rocha* (*The Rocha Street Cycle*, 1936), *Vagabundo en Tombuctú*

(*Vagabond in Timbuctu*,1956), *Domingo en el río* (*Sunday at the River*, 1960), *A punto de reventar* (*At the Bursting Point*,1971), *Alias Gardelito*, 1974, *Todos los cuentos* (*Complete Stories*, 1975), *Manía ambulatoria*, 1978) and *Adios pampa mía* (*Good-bye Pampa Mine*, 1978).

Hotel Commerce

by Bernardo Kordon

$\mathcal{H}$e entered with a firm step and flashed his salesman's toothy smile. From Chascomus to Bahia Blanca he could enter any grocery store and say hello with the same confident, secure tone, never forgetting any merchant's name. And he could do the same with hotel owners in the southern region.

"Good morning, Don Ramón! Do you have a room for me?"

The hotel keeper passed a worn rag over the counter and pursed his lips indicating a problem.

"Everyone chooses the same day to drop in on Colonel Fernández. The hotel is full."

"I just got in from Tandil to start work tomorrow morning. That way I can manage to get to Tres Arroyos tomorrow night. And now, what should I do, Don Ramón? Should I stay or leave?"

He thought for a few moments while the salesman continued holding the heavy sample case in his hand.

"There isn't a room available."

He pursed his lips again in a dubious gesture. He ran the cloth over the counter without taking his eyes from the worn leather case. Finally, he said: "I can get you a *bed*."

"It's all the same to me, a room or just a bed. What can you do?" the salesman asked, and softly deposited his case on the floor beside the umbrella rack.

"It's in the room at the back with another bed."

"What business is my colleague in?" the salesman asked, interested.

"He's not a colleague."

"A field worker?"

"No. I haven't the faintest idea."

The hotel keeper was being mysterious.

"Is there something special about this blessed bed? Will you reserve it for me or not?"

"But of course! Do you want to go to the room now?"

But before the salesman could answer, the hotel keeper added: "It would be better to let me speak to the other occupant first."

"What's the big deal with this blessed bed, Don Ramón? Is it made of gold or does the Queen of Sheba come with it?"

"Nothing special, really, friend. It's just that he came in on the noon bus and asked for a single room. Since the one I had left had two beds, he offered to pay me more for it so that I'd let him sleep alone. Clearly I can't leave you in the street? Now give me time to convince him that he should share the room."

The salesman didn't pay the least attention to him.

"I'm going to work a bit."

"The stores are already closed," the hotel keeper warned him. "Aren't you going to eat?"

"I already ate something on the road. Keep my bag; I'm going to visit Azcueta."

"He's out," the hotel keeper informed him.

The salesman snapped his fingers in an annoyed gesture.

"I came just to see him. Wasted trip!"

"He left yesterday for Buenos Aires."

"Will you make me some coffee, Don Ramón?"

While the hotel keeper made an expresso at the end of the counter, the salesman looked around the bar; two posters announcing a fair and an auction of new calves and a railroad schedule were on the wall. First he read the posters, then he went over to consult the schedule. This was the worst part of his traveling life: when sales were scarce, fatigue and tedium besieged him like ferocious enemies.

It was a pity not to be able to see Azcueta. He had been hopeful about the promises made on the last visit. He could have invited him to have a few drinks and formalized an important sale. He yawned sleepily and looked at his watch: nine o'clock. In the dining room the waiter was serving dessert. He didn't see anyone he recognized.

Don Ramón put his coffee on the counter. Then he went out to the patio. When he returned, the salesman had finished his coffee and was still studying the schedule as if it were some kind of oracle.

"I've just spoken with the man. Do you want to go the room now?"

"What for? It's still early." But he didn't know what the devil to do. It was impossible to chat with Don Ramón: the waiter had just asked him to make coffee for everyone, and the hotel keeper had entrenched himself behind the noisy fan.

"I'm going to stretch my legs."

"I'll put your suitcase in the room. It's the last one down the hall."

The salesman started walking down the dark street. He passed in front of the steamy windows of the bar where the bus from the Bahia Blanca line stopped. He didn't see any familiar faces there either. He looked at his watch again; ten minutes after nine. When he was like this, without any colleagues or friends around, the nights became interminable and it seemed as if his watch had stopped.

He walked toward San Martín Boulevard. There he found a movie theater. He went in before the show began. He avoided sitting among the boys with dark suits on and white handkerchiefs around their necks; he greeted Herziel the shopkeeper and his wife; and without taking off his overcoat, he sat beside two characters with earthy faces. It was cold and the floor was made of stone. He stamped his feet a while to warm them up, but when the show began, he stopped and let the cold climb up his legs. In a little while he could make no sense of the figures moving across the screen. He thought about Tandil's orders, forty percent less than the last trip. He had expected to lose sales in Colonel Fernández. Now he was hopeful about Tres Arroyos where the industries had turned it into an unsurpassable market and the harvest had been excellent. That Azcueta was away made his plans go awry. Of course he had to go around to the other businesses in the area. But Azcueta's absence gave him a feeling of failure.

Suddenly it occurred to him that Azcueta might be going to Buenos Aires to visit his company. And on the movie screen the only face he saw was that of his sales manager. Every time a client from the interior came to Buenos Aires—a client brought in by the traveling salesman, of course—the sales chief invited him to dinner and then presented him to the manager as his own client and personal friend.

The traveling salesman felt a cold that reached into his very bones. He renewed his foot tapping on the stone tiles. The movie—a musical comedy—didn't interest him in the least. He left halfway through it.

The Hotel Commerce was already closed. He pounded on the

door. At that moment he thought of his sales chief. He hated that face that followed him as if to watch him in the middle of the night in this isolated town in the plains.

Someone opened the door by pulling on a rope. The night desk clerk was on his army cot in the middle of the hall.

"Did you close the door?" he asked.

"I closed it tight. Sleep well, buddy."

He entered the last room from the dark hall and turned on the light. His suitcase was on one bed. On the other, he saw a figure stretched out with a blanket covering his head.

"Good evening," the salesman said. The other man didn't respond, although it was plain that he wasn't sleeping, given his strained position. The blankets were pulled taut over his protruding feet and head.

The salesman looked around the room. There was a sink in one corner and the walls exuded humidity. Two iron beds, hangers and nails on the walls, and a chair to put your clothes on, since there was no wardrobe.

Between the two beds, a rickety night table with a night lamp with no shade, a glass of water and a bottle wrapped in paper.

"Neither a colleague nor a field hand," the salesman thought, "just a sick man." And he began to get undressed. He put his coat on a hanger, folded his trousers carefully over his jacket on the back of the chair. When he was down to his wool undershirt, the man in the bed came out from under the sheets.

"Excuse me if I awakened you," said the salesman.

"I wasn't sleeping, just resting," the other responded with a shaky, hoarse voice like that of a child about to weep. He was a man of indefinite age, with a three-day-old beard and sad, dark eyes. He extended his hand—a small pale hand—to turn on the lamp, possibly because the ceiling light with its morbid yellowish color bothered him. The traveler thought he looked like a former bank clerk or a ruined storekeeper. That is to say, a decent and deplorable man. When he extended his hand to find the switch of the lamp, he took the opportunity to pick up the bottle and put it beside him.

"Are you traveling for business or pleasure?" the salesman asked.

"A bit of everything," the other responded, and attempted a sad smile.

"You're lucky to be able to travel for pleasure," the salesman commented. He got between the humid, cold sheets; the bed squeaked.

"Shall we turn off the light?" the salesman asked, and before the other could offer an opinion, he turned off the lamp and it was dark.

The faucet was dripping. The salesman closed his eyes and tried to sleep. He covered his head with the blanket, but it was useless; the water kept dripping into the sink and echoing in his brain. He raised his head in the darkness and finally decided; he turned on the light, jumped out of bed and went to the sink. He tightened it forcefully, but it didn't stop altogether; the drops kept falling. A strange vibration seemed to fill the room. The two men looked at one another. Now they both looked equally desolate, in their wool nightshirts and sleepless faces.

"Those damned drips always keep me awake," the salesman said.

"It's nerves. I suffer from insomnia too. Sometimes I don't sleep for a whole week," the other replied in his timid voice.

"And what's in the bottle helps?"

"Yes, a remedy. I think it's the best."

"To sleep?"

"Of course. But it's very strong. I don't recommend it."

The salesman understood that his roommate did not intend to invite him to share the contents of the bottle. He felt irritated at that, although he wouldn't have accepted a taste of it had he offered it. But he thought he should have offered as a courtesy.

He turned out the light, but kept his eyes open in the darkness. It occurred to him that if he'd had supper as usual, with a half bottle of wine, instead of eating those sandwiches on the road, he'd be sleepy. And moreover, he'd suffered from the cold in the theater; maybe he was catching a cold...too bad Azcueta had to be away just now.

He heard his roommate feeling around the night table for the bottle. He took a sip of water and fell back into bed.

"Now that he took some medicine he'll sleep peacefully" the salesman thought, "while I go on putting up with this insomnia." But the other began moving about in bed. The salesman waited for him to calm down, and then tried to list by memory all the sales slips he'd made out since leaving Buenos Aires. Monte, Las Flores, Azul... before getting to Tandil he fell asleep.

Not since childhood had the salesman felt the presence of the devil. This time, his old nightmare returned. He arrived in red with his trident, just as he had seen him at carnivals when he was young. He dreamed that he was sleeping in an immense room, surely one in an old hotel. There were an infinite number of beds. Was it a hotel or a hospital? Everyone there seemed to be colleagues of his; beside each bed was a chair, and on each of them was a case of samples. Suddenly Satan entered the room and began to go around to each of the beds. The salesman prayed that He would turn his attention elsewhere. And it seems that the prayer worked: the devil ended up choosing another patient. He raised the trident high and pierced him with it ferociously. In his dream he felt the cut of the metal and the total pain that burst into his ears like a bomb. And somehow he understood, while he was sinking in space, that all those bodies were none other than one body, and that one was none other than himself.

He woke up from the nightmare with a shout. He sat up in bed, panting as if he'd just finished running for miles. The dirty window was turning rosy; a new day was beginning. He looked at his roommate in the darkness, and barely made him out. There was something strange about his face.

"Did my shouting wake you? I had a nightmare…"

But the other didn't reply at all.

Then the salesman turned on the light. The other man's face looked contorted, his glazed eyes were turned up to the ceiling.

The traveler jumped out of bed and went out into the hall.

"Don Ramón!" he wanted to call, but he only managed a scream of horror. Down the hall he went, a crouching silhouette.

"There's a dead man in the room!"

The night desk clerk, a lame old man who was carrying wood to the kitchen, put it down on the floor and looked at the salesman in his underwear and his nightshirt with the tag sticking out in the front.

"A dead man in your room?"

"Yes, he just died."

The old man beat on the owner's door. Don Ramón came out, buttoning his trousers. He turned to the salesman with a conciliatory gesture, as if he were complaining about a dirty towel or a bug in his soup.

"How could I have known? He asked me for a single room for himself and that's all. But don't worry. It will all be taken care of. But you're going to catch cold, man, good God!" he indicated, when he noticed his bare feet.

The salesman didn't feel the icy floor under his feet, but he did feel the humiliation of being seen in his underclothes among people who were dressed. He returned to the room; he stopped for an instant at the door. Don Ramón was behind him.

"Go and get dressed, man."

He went in without looking at the dead man and began to get dressed. After putting on his shoes, he felt more sure of himself. When he put on his trousers he was in control of himself. On adjusting his necktie, he began to think lucidly again. He turned and rested his eyes on the cadaver.

Its stone-like rigidity surprised him. He had always imagined death as total abandonment, but here he found it to be an aggressive act against life. The corpse appeared to be under the control of some powerful force and it almost seemed as if this force still inhabited that intense marble-like face and those eyes, frightened, like those of a scared horse. The salesman remembered his dream and hesitated an instant. Weren't all the men in the dream the same person, and that person no other than himself? He looked at the dead man's face again and this time almost broke into tears. He felt sorrow, an immense sorrow for that "other" and for himself. Somehow, in a way, they had been almost like brothers when they exchanged those few words, both in their nightshirts and desperate for sleep.

At that instant a police official and a doctor came in. They both went directly to the night table. The doctor picked up the bottle and said: "Cyanide."

The official fixed on the salesman with a look.

"Do you know anything about this?"

"Nothing. He told me it was a remedy for insomnia."

"And it is."

He added with a smile: "Didn't he offer you any?"

The official and the doctor looked calmly at the man who'd slept beside the dead man.

"You can go to work," the official said. "Later, stop by the station to give a statement."

A policeman guarded the door of the Hotel Commerce. Curious people were pushing to get in. They assaulted the salesman with questions. He recognized a face: it was Efraín Gutiérrez, the owner of the Vasquito. They walked along together and exchanged ideas on the sickly and ferocious idea of taking one's own life. Both felt the fear and terror of death and they agreed that to kill oneself was an act of cowardice. Then they went on to talk about business. The children of the town followed with their berets pulled down over their eyes. And the pharmacist, Urpilleta, gave the salesman his best smile, gesturing a greeting from forty meters away. Then the salesman realized the importance he had acquired in this town. He could count on conversation with the merchants. He thought about the dead man as a free collaborator, a strange colleague whom he couldn't thank. "Maybe I can still win a hand in this damned town." With this thought he resumed his optimistic salesman's walk.

At lunch, he calculated three thousand dollars worth of sales, while in the dining room of the Hotel Commerce they talked of nothing but the suicide. They had found among the dead man's clothes an identification card issued by the Federal Police, a pocket watch, and some money; two ten-peso bills. One could say that this traveler had come to the city with the purpose of killing himself. That amount of money was not enough to pay for his room and continue on his way.

The salesman sat down at a table where he saw three of his colleagues. They looked at him curiously, he felt absurdly sad. He was served a bowl of soup and put two tablespoons of grated cheese on it.

Someone asked him, "And what can you tell us about your companion?"

He stopped with the spoon halfway to his lips.

"What companion?"

"The dead one, man," the other clarified, "Who was he?"

"What does he have to do with me?"

"Goodness, don't take offense! No one is accusing you of anything! I was just asking you what he seemed like, if he told you anything about his life. After all, didn't the poor fellow spend his last night with you?"

Finally the salesman got to the spoonful of soup. He found it bland and cold. He had no appetite.

Another person at the table intervened: "Didn't he say anything before he died?"

The traveler tried to remember: "We didn't exchange many words."

"That's a pity!" the other exclaimed.

"Didn't you ask him anything?"

"And what would I have asked him? It was very late, it was very cold. I'd just come back from the movie…"

"I don't mean to blame you, but as for me, I always start a conversation with my roommate," a third person at the table said seriously. "That way I always learn something about him and I often get interesting information…Once in González Chávez…"

"No, we never know if we should get involved or not," another salesman interrupted.

The waiter came to take away the soup.

"May I take this?" he asked, indicating the tureen.

The salesman nodded yes. Then he asked: "Get involved in what sense?"

"Well, you never know if he's a colleague or just some crazy person," the other responded. He was dressed in an irreproachable gray suit and when he spoke, he flashed the diamond ring on his finger. In general, this type of colleague, with his portentous facility with words and his visible future in politics, intimidated him.

"I don't know who he was, nor why he killed himself," the other interrupted with his mouth full.

"It could happen to any one of us," the man in the gray suit remarked emphatically.

"If he were a salesman, we'd have to have some sort of wake for him. Get together, go the mayor (I just happen to know him) and ask him if he'd allow us a final tribute to an unfortunate colleague. You, same as any one of us, could die tomorrow in a bed in the Hotel Commerce or the Italian Inn.

The salesman set aside his plate of ravioli. The thick sauce was dancing in his throat. He excused himself and got up from the table. He went to the counter at the bar and consulted the train schedule. Don Ramón made coffee and informed him: "There's no train until tomorrow."

He drank his coffee at the counter. He watched his chatting colleagues glance his way now and then.

He walked down the long hall and entered the room. Then he saw the twin iron beds and had the fleeting and confusing impression that it was impossible to differentiate them with their yellow blankets and red trim. Other traveling salesmen—and himself first of all—would sleep in the same bed as the dead man and it would be useless to ask Don Ramón if he had changed the sheets.

He left his sample case and went out to wander through the streets of the town.

At times the image of the dead man overcame him. That convulsed face with its protruding eyes didn't upset him as much as the face that he hadn't gotten to see very well; the face of his roommate, of the man he might possibly have saved with a few words. That man in bed with his head under the covers didn't seem the same as the one who was there at dawn with that violent and defiantly crazed look. That face transformed by death was the negation of the man who had drunk the cyanide. The salesman made an effort to picture him and could only see his own face. It was himself shrinking with cold under the weight of the icy night in the pampas, curling up in his loneliness like a terrified worm.

He tried to convince himself that he couldn't have done anything else. "How could he have started a conversation at midnight with a roommate who was a stranger?" They had exchanged a few words, true, but that hadn't been enough. Then doubt overwhelmed him and he felt blame for the death. He stopped at the corner; his heart pounding in his chest.

"Hey, but you've become important!" someone at his side exclaimed.

The salesman was surprised and turned his head. It was Urpilleta, the pharmacist, with his white apron and his amiably cynical smile.

"I didn't see you, doctor," the salesman excused himself.

"Of course, now you don't see me. Before you never missed stopping in to chat with me a while. But now I see you're very busy. You walked in front of my store three times and I didn't even get a greeting.

"Pardon me, Urpilleta."

"Pardon you nothing! I had to step into the street and block your way to beg you for a hello. But what's wrong with you? I don't suppose it's on account of what happened this morning? I'm referring to that vagabond who killed himself."

"Vagabond?" asked the traveler.

"Of course he was a vagabond! They only found a couple of pesos in his pockets. He didn't even have enough to pay for a common poison. Do you know what it's like to kill yourself with cyanide? It means you die like a dog. But why are we talking in the street? Why don't we get down to business?"

The pharmacy smelled of mint and disinfectant. Everything shone, the windows, the floor tiles and the beautifully stylized containers. In this cold and burnished atmosphere, anguish seemed to constrict his heart with nickel-plated fingers...the pharmacist's lips twisted into an uncomfortable smile over his gums.

"Well, it seems to me that you are worrying over this death."

The salesman hesitated a moment, and then stammered, "Of course, it made an impression."

"And what in the hell impressed you about it? Having death at your side? Come on now! We never know when it's going to happen. Sometimes we don't even think about it and we carry it on our shoulders. Of course it did! Death doesn't come around like a beggar, nor does it attack like a mugger, neither does it carry us away, it's not a rented car or a beast of burden. We carry death within us, in our souls and in our bones. What good is it to be scared if someone near us dies? It makes no more difference than if they had died a thousand miles away."

He paused to wait on a woman who bought some soap and a package of tea. He cut the roll of wrapping paper carefully so as not to miss the part printed with "Urpilleta Pharmacy."

He rang her up and then continued: "This vagabond that you are so worried about came in here."

"Did you wait on him?"

"Of course, I don't have any employees. He started to tell me a story about a garden plagued with ants. I understood what he wanted and I told him, 'Use cyanide. It's the best.' He stared hard at me with his bleary eyes. 'Ah yes...' he said, 'It is best. I'm going to spread out a lot of it.' The poor man came in here with death."

The pharmacist tapped his forehead with his knuckles and concluded: "He left calmer, with death in his pocket...But now I see you are worried. What are you thinking about?"

"I must not be getting enough sleep. I wanted to ask you about it. What can I take?"

The pharmacist opened a case in the counter and took out a bottle of pills. He held it out to him with a smile: "Take these. One or two and you will sleep better."

Still smiling, he pointed at him with an omniscient gesture. "But be careful! There are those who take seven or eight…"

He shook his head a little, still smiling.

"They go overboard and never wake up."

There was silence. They both smiled with the same cold and businesslike pleasantness. The salesman wanted to break this awkwardness. Generally, he would tell a few jokes and comment on the economic situation of the country. But now he felt confused like a child caught doing something he shouldn't. But what should he be ashamed of?

The pharmacist handed over the bottle. "Seven pesos."

The racket coming from the cash register made him come to himself.

"Your change, friend."

The salesman took the three pesos and put them in his pocket along with the bottle of pills. Then he attempted a fleeting nod and headed back toward the hotel.

He sat at the bar in front of the coffee maker watching how the waiter, a young man with joined eyebrows, set the tables for dinner. He set out the bread plates and bottles of wine. From the sideboard he took the plates and, slowly, in the darkness of the dining room, set the forks and knives at each place setting. All this was trivial, but wrenchingly sad and absurd to the point of making him want to scream. The waiter walked among the tables alone with a reluctant seriousness. He looked like a priest fulfilling a daily and fundamental ritual. And all this, the atmosphere, was saturated with a hidden horror that before long swelled like a gust of wind, inflating the dirty metal of the silverware and making the country biscuits dance under the influence of this impassive witch.

The salesman felt convinced that he had come to the culmination of his work. The Hotel Commerce, the town of Colonel Fernández and the whole world had set themselves to devouring the corpse of his roommate. Each one of these dishes contained a piece of him, toughened by death and tenderized by a Creole cook. A sad little feast for a sad people. Now he understood the grave and ashamed silence of his table companions in hotels around the province.

"Don Ramón!"

The owner of the hotel appeared with a tray on his arm. "Could I bring you an appetizer?"

"I'm really not all that hungry. But what I do want is to get to sleep early. I don't feel well."

"But I imagine you would want to eat first. And they will serve you."

A strange repugnance turned his stomach. How could he sit in this sad dining room where they were already setting out the plates to serve a suicide's flesh? It could have been that of a traveler, a truck driver, a traveling salesman or an artist of the area. The road ate up one of its children and all his brothers shared the banquet of his remains.

"No, I'm really not hungry at all, Don Ramón. I'm going to get some sleep."

"You aren't feeling ill, are you?" the hotel keeper asked concerned.

"Ill, no. But I do feel tired, very tired."

"Well, your room is ready."

"Which room?"

The hotel keeper hesitated a moment and explained: "There hasn't been any change of guests, so you'll have to stay in the same room you had last night."

An attendant accompanied him to his room. The salesman opened the door and paused before the darkness of the room. He turned on the light. The beds were made; they looked the same, impeccable in their cold poverty, between the peeling walls with large water stains. The faucet was still dripping. One two three…one, two, three…

He filled a glass with water and left it on the night table next to the bottle of pills. Afterwards, slowly, he began to undress. He got between the cold sheets curled up, with his knees nearly touching his stomach. He stretched out his arm, found the switch and turned off the light. But he couldn't sleep. He added and then added again the orders he'd gotten that day. He remembered all of them, down to the fraction of a cent. Their total value exceeded the sum of all the checks. When he finished counting, the image of his dead roommate surged into his mind. Then he realized that he could not remember if he had gotten into the dead man's bed or the other. How could he have forgotten this detail? He rose up and looked for the switch to turn on the light. At that moment, someone opened the door. The salesman turned to get into bed and hide his head before that someone turned on the light.

"Good evening," said the person who had just entered.

The salesman showed his face from between the sheets. By the yellowish light, he could see an older colleague. The man put his suitcase on the floor and rubbed his hands together energetically. "It's terribly cold, friend! Only *I* would think of coming in at this hour!"

"I came in last night on the same bus."

"What end of the business are you in?"

"Wholesale, grocery."

The other man put his clothes on the back of the chair and got into bed. He coughed a little, cleared his throat and said: "Ah, the noble grocery line. It brings in good orders, right?"

"That's true more or less."

"I always said that what ever happens, everyone has to eat. Is that the truth or what?"

"It's the truth," the salesman admitted. "I've always had good accounts."

And he thought again of the amount of his last check and still, again, he associated it with the clear, terrible and painful thought of the dead man at his side.

The new arrival had turned off the light while the salesman was remembering his dream of the night before. He hadn't any doubt that all the beds were the same, that all those who slept there were the same person, that he had died the night before, and that he too had just finished coming into the same room in order to sleep in the other bed.

He reached out his hand to find the glass of water and the bottle of pills.

The new arrival began to explain in an apologetic manner: "The hotel keeper told me that you seemed a little sick, but because there wasn't any other room available…"

"I'm not really ill, but I haven't been feeling all that well."

"I'm sorry if I woke you up."

"I hadn't been able to close my eyes. I'm going to take some of these pills."

"Are they sleeping pills?" the other man asked in the darkness. He showed a cordial and courteous curiosity.

At this moment, the salesman had the thought that the dialogue of the previous night was being repeated. He opened the bottle, took out seven pills and swallowed them with a sip of water.

"Good night, colleague," said the other man, "I hope you'll feel better in the morning."

They both turned over, each toward his own wall. And the words of the new arrival continued floating in the air with an extraordinary mix of solidarity and condemnation.

The salesman sighed and closed his eyes. The following day the ritual of sacrifice, the sad celebration of the Hotel Commerce would continue.

He heard the maddening tick-tock of the dripping faucet. But he knew that in a moment he would hear it no more.

Beat It, Paraguayan!

by Bernardo Kordon

*I*n the evening, the postman and the doorman would meet, and later on the salesman would appear. He was the one who ran the show: everyone recognized his eloquence and experience. Once he had been a fruit vendor in Abasto, then a truck driver, until he finally sold the truck to install himself in a kiosk selling cigarettes and sweets, but then he had to close it on account of the demolition in the area. He started to sell contraband, especially the kinds of things no one needed and everyone bought: cigarette lighters, compressed air rifles, mechanical toys from Japan and a black puppet that tap-danced.

He nodded to his friends, then leisurely walked around all the tables in the cafe before sitting down. As he offered his special of the day—a yo-yo that flashed red and blue lights while going up and down—his stooped posture and smile could mean one more sale to him at the end of a long day of making the rounds in the city.

When he sat down, he placed his bag of goods on a chair, and began to lead a discussion raising his voice so that everyone in the cafe could hear, so that when the taxi driver came running in on his way to the bathroom he would be able to pick up the topic of conversation while he was peeing. When he sat down he ordered a coffee, as usual, a piss and a coffee, that's the only way you can add on a few more hours in the taxi, he'd always say, and hurrying as usual, he burned the roof of his mouth with the coffee and then gave his opinion:

"I say that a man who really wears the pants does whatever he wants with his money, that's why he earned it. Whether it's a thousand pesos or this Negrete's 320 million. He should spend it the way he wants to!"

Calmly and irresistibly the vendor turned his smile on him:

"You're wrong, I tell you. We're not dealing here with money someone has earned by working. The problem is something else: use your head and think for a minute. Whose money is it this Paraguayan is taking? It belongs to all of us who play the soccer lottery, isn't that so? The money is yours, mine, everyone's. So then, it's not only the Paraguayan's problem. It's our business too. Or isn't it?"

The vendor pointed his index finger at the taxi driver:

"And now you're going to take all of us down to the courthouse. They're going to hear from us there."

The taxi driver gulped his coffee down and asked for another.

"A piss and a coffee," he explained as usual. "Every day I drink more coffee but piss less, and sometimes it's an effort. It's my kidneys, right?"

"Of course," the vendor smiled, "I had a reason for saying to hell with the truck."

"And now you're going around as red as a baby," the doorman interjected.

"I got a bit of sun," the vendor continued, still smiling. "Today, I spent the afternoon in the Palermo district. "I chatted with half the world. A lot of girls, you know? Grandmothers, mothers, aunts, maids, whatever. They go strolling with the babies and want to enjoy themselves too. I show the toys to the babies, and talk to the ladies about any old thing. In the end they buy something from me and we're all pretty satisfied warming ourselves in the sun. The truth is that it turned out fine for me, I can't complain. There was a spring sun in midwinter and a lot of people in the park. Everyone was talking about the same thing, about the Paraguayan and Fabiana. That's why I say we have to go to the courthouse. It is, as they say, a matter of honor."

Like a picture out of focus the burnished and angular face of the Paraguayan, Mercedes Ramón Negrete, took form. Above it like a rosy cloud floated the image of Fabiana López, an Argentine with a round face and meek smile, the warm companion that God (always Argentine) had placed at the side of the cold-faced Paraguayan to wash his shirts and offer a bit of homey warmth. How could he abandon her now for those millions that came to him out of the blue? Fabiana was on television now several times a day. She wasn't claiming part of his fortune. She was merely making inquiries about him and begging for a meeting so she would know how he was getting along. Fabiana never tired of saying that Mercedes Ramón was a big-hearted man. If he had abandoned her, it was surely because of the bad advice of people with bad intentions. Both the newspapers and television harped on Fabiana and the Paraguayan, constantly pointing out that money had nothing to do with happiness: an innocent romantic from the slums had shipwrecked onto the infected morass of 320 million pesos. Luckily, there were still a lot of pure hearts in Villa Corina, the place the Paraguayan had just deserted. It wasn't just Fabiana. The whole slum was replete with kindred souls. Friends were disillusioned because the Paraguayan never visited them the way he'd promised the night he won the prize. Although deeply wounded, they nevertheless declared before the cameras that after he'd spent the 320 million, however he did it, the Paraguayan could return to Villa Corina and find his former friends ready to give him a hand, a little job to help him live and even help with building another shack. It wasn't just Fabiana but the immense heart and the bountiful goodness of the pampas that would warm up to the needs of this chance millionaire—why, he didn't even know anything about soccer!—he was so defenseless—he didn't even know how to talk! He was surrounded by lawyers and bank managers always so ready to ensnare the unsuspecting.

"Are we going to the courthouse or not?" the vendor fretted.

The taxi driver begged them to let the motor (overheated by the lousy traffic that worsened every day) cool off, but afraid of getting there late, they all piled into the taxi and demanded the driver's presence by blasting the horn continuously.

Down San Luis Street and then down Jean Jaures, they proceeded toward Corrientes Avenue.

Doorman: "Now we're passing the Carlos Gardel[1] house."

Mailman: "Just one of the millions; a house the same as all the rest. I can tell you so because I deliver the mail there: all bills, same as in any other place of business."

Vendor: "What do you expect? That Gardel would write? He can't.

Taxi driver: "So anyone at all can buy a house and call it

[1] Carlos Gardel: Argentina's foremost tango singer and composer who died in a plane crash in 1935.

whatever he likes and that's all there is to it? I don't think it's that easy. There are news reporters who know a lot, without mentioning the police who are there to clear up any nonsense."

Mailman: "I know this neighborhood better than anyone else and I can tell you it was a house just like any other house. As for the newspapers, they shouldn't even open their mouths. They should publish ads and get on with it."

Doorman: "It doesn't matter whether it was Gardel's house or not. It's sort of like a statue now, I mean, a homage. And that's why I take my hat off now."

Mailman: "It's just a business, nothing else."

Taxi driver: "If they have money they'll make more. If not, they'll have a hard time. Money makes money, you know? Riding in a taxi, you know when things are going well or not in the country."

Vendor: "Whether or not there's money isn't the main thing. Whenever I try to sell something, they always start off by telling me there's no money, but I don't give up, and finally a thousand peso bill appears. The important thing is to take some happiness home every day, that's what I tell them and then they buy something from me."

Mailman: "And what happiness do you take home?"

Vendor: "I do my part every day. Every morning I count out a thousand pesos and hand them to my wife for her food and the baby's, and I take the rest because I almost always eat out, and moreover I need money in case anything turns up, let's say a merchandise sample, or one of those appealing girls who turns up suddenly, but I tell you my home comes first, whatever house of Gardel's you're talking about, to me, my home is sacred. I never leave a bill unpaid, family and friends and all that come first. That's why this Paraguayan thing makes me furious. Didn't he have a wife and home after all? He had all kinds of friends and didn't even buy them a drink. Really, wasn't that wrong?"

Taxi driver: "And now I'm the scapegoat. I'll take you to the courthouse, but I'll keep going."

Vendor: "Now you're backing down."

Taxi driver: "I promised to bring you and here we are. But I can't park here. And it's prime time for my work. I still owe three payments on the taxi. Are all of you going to pay them for me?"

He turned into Libertad, stopped at the corner of Lavalle and

Talcahuano. They got out and a man promptly took the cab.

"He's gone, that's that," the porter said. "And now where do we go from here?"

They began to traverse the halls of the courthouse, an immense sooty-colored fortress, with enormous, grimy windows, an overwhelming mass of stone unlike any other in the whole city, oppressive when seen from the outside and sinister when seen from within.

I'm Norma Morello. For eight years I was active in the Rural Movement. I've been a rural teacher since September 1971. First in school 497 in the third section of Goya (in Corrientes) a neighborhood where the economic condition of the people is bad. Because some are sharecroppers, they have to give a third of their harvest to their landowner with no help from him (I shared their homes and food, I assure you that no one would choose this Western and Christian way of life). Some, on the other hand, are small land owners who don't have enough to live with dignity or educate their children beyond second or third grade. In the second school, at La Marta ranch, the situation was no better; I had about four students, who were retarded because of being underfed.

The thirtieth of November at night, they broke into my house. They didn't find evidence of any connection with the guerrilla movement although they tried to change some documents, including a mimeographed map of the city of Resistance.

They detained me in school number 534 at half past one in the morning.

In the subprefecture I was informed that I was at the disposal of Federal Coordination, they didn't know why. But the military officer who detained me commented: 'There's a big organization behind it.' He talked now and then about the Argentine situation: there is no hunger, he once lived in the woods for three months with a knife and some matches. He told me he would give me a test to see if I were Marxist or not. I told him I was a rebel student. He asked me, jokingly, 'Don't you want to go out and get some sun?' After I was there seven days, someone came who said he was from Federal Coordination and asked me some questions. Right away I realized it was a farce prepared by the secret police in Goya and Buenos Aires. They asked me questions about arms and about people from Tucumán whom I didn't know, except incidentally from having been in the movement.

They didn't have sufficient proof in their hands to justify the test that the military officer who detained me had talked about, and that I would soon have to face. This man made it impossible for me to defend myself since he accused me of things I didn't know about, about which there did not and does not exist any proof whatsoever: arms they sent me by mail from Tucumán, people, places, etc. When he left I realized what awaited me: the torture chamber.

On the morning of the ninth an official appeared who told me: 'Get your things ready; we're leaving right away.' I asked: 'Where to?' He told me he didn't know anything. They took me; a package went with me and an envelope that said: 'Coronel...'

The plane landed before getting to Rosario. As the plane descended, a long blue car immediately drew up, with various men who circled the plane. Two of them got on. One blindfolded me. The other handcuffed me. They put me in the trunk of a car and said 'If you touch the blindfold I'll shoot you.' We traveled some twenty or thirty minutes. They let me out at a house on the outskirts of town (we walked down a dirt road). They made me walk through a tunnel; I was the only one who fit and that was sideways. Coming out I began to hear loud metallic noises and things moving around. A radio was playing classical music and a loud voice told me: 'Opera music...for the operation...for the four whole days you've got to live...Get undressed.' When I wouldn't undress they took my clothes off. 'You're not the first one to get undressed,' they told me along with other rude comments.

No one could remember ever having seen such a crowd at the courthouse doors ever before. Men and women kept coming from everywhere and they got all fired up commenting on the news in the newspapers and magazines. Some were holding up placards like, "FABIANA'S LOVE DROWNED IN SOCCER LOTTERY MILLIONS." In one photo, she was shown weeping, pounding on the residence of the Paraguayan consul: "Why don't you let me see Ramón? I don't want his money, I just want to see him." The new millionaire had declared that Fabiana wasn't his lover, but merely a friend. She replied: "The people who are holding him are dictating these things to him. How could he say that I didn't wash his shirts! Anyway, doesn't everyone know that I washed them for him?"

"Did you see Fabiana on television yesterday? She was great! They say they're going to give her a contract starring in a television series they're making of her life."

"I heard that. But someone also said that first they're going to make her lose weight, about forty-five pounds, and they'll have to teach her to read and write, because the poor thing was raised out there in the country, in Chaco, and never could go to school. In order to be an actress you have to know how to read, I think, because everything is written down in those scripts."

"That's the least of it: to be an actress you have to have heart, a lot of heart, and Fabiana has a really big one. Or don't you think so?"

"I got here early and saw her go into the courthouse. We recognized her right away. And how we applauded her! She seemed very happy as she walked along with her attorney and other people, and all the photographers and television cameras."

"Why shouldn't she be happy! The only thing she's been asking for was to see him!"

"And the Paraguayan, didn't you see him going in?"

"Him, no. I'm sure he came in undercover."

"They're together inside now. It's been about an hour. I just heard it on the radio."

"Let us know of any new developments."

They laid me on a low bed, stretched out, with my arms and legs spread. The deep voice told me: 'All right, you disappeared from Corrientes, you're going to be here as long as it takes you to sing. We're not in a hurry, a week, a month, it's all the same. Now I advise you to start and really talk, because if you don't, do you know what this is?' and he passed a prod over my skin, without electricity. You tell us everything right now and tomorrow straightaway we'll send you abroad, to whatever country you choose.'

Because I said I didn't have any information that was anything the whole country didn't already know, they stuffed my mouth with a rag and began to run the prod over my body with the electricity on; my right side, my leg, my arm, my groin. Someone came in who busied himself with the verbal interrogation: 'Montoneros, ERP, communist, arms, members of the resistance, contacts; nothing on these topics?'

Again they go over my mouth, side, arm, leg, groin. Then they started asking about sex: 'Who slept with you? Which one of the priests? How?' They began to touch me threateningly on my breasts, my genitals. I was filled with loathing; I thought about the other things that could happen. I begged them to kill me quickly. They told me 'When you leave here you'll be useless as a woman for any man. Talk or we'll fry you,' and they started putting the prod with the electricity off into my vagina over and over.

They covered my mouth again and started the electric prod: breasts, abdomen. They were running it from my throat down to my genitals, from my arms down to my groin and legs. They stopped. They asked, 'Nothing?' Because I answered no, they did it again and again. Then all the voices and noises stopped. It seemed as if they had all gone. I relaxed. At that moment, I felt something fall on my stomach savagely, an object that seemed like a heavy ball or something.

Suddenly the doorman found himself alone and lost amid all the people and looked around for a familiar face. He saw a space in the center of the thirty-meter-long courthouse stairs jammed with people. He elbowed his way through and there was the salesman making his dancing puppet perform. Just then, someone bought two dolls from him and he took another two out of the sack he had left on the ground.

"What are you doing? Is that why you came? To sell your dolls?"

"I still have two left," he said. "And when it gets dark, the luminous yo-yos will look great."

"That's why you brought us?"

"I'm entertaining people and earning my money for the day. I'm not hurting anyone."

"And the others?"

"They're around," he shrugged his shoulders. "I'm doing my own thing."

The mailman appeared at the top of the stairs. Thanks to his post office uniform he had gotten himself into the hall in search of news.

"I was with the reporters and cameramen from all the television stations," he informed them, "They told me that the Paraguayan settled for sixteen million: ten for Fabiana and six for her attorneys."

"They're saying the same thing on the radio," said the woman who was holding the speaker to her ear. "They say it's all settled."

Someone is coming to 'talk.' 'Where will you go when we free you? To Goya? And what do you say to staying here forever? Do you know how to...the French way? No? You'll have to learn that! Not those filthy things you read. Look, I don't even read the papers.'

Someone else comes; he begins to pluck hairs from my stomach with tweezers. I feel an awful pain in my arms and legs...The worst was yet to come.

Someone comes in who says: 'Hasn't she said anything yet?' It was a new voice. The interrogation started over again. They stopped. They asked if I wanted to be raped by the twenty-five of them there or by the prod. They passed the prod over me. If I wanted ten. They used the prod again. They started in the vagina. They wanted me to admit that I had had sexual relations with priests. They ended up agreeing that I had had relations with a companion from Central America from whom they themselves had letters, as did I, testifying to the absolutely fraternal relationship that had existed. At no time did I make the effort to deny it. Their judgment didn't interest me.

By mid-afternoon (they had started at twelve o'clock) I was desperately thirsty. I wanted to shout 'Water!' They passed a glass dripping with condensation over my face. No water. They opened a faucet so that a heavy stream of water poured out; I thought I would go mad. I get dehydrated easily, it's a problem I've had since childhood: thirst.

At some point someone dried me off and told me in a soft voice, 'Talk, I'm telling you to talk because I know they're going to destroy you; the worst part's coming.'

From then on the pain of the interrogation was unspeakable; from the 110 volt prod they went to the 220 volt one. More and more they concentrated on my breasts, my groin, my vagina. They said to me: 'Look when it gets up to here, up to here on you...'

Someone else said: 'All these mares coming in here are the same. Break her...'

They put it under my nails, on my feet, provoking twitching muscular reactions all over my body with the prod. They applied it to my stomach, my spinal column.

Thirty-five journalists with their photographers and cameramen were waiting and jumped in front of Mercedes Ramón Negrete. He was wearing a shiny Pierre Cardin suit, a powder blue embroidered shirt and a burgundy tie. He walked on down the corridor as if he didn't see anyone around, as if he couldn't hear the journalists' shouts and calls. The spotlights and flashes bewildered him and he gave a timid smile, and flanked by his attorney, some policemen, and a private bodyguard, quickened his pace, but they had already blocked him. "Can you tell us what you talked about with Fabiana López?"

"That's a personal question. I don't have anything to say."

"Are you planning to give Miss Fabiana everything she asked for?"

"I don't have any reason to tell you that. I repeat this is a personal matter."

"Do you think you can leave just like this?" a journalist warned the attorney. "Too many people are waiting for you outside!"

After I'd been tortured for ten hours, except for brief intervals, I thought my heart wouldn't hold out much longer and I was glad. Then the guard left; someone said 'I admire you for your silence!' He moistened my lips with cotton dipped in water, he told me he couldn't give me water because of the amount of electricity I had inside me. He loosened my arms and legs and gave me permission to accommodate myself as I wished. I was completely broken, I couldn't move by myself. He told me that that night they would keep on beating me.

The second day someone began to doubt the accusations that had been written from Goya. I heard 'But man, these are only suppositions; there's nothing concrete here!' This same person was saying to me 'I believe you must be an ideologist; you don't look like a guerrilla fighter.'

At some point I heard: 'Whoever ordered this is a son of a bitch; whoever sold you out is a son of a bitch. What happened is they've filled the heads of the higher ups so much we have to keep going.' I had the sensation that there was a human being among the jackals.

The fourth and fifth days they interrogated me in conversations only; there was no torture. On the fifth, at night, a transfer.

The transfer was tortuous. In the condition I was in, the situation was doubly serious. On the way they said to me: 'Can you swim? We're going to have to tie a stone to her.' I was convinced they were going to throw me in the river.

The crowd broke into cheers and hurrahs when Fabiana López appeared at the top of the stairs. She stopped. She smiled and greeted them, waving her hand. She held that pose for a moment, to give the photographers time. Surrounded by journalists, she turned toward the three automobiles with press signs that were waiting for her at the foot of the stairs.

"How'd it go, chubby?" Someone shouted impulsively. "See how he gave you something after all?"

She didn't stop smiling, but walked a little faster. A woman caught her arm:

"Is it all arranged, Fabiana? I prayed so much for you!"

"I already told all about it on television," Fabiana said, pulling her arm away.

"Listen to the next news broadcast," a bearded journalist said, "live and in color."

The crowd let the automobiles of Fabiana López and her entourage take off and stayed there watching the opposite end of the stairway.

"And the Paraguayan? Is he staying inside?"

Someone who knew said no, that the Paraguayan would surely leave through another exit.

"He's getting away!" shouted a gray haired woman wearing an embroidered poncho, "And I came so far to tell him off!"

The postman brought the news from inside:

"They're saying in there that the Paraguayan is going to leave through the door for detainees."

They took me to a house. They told me I'd be there a few days under discipline, that my life depended on the blindfold; if I touched it they'd shoot me.

In three days or so a doctor came. He gave me antibiotics; I remember 'amplicicline' I was terribly swollen from the waist down, especially my thighs. I still couldn't walk without help for a few days. About the eighth day they took off the blindfold and made me look at the wall; my sight was blurry from not having been used. I washed my eyes, put on talcum powder and then they bandaged me with gauze.

At the same time, they started an oral interrogation about the Rural Movement. My trip to Central America. If I'd been to Cuba, the letters I had, the Rural Movement's plans.

Then some men began to arrive that one could tell were from the secret police (confirmed by the questions I was asked). Some began the interrogation in a normal way, and ended with exclamations like:

'You know very well what you're not telling us; you're going to be asked now…!' Someone else started in directly: 'Don't fold your hands, you're no saint!' an instant later, again, 'Don't fold your hands!' Another one started out slapping me in the face, the abdomen, the stomach, he grabbed me by the hair and threw me back while he said: 'You son of a bitch, tell us about when you were in Spain! You rotten bitch, you made out with…! I'm going to take you to a place you won't come back from, where I'll show you a muzzle, because I'm going to muzzle you!' I had to risk looking over at it because he didn't show it to me; 'I'm going to sit you on an ant hill the way I did to your friend; he's the one who sold you out, stupid. Him. We're going to keep him a month before we kill him, but you I'm going to blast now, and I know how to kill slowly…' He started to beat me again. He asked me about associations, unions, especially one. He told me he wanted maps, that he'd take me right away. Someone opened the door and said: 'The ambulance will be here in ten minutes.'

"You have no right to do that to an Argentine woman!" the salesman shouted in a hoarse tremulous voice he didn't recognize as his own. Voices seemed to burst from everyone's lungs and reverberate strong and sonorous like stones against the filthy walls of the Palace of Justice.

Two paddy wagons with an entourage of motorcyclists and two assault cars with machine guns poking out of their roofs stopped by the door that faced Lavalle Street. They were transferring men and women detained for subversive activities.

"Move it!" an official shouted. But the crowd remained still, their gaze fixed on the door where the millionaire Negrete was expected to slip out.

He tried to escape precisely at the moment the swirling assault cars and motorcyclists took off, returning the men and women to prison who had just testified about the way they had been tortured. They were handcuffed and isolated in individual cells which were more like vertical coffins. The echo of the indignant crowd reached them, and some might even have thought that it had to do with something on their behalf.

"Beat it, Paraguayan!" screamed the woman with the embroidered poncho. "Enjoy your money, but get out of this country!"

"You have no right!" another shouted. "Why did you do that to Fabiana?"

"I didn't do anything to her," the millionaire Negrete smiled timidly. His attorney gripped him by the arm protecting him, and several policemen opened a path for him between the curious onlookers.

"Beat it, darky!"

He was taken away in a shiny Mercedes with diplomatic license plates.

EUGENIA CALNY (1929-)

Born in the province of San Juan, Calny (whose real name is Fany Kalnitzky de Brener) grew up in Buenos Aires. A born author who began making up stories even before she learned to write, Calny has also done editorial work for literary and women's magazines and for literary supplements at *La Prensa* (*The Press*), *Clarín*, and *Editorial Abril* as well as a children's supplement for *La Nación* (*The Nation*).

In her quietly understated style, Calny presents the commonplace, seemingly small tragedies experienced by women struggling with their perceived obligations to fulfill the expectations of others and play the secondary and subservient roles traditionally assigned to them as dutiful wives, mothers, and daughters. By describing the repressed resentment that this sublimation and lack of appreciation causes in her protagonists, the restlessness and growing self and social awareness they experience, by sensitively revealing their sensual and sexual desires and feelings, Calny helps the reader understand the inevitable change and revolution in women's attitudes that finally brought about the women's liberation movement.

Her works include five book of short stories, *El agua y la sed* (*Water and Thirst*, 1960) which won Municipal Honorary Mention; *Las mujeres virtuosas* (*Virtuous Women*, 1967); *La tarde de los ocres dorados* (*Afternoon of Gilded Ochre*, 1978) which received Honorable Mention and SADE (Sociedad Argentina de Escritores/ Society of Argentine Writers) awards; *A los 33 años* (*At Age 33*, 1992) and *El angel, el diablo y la muerte* (*The Angel, the Devil, and Death*, 1994); a play, *La madriguera* (*The Burrow*, 1967), a book of poems, *La clépsidra* (*The Water Clock*, 1989), and two books of children's stories: *Cuentos con música* (*Stories with Music*, 1994) and *La Torre de Babel* (*The Tower of Babel*, 1987). Since 1976, Calny has written over thirty works for children and adolescents, including *La gaviota perdida* (*The Lost Sea Gull*) which is considered a children's classic.

Drifting Balloons

by Eugenia Calny

"Like a balloon, civilized man would be lost in space were it not for woman, representing ballast and ties that prudently keep him close."

In my family no one had read Santiago Ramón y Cajal; but all the men without exception fulfilled their role as balloons…Balloons of all colors—swarthy, blond, dark, auburn—always barely held captive by feminine hands…a navy balloon, cap cocked to one side. An adventurous balloon with a fragrant pipe. A bohemian balloon with beard and brushes. An intellectual balloon with books and glasses. A balloon behind bars, baffled and imprisoned. They all, for generations, drifted off into the blue….

We: ballast, cord, pillar and seed, stayed behind.

Unfortunately the women in my family all resembled one another. "The three Ss," as my Luis used to tease. Sad-faced, stolid, stable. However, when he said it I would be close to his skin, his look, his smile, his rhythm and "sad-faced" was a bitter-sweet compliment whose sweetness I swallowed, carelessly discarding the bitter part, because of the symmetry of loving lips….

We women were a clan apart, independent, made of iron. United by ties of blood that were not always identifiable. My mother and I shared with my grandmother the old house she had built with arduous, and herculean efforts. We had all been legitimate for three generations and by some family law, all gave birth to other females. We were always growing in numbers, whether in passing, on vacation for a season, or just abandoned, a second cousin, an aunt we barely knew, or some needy young woman.

What united all of us was the fatality of our blind destiny, severe and austere as a religion. And the blind, severe and austere acceptance of it.

We lived in a matriarchy. Actually, a very special matriarchy. Our men were names, memories, dates, disturbances. Sowers who never bothered to reap their harvest.

The only one who had left us in the normal way was my greatgrandfather. And he went grumbling, resisting, cursing and fighting all the way.

From five in the morning on he would put away miles on horseback. He would put away food the same way, almost without chewing, and wine and distilled *grappa*, anything. The only thing he didn't swallow was his rage; this he distributed democratically among his children, his wife, the dogs, and the servants. But when he was ninety-eight years old...

"There are more widows than widowers," my Luis would laugh. "Statistics say so." And statistics are irrefutable...

"You never lose your heads, you have no inhibitions or complexes. You always know what you want and where you're going," Luis would tease...or say admiringly. "It's your rural heritage..."

Rural heritage...Yes, Luis, my great-grandfather used to growl and shout. But the one who stood alone to face the locusts and the droughts and the children who came and went before their time was Great-grandmother.

When Great-grandmother could have enjoyed the countryside a little, the good part of it, the clear and dreamy-eyed thistles, the sweet blood-red juice of the dwarf vines, the landscape of cactus bristling with burrs in their pathetic defense of water, the festive and burning sun, giving us pure air for generations to come, he decided to pack his bags and his children and come to the capital.

Naturally, he gave back the parcel of dry, cracked land that had never become entirely his. And he brought along all his savings tied in rags, stuffed in the copper kettle that a globe-trotting gypsy had sold him long ago, in his youth, scratching his rough palm, his long life line.

There, though stingily, the earth had offered flowers and fruit. True, one had to dig deep into its entrails with a plow or hoe to feel it turn over and shudder. In turn, one had to submerge oneself in it, half bury oneself, kneel as if before an altar, break one's back, calcify one's bones, scold it, shout at it, or bless it. But in the end, the earth produced.

Here, nothing grew from the pavement or the sterile mud. There weren't even lemon trees bursting with fragrant blossoms. Nor *prisco* peaches splitting in two. Nor homey twining grapevines. One had to buy *everything*.

(The coins rattled against the kettle.) The children went like deflated balloons in one or other of the epidemics the authorities ascribed to them. Beaten, dried as a raisin, Great-grandmother followed them not before leaving an inheritance to her only survivor: Grandmother. (And the copper became wood.)

"Kettles are no good as banks," declared the then young woman.

She chose a calling for herself: washerwoman. And consequently, ironing woman. Who could compare to her in starching shirt collars and cuffs? And linen sheets with Richelieu borders and elegantly intertwined initials...Washing and ironing bridal trousseaus, in full youthful bloom how could she not fall in love?...

Grandfather had blue eyes and no real job. He had been a sailor on cargo ships. A lover of sirens who were worn out from the fumes of the port. A soldier at some front with old scouting posts made of barbed wire. A prisoner of thirst and drink. A good dancer. A wood carver in whose unusual artisan's hands filigreed sighs and flights of tireless birds would come to life...A singer of Christmas carols, sailor's songs, obscene songs. An aquatic vagabond anchored by idleness or miracle. What difference did it make?

Her hands hardened to the bleach and her back conformed to the ironing board. And she saved. She would walk any number of blocks to save the cost of a ride. And when the mileage exceeded even her will, she traveled at hours of dawn and mist to take advantage of worker's rates on the streetcars.

She was tall, bony and vinelike. (Oh, pardon me, I should say, tall, slender and with no superfluous fat.) (Why didn't I stand up for her when, sure of her deafness, because of her mummified presence in a corner of the kitchen, Luis would say, dying of laughter, that Grandfather had acted out of good taste, of aesthetics? Why is it hard for me to see in her furrowed face some smoothness, if not from beauty at least from the youth that must once have been hers?)

She and Grandfather lived together for five months. At night she was never hungry and fed her cardboard box its daily ration of coins.

And she sat, contentedly, tranquilly, hands folded quietly over the curve of her womb.

One night when she had prepared dinner for both of them because it was a holiday and one of her clients had given her some hardly used baby clothes, she fell asleep in front of her plate. She was awakened by who knows what morning bell and saw grandfather in the doorway. Staggering, grotesque, babbling incoherent words. He had papers in his hands and he was rummaging through the drawers looking for things, tossing things. Grandmother sighed at the uneaten dinner that would turn bad without even a touch of ice in the pan, and, drained of energy, drowsy in the heat of the night, closed her eyes again to drive away the bad dream.

Grandfather never came back. He left her only one thing, a small wood carving: a condor with feathers skillfully marked, curved raptor's beak, and useless wings folded in a tragic gesture of immobility: its drive to heights, to immensity, would never go beyond the truncated gesture which both urged him on and retained him in space...And which he seemed to feel within his bitter, savage, uselessly varnished fibers.

Grandmother convinced herself of his departure and accepted it after a few practical inquiries. Someone, a neighbor, murmured that the fugitive had talked about sailing away. Years later, someone said that he was living in Brazil. When I was small, it used to amuse me to imagine that I might have black relatives with freckles. (That he'd formed another home. That he'd made a fortune.)

After Grandmother had made sure that he was not included on any hospital lists or accident cases, she opened the cardboard box—damp and covered with green moss—and counted her coins.

"I'll have to save," I'm sure she said or thought in her solitude.

Fortunately, she was an artisan of foam and scouring. And in the final months, her neighbors came to help her. When my mother announced her imminent arrival, grandmother walked to the hospital, carrying her own small bundle of clothing.

"It will be a female," she told the midwife, "because she has to help me."

By the time she was nine years old, the child was earning her first coins running errands in the neighborhood. Sometimes, instead of money, she would accept a piece of cake. Then Grandmother would scold her. You had to save…in a little painted clay doll that might have been a little gaucho or anything else, because just as soon as you put something into it, it became shamelessly deformed.

Grandmother took out a savings account book (they were bigger then than they are now) and every time the doll's insides would fill up, she'd make a deposit. Going to the bank branch at the post office was a nice outing for momma. On Sundays, the streetcar would take them for a ride to get some fresh air along the coastal road. You could look at the sea (I wanted to call it the "lion colored" river) and dream….

One day, in the grocery store, while he was weighing sugar on the scale closely watched by Grandmother, the shop owner commented: "*Caramba*, lady; this child seems to grow with the rain."

Since it had been raining a lot in recent winters, Grandmother was startled. Her daughter's thin body was beginning to reveal some womanly attributes.

When you spend a lot of time in the city (in addition to running errands the girl had also started learning to sew), you usually come to know love—or its substitute—prematurely. My future father worked in the same tailor shop as my mother. He worked seasonally of course. The irons with their hot coals bent their backs and warmed their faces.

Father was alone. He had arrived in this country as an immigrant, from who knows what city razed by which revolution or atrocity. He liked to tell my mother how, when he first went to work as an apprentice, in tailoring of course, and went proud and expectantly to receive his first wages, the owner threw him out, slammed the door in his face and threatened him for his absurd pretensions.

Of course after that, he grew up. He got big, strong. He learned to swallow his tears inside. He took part in a strike and ended up out of work. They exchanged their first kiss through bars, with a policeman and a homemade beef roulade as witnesses. He had no previous record and was soon free, a hero. My mother, despite tenacious maternal opposition, fell madly in love—which is the only sane way to fall in love—and ran off to marry him.

They had a measure of years and whatever they were wearing. Naturally, they came back to the big old house. And Grandmother took them in without comment, with a bowl of hot soup. She didn't ask any questions and she looked carefully at the girl's loose blouse.

Momma didn't have an easy time carrying me. Grandmother says they were afraid they'd lose me. But…now, well. In my family the women always were inclined to love. Whole, blind, unparalleled love. Fruitful love too.

My father had great plans. His mind was continually bubbling, in danger of exploding. The capital came to seem too small for him and he decided to roam through the outskirts. Then greater Buenos Aires became too confining for him, uncomfortable as a shrunken suit and he looked toward the interior (I must have traveled too, without a ticket…).

Exactly at the end of her nine months, Momma returned to the old house. She had set up and undone four houses in a year. She had stolen pesos out of fatigue and hunger. Bringing things…broken dishes, old rags, new little nightgowns. And a little bank she'd been given as a gift: a pink plastic piglet, with lively, protruding eyes.

"Female," the doctor said, and surely Momma and Grandmother clasped their hands fervently. It couldn't help but be a blessing. My father, pleased and irresponsible, sent a congratulatory telegram…

It was the only thing he sent me. Although when he came to visit once in a while, he'd bring presents. Useless, expensive presents. Grandmother would look at him sternly. But Momma…her eyes would light up. (Have you ever seen that special glow of loving eyes?) Father had a unique sense of humor. He was biting, ironic, mocking. He resembled my Luis…Sometimes, caught up in the captivating mist of his own words, it seemed that he might finally drop anchor at our side. With all my might I used to help Momma tug on the weak thread that might possibly hold him. But only for a few months. Because everything always depended on a harvest, a future business deal, an associate, a promise. An idealist, unaware, crazy. He used to like to read us fragments of books and poems that we scarcely understood. But the days he spent with us were happy ones. Although I'll probably always remember him with a suitcase in his hand, waving good-bye.

Grandmother used to say he went the same way he'd lived. In a train wreck, because the crossing guard was in a drunken sleep. Had he been able to express an opinion, I know he would have said, "Poor boy. Not drunk, no; he just fell asleep…" And we never knew if he was in the train going north or in the one coming to Buenos Aires.

Momma put a black ribbon on his picture. The neighbors and the clients that brought their sewing to her all expressed their sympathy with proper solemnity. None of them let on they knew that she had been a widow almost all her life.

I was fourteen when I read the ad in the newspaper: "Needed, girl who knows how to paint." It was two blocks away from home; that would save transportation and I was crazy about painting. If I could have studied…Enough. Luis reproaches me for that: life is not built on "could haves." The employer wanted a sample of my painting. "I don't like to deal with minors," he mumbled. He gave me a small glass vase and flower motif to copy. My sable-hair paint brush trembled when I daubed it into the red paint. But the employer smiled with satisfaction. "By the way you pick up the brush, it's clear you know how to paint," he asserted. (Why correct his error?)

Six hours of work for seventy pesos pay. I would stay after hours, voluntarily, to learn more. Momma and Grandmother looked at me with surprise bordering on admiration. That I would seek work on my own initiative, was more than they could dare ask. It was promising. Their admiration rapidly dissolved in tears.

I had at least ten ideas on how to spend my first earnings. Number one was that first pair of nylon stockings so languidly exhibited in the shop windows. But my entire first salary had to be saved. By law, by tradition, by inheritance.

The echo of the war, the wildness of the "boogie-woogie," the unattainable nylon stockings, the rush for vitamins, Clark Gable's robust smile, the changing geography of Europe…The whole world was vibrating around us. It trembled, it was swallowed up in the convulsions of a monster about to give birth, painfully, to a new era: with all its weaknesses, its faults, and scars, its scientific and technical advances, its illusions. The post-war period. But inside the big old house; silence, refuge, peace. The solitude began to weigh on me. The years.

Adolescence and the war ended. How many refugees passed through the house splashing us with their fresh sorrows, their memories, their hidden secrets, pregnant with phantoms? Time. In this house of women there was always space for another cot, another place at the table, the warm gesture of listening. For the most part, women. In their stories there were always balloon-men. Prisoner balloons. Balloons snatched away. Balloons hungering crazily for immortality.

The neighborhood changed so much in fifteen years. But we still continued to paint the small wooden door green. "Boogie" was followed by "rock and roll," the "twist." Giant figures rose up and fell into light or obscurity. Girls lengthened their skirts, shortened their skirts, feathered their hair, wore ponytails, uncombed manes, dashed their hair with spray, painted their eyes like Cleopatra's. There was an old wave and a new wave. Television, round tables, psychology, tests and traumas. And the world was anguishing amidst cold wars and old-new fevers and new-old hopes. Hopes...

(Painting the door green again?)

I made the decision without asking. And when the little room upstairs became empty again, that room which had always sheltered someone who was disinherited, cast away by life, I decided to rent it ...to a man. (I was like a bush without flowers: roots, bark, needles, branch-like arms. Or vice versa. Thirty years and not even one rose...)

By then Grandmother was already scarcely speaking. She would just move her head in a corner of the kitchen, she seemed like one more object, a mended old casserole. Momma was sewing only for a group of friends to whom she couldn't say no.

I was head of the clan. My salary had grown along with my skill with paintbrushes. Oh, never anything good; just decorations on the glass and crockery that my employer insisted on calling crystal and porcelain...But I allowed myself some eccentricities. One night, for example, on returning from work, it occurred to me to buy a rare candy: coconut candy, imported from Brazil. They raised such a fuss...that Luis, our roomer, looked into the kitchen. The two women were accusing me of waste, and he defended me on grounds of my youth....

(Was that the moment he dazzled me? He suddenly balanced our ages that way. And love after thirty...)

We ate the coconut candy between the two of us in successive after-dinner chats that summer. After supper—he ate at an inn—he started coming down from upstairs to have coffee with us.

"Be careful," my mother's tired eyes seemed to warn me.

"Be careful," warned my grandmother's sunken almost lifeless eyes.

Be careful? I would have wanted to be prudent, reasonable, cold. I would have wanted to usurp all the feminine experiences of the family...and *absorb them*. (But love after thirty!)

The longer summer wore on, the more immersed I was in his clarity, in the magic of his voice, his contagious laugh. And one night, from so often drawing near his gaze to see the truth clearly, to discover his secret, to shout voicelessly at him that I needed a "stable husband," or at least a "stable man," I received the full impact of his magic stiletto, and I self-destructed.

Vacation time came. Luis packed his bags because he had come to the capital just to study, to improve himself, and love hadn't entered his plans. (Love never enters men's plans.) He had his degree now. Why not a girlfriend in the provinces too? Why not a warm, cozy nest-like office set up by his parents?

He promised to come back, because *he knew*. But first he had to check on so many details, so many transactions, change so many plans! His parents had done so much for him. Spent all their savings so that he could study. How could he disappoint them? When I saw him leave, I was crystallized by tears. I think that had he touched me, dared even to look at me, I would have shattered like crystal.

I went into the kitchen, and without looking at me Mother asked: "How many months of vacation will they give you at work, Lia?" and without waiting for a reply, "nowadays, it's not like it used to be."

"We'll have to save," Grandmother spoke half asleep, as if she had awakened only to speak to a memory.

And it's as if, suddenly, the copper kettle, the cardboard box, the little clay gaucho, the plastic pig, are all crashing down on me. I explode. Later, I scarcely feel her hand on my hair. She must have been speaking for a while, but I'm just now making sense of her words.

" ...painless birth, why not? It doesn't cost any more. And there's already enough pain," she pursed her lips. In the new maternity ward where they turn on a red or blue light according..." She dries my broken crystals. Why don't they tinkle? "After all, you're not in the street. We're not in the street..."

Sad-faced. Stolid. Stable. Made with the good stuff of the old days, the big old house stands, fruit of the savings of generations of women. Because they have all added something to it as they came along. Because they all...

Letters come. They are nice, simple, promising. He'll come back. Is it true that my Luis will come back? Yesterday a strange man came and asked for shelter for the night. We found out that he is the husband of the woman who takes turns at caring for Grandmother. In reality, we have to feed and care for both of them. We allowed him to come in. He set some depressing drawings and canvases in the corner, but after looking at us he turned them to face the wall. They exchanged almost no words. It had been so many years. The next morning he wasn't there. The woman carefully cleaned up the room.

(Drifting balloons, climbing up into the blue…)

I have savings. My fingers are pulling so hard on the string that they hurt. I've gotten caught up in the srings, they cut into me, leaving their red marks: fine, cutting scars on me. I hold the string tense, clutched between my teeth. It catches on a cloud, but the clouds are air, and I don't let go of it, don't let go of it, I feel it's still mine, as long as it doesn't burst in the light…

In the Hero's Shadow

by Eugenia Calny

*I*t was the high point of the celebration. *Sixty glorious years*…her thoughts plagiarized the title of an old movie about the life of Queen Victoria. In it there'd been a queen and a prince consort. Here it was the reverse: there'd been a public figure, a winner, a hero…Her husband. And she was in his shadow. She was nothing, but *his wife*.

Once more they raised their glasses to toast him. She raised hers: felt the tickling sensation of the cider, the tears, the memories.

Another speaker stood up, cleared his throat and said that few men in their lifetime had been privileged enough to reach the point where others recognized their merits. And Manuel Andrade had achieved that. She remembered a verse she'd read somewhere:

Ah, it is not always true that death herself
determines the measures of a man's greatness.
After she covers him with earth,
his name rises up again from the grave.

This was not one of those posthumous tributes that makes you sigh: "Poor fellow, so much talk, so much praise, but it's all the same to him now…"

No. There was Manuel Andrade, sixty years of age, bald, obese, imposing. Full of life, surrounded by life. There were his children and his children's children. His friends and their children. His current friends and the friends of his early years. Even some dignitaries had been invited to the celebration and were stiffly, appropriately, fraternizing with the public, conscious of the importance their very presence created.

María felt that genuine pride a woman feels at the side of a strong man everyone admires. As a *person*, as herself, her pride was weaker: bits and fragments of her were less noble.

While he was expressing his thanks for yet another gift—a briefcase wrapped in cellophane—Andrade turned toward his wife with a low voice.

"They're flat. They need a little more spice. You usually make them better. At a time like this…" and he indicated, with a vague gesture, the platter of *empanadas*[1] that the guests were devouring.

His two elder daughters made a really triumphant entrance carrying in huge trays of roasted chicken. A tempting aroma spread throughout the hall. The obese woman sitting across from Don Manuel removed her belt; held her wine glass with one hand, grasped an *empanada* with the other and said, to everyone in general:

"And all this was prepared by doña María!…You can eat with confidence, gentlemen! It's all homemade! Ah, doña María has a golden touch! Congratulations, dear."

María thanked her with a gentle nod. Memories of countless weddings, baptisms, family and other birthdays paraded through her mind. She saw herself working from morning until night, for days beforehand, among stacks of plates and pans back in the days when gas, pressure cookers or soup concentrates, pre-baked pizzas and cake mixes still did not exist. Suffering from a cold, standing beside the open mouth of the red-hot crackling oven and kneading dough. With her hands stained with blood from the chickens and dirty with flour and dust, her face fiery, and a burning pain in her waist, preparing banquets for fifty, one hundred, two hundred people. And she saw herself, blond and fresh faced when she was twenty. With a child in her arms and another in her womb and her first gray hairs when she was thirty. With wrinkles and glasses at forty, with her first grandchild and her tiredness at fifty and now…

At sixty years of age, *her* obscure, anonymous, uncelebrated sixty years of age; lusterless years without any identity of their own, María would have hoped things would be different…But Manuel hated any

---

[1] empanadas: fried pastries stuffed with meat or vegetables

kind of food that wasn't homemade. As far as he was concerned, any food that could be bought ready-made was toxic; at the very least, inedible.

The children, dazzled, as usual, by the sun of their world's solar system, took their father's side.

"But Mom, remember that it's Dad's birthday! Aren't you going to give him that satisfaction?…You're only sixty once in your life, Mom!"

Only once in a lifetime. For her too.

The children had promised to help her; but the oldest one's children had measles and the other one left work so late. María made a fan of the paper napkin. She felt so exhausted that she would gladly have slipped away to go and lie down for a while. But she couldn't leave her husband alone. She couldn't let the public down. She had to play her role to the end.

A group of old friends—gray, wrinkled, balding, unconditional admiration and deeply rooted affection—gave him a certificate. Everyone applauded. One of them asked permission to tell a story about him. He'd known him well for thirty years. And then another and another. As the attentive audience listened, Don Manuel, founder of the Volunteer Firemen and the city library, and the Neighborhood Fund for Street Repair was paraded before them. About Don Manuel as husband, father, or simply man, there were no anecdotes.

"…thanks to his thirst for learning and his love for books, even though he had no degrees or formal learning, Don Manuel founded our library and donated its first seven books…"

A small laugh escaped María and surprised, accusing eyes turned on her. It would have been almost funny to tell them, for example, that of those seven books he'd donated, five had been hers when she was still single, they even contained dedicatory notes to her. And when he used to read over the children's homework it was always "Keep still! You all know that when Papa reads, you have to keep dead still," which was the same as ordering them to keep perfect silence—an order the children, two daughters and a son—tried to obey in order to avoid the risk of getting hit or injured by flying objects.

Once the oldest girl—ten years old, lanky and freckled—had dared to interrupt him when he was reading the paper, and the sewing scissors flew at her, decorating her cheek with a small scar…

María turned misty eyes toward her daughter. Through her cream base and powder she discerned the slight trace of that scar…The girl interpreted her glance to mean something else and answered: "He's ready now," referring to her son, who, a few minutes later, standing on a chair—his knees hopelessly dirty—recited his "Poem for my Grandfather."

Applause, kisses on both cheeks, and the threat of an unbearable repetition.

"Don't embarrass him anymore," Don Manuel's voice intervened, rescuing him. "He's just had measles and he's weak…"

The child happily slipped away among the tables.

Don Manuel began a conversation about childhood diseases with the woman seated next to him.

"My children were never sick. In my home we didn't know what sickness was," he stated proudly. "Not like today's generation."

Naturally. As far as he was concerned, the children had never been sick. Because he had never had time to pay attention or find out about such trifles. But she certainly had known about fevers, sore throats, diptheria, whooping cough. About sleepless nights, doctor's calls, temperatures that wouldn't break, tonics, weakness, and anxiety. She alone. Don Manuel had demanded that they let him sleep in peace, "That's why I work all day." And when the children, whether small or sick or well, broke the silence of the night with the intemperate cries of their fragmented nightmares, she would see his violent reactions, his fury, his fist banging on the furniture, his insults, the blind menace he directed toward the cradle.

"Don Cosme, my father, may he rest in peace, used to say that when you donated the land across from the plaza…," one of the guests was saying just then.

The land across from the plaza. She had bought it, saving (why did that sound so ridiculous now?) one coin after another, one dollar after another. That was the time when crisis had threatened their already scanty household budget and that was when she bought the small machine to sheath buttons and began to do a little sewing. The plot—a minuscule one where weeds grew happily—had given her a feeling of security. It was her own little piece of land where some distant day, she would raise a scaffolding of mud and dreams.

Then…

She remembered the eviction, the generosity of others. And if now they lived without fear of losing the roof over their heads, it was thanks to their children. Thanks to the closeness of their children.

"Come on, old girl, what's the matter with you? You haven't opened your mouth all night."

"It's just that…I don't feel very well," and suddenly, she knew that it was true. Those memories, reactivated, were producing an almost physical malaise. "I'd like…if I could leave for a little while…"

"Come on, old girl, you've always been right there beside me. What will people say if you disappear in the middle of the party? Don't let me down now…"

She nodded her assent, giving him the mute assurance that she would not let him down.

Now the guests were calling Don Manuel's name in chorus, asking him to speak. Heavily, he rose to his feet.

"My God, he ate too much," she thought. Before long his liver would begin to protest. She trembled. When he didn't feel well, he always took it out on her. Between the old family doctor and María, they coddled him like a child to make him take his medicine and follow a diet.

"The time has come to say thank you. To those old friends who are present and to those who are not…"

"Now," María said to herself, "*now*," without knowing exactly what she expected.

The thank you list was long and replete with personal names. But hers was not included.

The tears that she had tried so hard to hold back all day rolled down her face. The heavy woman handed her a handkerchief, meanwhile taking it upon herself to explain to the kindly guests:

"It's emotion, you know? Emotion…"

She looked at them through two unsteady lenses. Everyone loved and admired him; they owed him a lot. Those who love in general cannot love—and even less show love—to just one person.

She was the only one who knew this. She held fast to the last threads of that conviction, sighing deeply to drink in the pride, the appreciation of life which at this late stage still allowed them to be together. She should be happy. (She was tired, that was all.)

She was happy. She had always done it before, through all her sixty years without glory. In the last stretch…"Weakness is forbidden."

The three children came up to her, seeking maternal refuge as they usually did in those great moments of joy, or pain.

"Yes, it's emotion…" she repeated, aloud, a little disconcerted now by the conversation of the others. And she dried away her last rebellious tear.

ISIDORO BLAISTEN (1933-)

Born in 1933 in Concordia, Entre Ríos, but raised in Buenos Aires, Blaisten was the son of Ukranian immigrants who both died before he was ten. He grew up poor, lived in tenement houses, and witnessed the violence in the city first hand when his only brother was shot and killed in 1945. Although his early ambition was to be a painter or a poet, Blaisten has been at various times, an artist, poet, photographer, conference speaker, salesman, bookstore manager, essay and feature writer, columnist, presenter of literary workshops, and short story writer. Essentially apolitical, Blaisten who nevertheless appreciates the freedom of expression democracy provides the creative writer, actively promotes many of Asociación Mutual Israelita Argentina's (Argentine Israelite Federation) cultural events.

Best known for his wit and originality, his use of colloquial *porteño* language, and his verbal inventiveness, Blaisten uses humor as a camouflage for the anxiety and desperation of the poor or marginal types he typically portrays. He paints acerbic pictures of proud *porteño* types more afraid of ridicule than failure, and creates absurd situations inverting, distorting, or exaggerating reality, creating whimsical and sometimes harsh parodies of our bizarre, irrational, sometimes poetic world. His most recent collection of stories, *Al acecho* (Stalking, 1995), is written with a somber, almost morbid tone that demonstrates his tendency to experiment.

Blaisten's first book, *Sucedió en la lluvia* (*It Happened in the Rain*, 1965), was a collection of poems to his mother expressing the loss and desolation he experienced at her death. His other books: *La felicidad* (*Happiness*, 1969), *La salvación* (*Salvation*, 1972), *El mago* (*The Magician*, 1974), *Dublin al Sur*, (*Dublin South*, 1980, 1992), *Cerrado por melancolía*, (*Closed on Account of Melancholy*, 1981), *Cuentos anteriores*, (*Previous Stories*,1982), *Carroza y reina* (*Queen and Carriage*,1986) *Cuando éramos felices*, (*When We Were Happy*, 1992), and *Al acecho*, (Stalking, 1995) are all collections of short stories; *Anticonferencias*, (Anticonferences, 1983) contains a selection of his essays.

His has been awarded the National Arts Award, First and Second Place Muncipal Awards of Buenos Aires; the National Literary

Award, the National Award for Essay and Literary Criticism, the Esteban Echeverría Award and the Konix Platinum Award. His stories have been translated into English, French and German, and have appeared in numerous anthologies in Argentina and abroad.

The Tarmites

by Isidoro Blaisten

*I*t's not really "tarmites," but "termites" with an *e*, because the name really comes to us from those insects, termites, that terminate everything they encounter.

I don't know why, but that's what they all call us: "the tarmites."

I don't know exactly how one gets to be a tarmite. It's hard to explain. Now, after so many years, it seems to me it happens in a number of ways: from disillusionment or boredom; habit or imitation. But there always has to be something inside first. You are born with it and there's nothing you can do about it. Take Tuderi's case, for example. The poor fellow has no class and he'll never learn, no matter how much you try to teach him.

In Margarita's case, it's easy to explain. My old lady enjoys it because of the excitement it always gives her. "I don't know why I go along with you," she used to tell me, "most likely because I'm stupid, but I like the excitement you bring me."

As for me, on the other hand, it organizes my life. I alone know what it means to get up in the morning knowing what you have to do: to have a plan and an obligation and at the same time be free and know that every day will be different. Sometimes I think about the unfortunate laborers, the policemen, the traveling salesmen and then I smile. Let's be honest. It's not all roses. But Margarita says that in order to choose one thing, you always have to reject another and, since I've been struggling for years, I know she's right. I know lots of other things too: I know that now we can never start over again, that the years have passed, I know that we're out of time and that it's irrevocable. I know all this, I know that it's too late now, that I'm going downhill, that the kids are going to be very unhappy. I know lots of other things too, but my life is organized.

Early in the morning, Margarita brings me coffee and the borrowed newspaper. The first step in getting organized is to write down the death notices so that we can be well dressed. We tarmites all dress well, because, as Margarita says: "In this country, when you go around well dressed, you show your talent." That's why, as soon as I've finished writing down a name from some upper class family, I rush off to be one of the first to arrive at the home of the deceased.

On the way, I practice. My memory is in good shape now, that's sure. Not like Tuderi, who always mixes up the family names and more than once has had a rough time. Not me. When I'm facing the doorman, I spit out all the necessary first and last names for him without skipping any.

I should make it clear that doormen are the vilest things God put on earth. They sniff us out right off and have the soul of rats. Since they're nobodies, they're servile and prudish. They're like women with property. They defend things that even their owners disdain. They want to get ahead, and they don't know how to, they can't. They have no class and they make themselves feel important by humiliating people. They enjoy it when they catch us, their eyes shine, they get so riled up it seems as if they've waited all their lives, as if they were born just for this moment…It's better not to talk about it. The maids, butlers and self-seeking relatives are dangerous too, but they've been around more, and after all (modesty aside), one doesn't get to be a tarmite by accident.

Once I've passed the sound barrier, the real test comes: the attack on the widow. Here everything has to be well gauged, from removing your hat with a somber gesture to asking about the belongings of "our philanthropist" or "our philanthropist who's left us," as the case may be. I always say "philanthropist" and not "deceased." Like poor Tuderi, who more than once came out with "the decedent" and another time, when he wanted to act refined, said "the defunct." Fortunately, he has such a sad face it's pitiful, and sometimes he works the silences so well there's nothing more to do. As Margarita says: "He may not have talent, but grief speaks to grief."

But the best approach with widows is a discreet solemnity. Don't exaggerate, get right to the point like a mailman and immediately invoke "Don Orione," "The Penny Association," "The Little Followers of Mary," "The Ragmen of Emmaus," "Help me out," anything at all. Prepare the credentials right away, then all the first and last names, and then the silences. The silences are very important. People are disturbed by them and want to get them over with right away. Then you stand there like a judge although you're not judging anything and to get rid of you they give you anything. But the main thing is to know how to soften them up with the dead person's name and with the suits he wasn't using and had promised to the association and to notice carefully if it's all right to say "poor thing," "unbelievable," "how unfair fate is," or "he would have wanted it this way." "A philanthropist like him," almost never fails. On the other hand: "A man like him, always helping the needy," sometimes works and sometimes doesn't. Often the widow has stopped crying to stare at me surprised when I've said that. But usually the most effective thing is to keep repeating "philanthropist," and finish her off with "I understand your grief, ma'am," and keep still. Then the woman covers her face with her handkerchief and tells them to bundle something up for me. I keep the suits that fit me. The rest I sell to the Jews on Liberty Street. Two mornings a week Margarita does the same with dead women. But nobody can compare with Margarita. She can get anything. She makes people cry, she takes over, she actually suffers. She consoles the sisters, they serve her coffee, she kisses the children, she really gets emotional. Once she came back home in tears with a taxi full of clothes. An incredible "booty" nobody else would have attempted. All the judge's clothes, almost all his wife's belongings and the children's wardrobe. Lucky it was a hasty donation. Some poor, obliging relative, one of those who never counts for anything. We laughed a lot with Margarita, imagining the uproar that must have followed later. But the thing is that we made some great selections, and Martin and Alex have two lovely uniforms for English school that will last awhile.

It's just that Margarita is incomparable. Sometimes I realize how much I love her and wonder how far she might have gone with that talent, that grace, that class and bearing of hers. But, in brief, as Margarita says: "Don't look back old man, or you'll turn into a pillar of salt."

Once the clothes are taken care of, we have to decide how to crash press conferences and manage the food. First we read all the papers, note the places, and prepare our business cards. Then I lead the way.

When the stingy doorman is overwhelmed with three or more guests, I take advantage of his confusion with the cards and go in. With great dignity, of course, but still almost running until I reach the middle of the hall. In the middle of the hall I'm safe. There you find the best tables, the big shots, the most distinguished personalities and all the people who want to be seen (and who, if they're smart, take our side when danger comes around or when things get sticky). In the middle of the room it's easier to shake off the miserable doorman yelling that you're a rabble rouser, a Peronist, crude, stupid and scum. I can always find Natalio, Tuderi, the Angladas, and Crespi there as well as some other tarms I know who'll come to my aid when there's trouble.

Crespi's made to order for these occasions. Tall, with white hair, very elegant, he's a perfect gentleman. His presence alone commands respect. He treats doormen with olympic disdain. He never shouts. "Do me a favor, you impertinent fellow and don't bother the doctor," he warns them, lightly pulling on their lapels. "You have one minute to disappear," he tells them when everybody's looking at them. And he starts to mark the time on his watch. Right after that he introduces me to the head of public relations, asks me about my little polo ponies, and he begins to complain about household help in Europe. What a gentleman Crespi is! And a great friend. Margarita and I dearly love him. Crespi has saved me a number of times, but fortunately, except for two or three times, I haven't had any major difficulties getting in, even though, to start with I don't like to make a show of my credentials like Neftalio. I always use them as a last resort, no matter how much trouble there is.

We tarmites have credentials from the most disparate publications, almost all of which are nonexistent. Tuderi's, for example, has my signature and Crespi's. I signed it as president and Crespi as secretary. We had to recommend a print shop to him because the poor thing (in spite of being a great guy) just can't manage and has no class. A number of times the concierge carried him off toward the exit. We had to teach Tuderi how to take him by the arm and exit with dignity, talking to him as if he were a friend, slapping him on the shoulder when everyone was looking, trying to give the impression that we are condescendingly taking a subordinate by the arm.

But to have to resort to your credentials is like calling the police. Like admitting you're a cuckold. It's almost like admitting defeat.

It pains me to confess that I've sometimes had to do it. There was no other way to avoid an unfortunate ousting. But I always get in. Well, almost always. I and all the tarmites. Certain maitre d's at a, the Alvear, and the City Hotel respect us because we make them look good. Sometimes the managers even look for us to boost attendance when there's an event.

Once I've gotten in, the rest is easy. Greet people, introduce yourself, yes, but above all a lot of talk, laying it on. As Margarita says, "Style makes the man, old boy." And everyone has his technique. I always talk about "my little get-away place at General Vellegas," which has worked fairly well up until now. "Just a little place, a mere 1500 acres," I always begin by saying (rather, that's where I stop, for I always work the silences). Then I continue mentioning the offers, "I've had so many offers for it," I say, "that I don't know what to do…raising Zeus brand cattle might be interesting" (here a small silence). "Although lately I've gotten enthusiastic about that blessed complex of refractory bricks…but look, after all, what can I say, doctor, family memories are like those cameos, they don't come in use much anymore and that, nevertheless one…"

And here I break off leaving a touch of mystery. It's never good to lay it on too thick. Then, moving on, I help out the photographer. Photographers. Our only friends. It's a task I undertake with pleasure. I form groups, smile, make jokes. Truly, I take them under my wing. I never say, "Let's take a picture," but, "Come, let's immortalize ourselves." I never address the man as a photographer but "Dear Journalist." You can recognize the ordinary types, the half bald ones and the ones who want to run the show because they yell: "How about a picture, boss?" We always say: "A photograph, if you please."

That's why there's such a communion of ideals between tarmites and photographers. Like us they also work by "assault" without having been called on. But even "the officials," "the exclusives," and "the ones under contract," see us as a possible sale. That's why we always seem familiar to them and they always remember us; they're not sure whether it was at the reception for President Arosemena or the one at the Ministry of Ghana. Finally, the journalist places us. "Yes, it was at the reception for President Arosemena," and they ask us again if they can bring the whole set of proofs by our office and we answer, "of course, as usual." Then after someone else has paid, I disappear, moving on to greet the "attaché," who almost always is Natalio who's devouring the canapés by the handful and telling humorous tales to the public relations manager of the Propaganda Graphic.

This is the time to eat. First I replace Neftalio in the conversation giving him time to swallow and then comes my turn.

By now there's nothing left. The devastation begins. That's where we get our name. When the crowd's tipsy with whiskey, we make everything in sight disappear.

I don't know why there's always some dimwit who watches me while I eat. It's inevitable. Then I put on a nauseated expression and go up to him with the plate in my hand asking him to taste one and see if the hors d'oeuvres are bad. The dimwit never knows what to say and shows his manliness by calling the waiter. At this point, I take the opportunity to compliment him on the lunch, and hand him the plate that someone in the kitchen "was careless about." When he comes back with fresh hors d'oeuvres I taste one, make the dimwit try another and then indeed we both agree that the hors d'oeuvres are sensational. And when the waiter leaves, glaring angrily at the other fellow I pat him on the back and congratulate him.

Because we're always congratulating, smiling, and celebrating. We approve of whatever they say and observe everyone attentively. We always nod "isn't that so" with our heads and act expectant even when they're speaking nonsense.

That's when, if the cocktail gets friendly, if the hicks laugh a little louder, if then they start inviting us to visit, if we've managed to create an atmosphere where everything is pleasant and possible and the wives of the so and so's and the wives of the poor clerical nobodies begin to feel like somebody and everyone thinks he's no longer fat, and the executives with no manners laugh and forget to be pedantic for a moment, if by now they're all set, then the time has come to suddenly remember that your wife is about to close her shop.

"I bought it for her so she'd have something to keep her busy," I explain.

"Would you like to meet her?" I ask, "I'll call her right now."

"Yes! Yes!" they all say enthusiastically.

Then I dial the number of our boarding house where no meals are served and when Margarita answers, say:

"How're you doing, Margara. I'm at the reception. Why don't you come on over? Look, close up and come on over because it's fabulous. You have the children with you? Well bring them along, Margara, bring them along."

"How's the food old boy?" Margarita asks me.

"Yes, some great people, wonderful," I answer her. "All right then, come as soon as you can. We're waiting for you."

And when Margarita arrives, wearing the dead lady's exclusive designer dress for the first time, holding Martin and Alex by the hand, it's as if a queen were entering with two princes.

Margarita comes in and it's as if everything were illuminated with a different light. Sober, precise, perfect. Majestic. Margarita could have been anything!

"The main thing, old boy," Margarita always tells me, "Is not to make the ladies jealous." And in five minutes they're all friends and arguing over her. They want to tell her about their lives, they level with her, reveal themselves, tell her if they're having affairs behind their husbands' backs, whether or not the maid knows about it, whether she helps them out or blackmails them, if their husbands are fooling around, their abortions, everything.

The curious thing is that Margarita merely listens. The most I've ever heard her say is, "How terrible!" "Worse than animals!" "He's leading a double life." True, sometimes, she's so overcome she weeps.

But when she starts to speak with that deep angelic voice of hers, with that class, with those majestic gestures, when her glance crosses mine and I nod assent to her and she begins to tell the story about the boat, the one about the Danish student from the Dante Alighieri school, or the one about Mussolini's intimate friend, then I love her more than ever and imagine how far Margarita might have gone.

It's enough just to see the silence she produces. It's total and almost obedient and there never fails to be some old man with his mouth open, a drooling manager, or some other lustful fellow eating her up with his eyes. Especially when she makes that pause after a moment of suspense, looks around at everyone, sighs and says:

"Then, Il Duce didn't say anything to him and let him go…But one fine day they knocked at his door. When he went to answer, he found an officer who handed him an envelope. It was a letter from Mussolini. There were only two lines written in it. It said: 'Either change your country. Or change your shirt.'"

I've heard Margarita tell this a thousand times.

I know every inflection of her voice, each one of her gestures by memory, but I am still captivated by the influence she has over them, the style with which she delivers the punch line, that sense of well-being she creates.

The children, on the other hand are mournful. Martin and Alex have sad eyes. They are sad even when they eat. They're obedient, that's true. We can't complain. They know they're never supposed to speak except to answer questions and they're to eat as much as they can hold. They have a certain style and there's always someone who tells us, "They're so well behaved!" But they are sad. Sometimes I look at them and a profound sense of sadness invades even me because I know they're going to be very unhappy. They don't realize it yet and they do well enough at things. They know that they have to stuff everything they can into their pockets and smile. Whatever can be sold or traded and always smile. When they eat, they're to smile first and then chew; smile first, then swallow. They also know they're not to start eating until Papa pulls on his ear three times in a row. They know that Papa has a little place at General Villegas, that Mama is a professor of Italian and has a little shop at Cañuelas. They know that if there are other children they're not to go up to them, but when the others approach them I've seen how they tell them that papa has a sword like a rapier, explaining to them what a rapier is, that it once belonged to their grandfather and that their grandfather fought against the Indians, leaving them with eyes as round as owls. Alex takes after his mother that way. He doesn't talk much but when he does, he turns them on. Martin, on the other hand is always more outgoing and between the two of them they complement one another rather nicely.

But unfortunately they are sad and I'm afraid they'll turn out to be heartless.

The thing is that they're oblivious. Margarita says that they're "stone statues in short pants" and she's right. Sometimes I watch them eat amidst all this false luxury and think about a little merry-go-round that they'll never go around on and I understand why, in spite of the training one gives them, there are killers, thieves, prostitutes— tarmites' children—who occasionally, before they die, stand quietly in front of some toy store window gazing at a train or a baby doll with inscrutable expressions.

When the party's over, we're the last to leave because we have to organize the real harvest. While Margarita and the children gather enormous armfuls of flowers, I open fire on the waiter I've been studying since the beginning.

"Waiter," or "waiter, sir," or "sir" (according to the situation and his age), I say to him, "allow me to congratulate you. No. Don't say anything or thank me for anything. I want to congratulate you because you're very correct, very correct...And I'll tell you something else: I've been noticing you all night. There's something about you I like a lot and I'll tell you what it is..." there I insert a long, really long silence, with a hand on his shoulder and finally I say, "You don't seem to be a waiter from here, but a European sort of waiter. Yes sir. Because you're obliging without being obsequious, you're not de- meaned, you don't go around begging for a tip. You are a man who shows some class, a gentleman waiter!"

I congratulate him and then I have to wait while the waiter tells me two or three stories about distinguished places, and that I shouldn't think, just because he's here as a mere waiter that he doesn't know what it is to work in aristocratic places and in very *special* places where you had to see, forget, keep quiet and forget. I listen to him attentively, I let him savor the sweetness of it for a moment and after he's really built up and confident, I attack:

"Can you imagine what luck! Just in the last few days I've been thinking about giving a bash, a little celebration, well...a party. A little old great-aunt. She's going to be seventy-nine, what do you say? She has a big old house in Barrancas, and it occurs to me that you, sort of on your own, could handle the serving, always assuming, of course, that the price is right."

And as he's willing, and as I'd like my aunt to taste the goodies, I ask him to pack up some of the left-over sandwiches, cocktail sandwiches, varied canapés and sweets. I've never understood why they all ask, "Cashews too?"

As if it cost them anything! The greasers! Poor nobodies! Ah, well.

"Yes, yes, the cashews too," I always have to say praising them and making an imbecile of myself:

"How well toasted they are! Did you toast them, waiter? No, really, it's not easy to toast cashews." And as soon as I finish tasting one, I take out my wallet and wait for him to tell me: "But what are you doing sir? Please. There's no need! And here again I start to talk about European servants and take down his phone number which almost always is at a grocery in Villa Dominico or thereabouts, and you'll have to ask them to fetch him. Ah, well.

We always leave when they're about to turn off the lights. Walking back to the boarding house with the food, walking to help our digestion, with the children ahead of us and Margarita and I following slowly, commenting on the ice cream, cassatas and our friends, how emaciated and baggy-eyed the oldest Anglada boy is, how that fellow lacked a flair for making speeches, that this time the whiskey wasn't bad, or how dirty the carpets were.

This is one of the sweetest times. Everything seems good and restful with something charming about the lights of the nearly deserted streets. Or maybe because its just a brief interval before the abrupt change to come later.

Because when we get to our door, the first thing we'll do before going upstairs will be to give the newspaper vendor a small gift or some toothpaste, gather up some borrowed newspaper, go up the stairs, enter those wretchedly sordid rooms, turn the porcelain key and turn on the sickeningly yellowish light bulb coming out of a small tulip, edged with stripes, hanging there since 1922, and giving the furniture and us the appearance of something past and obsolete, finished and done with like our lives. Then we see ourselves badly reflected in the round mirror of the dresser that's overflowing with jars, trays, almanacs, ship menus, ballpoint pens, ashtrays, a bronze ball unscrewed from a stairway, cylindrical matchboxes, lumps of sugar from countries everywhere, small cans of beer, loose cigarettes, wrinkled grapefruits, pieces of cake, sandwiches with bites taken out of them, dark bottles fighting the onslaught of encrustation, stylized ceramic containers filled with apricot, and cheap whiskey, hamburgers, and memo books and whatever else.

On top of all this we put the flowers that Margarita will sell tomorrow. But before going to bed, we have to get organized. Organize the whole next day. Each one has his newspaper already assigned. The children too. We spread them out on the table and sit down around them. Everything has to be organized. All the addresses from the gossip columns have to be copied. Special notes of deaths and openings have to be made. You have to hunt, hunt urgently. The littlest bit of news left uncircled could be a real score. You have to scan without missing anything. Hurriedly, it's true, because we have to return the newspapers. But suddenly Margarita gives a happy shout:

"Look, old boy, pay dirt!"

And we all run to read over her shoulder because a Greek ship has come in and the Greek Chamber of Commerce will give a banquet on board, and the possibilities on board a ship are limitless. People want to take souvenirs from a ship. I pat her on the head, and rush to get the cookie box where Margarita has left our name cards and think about how much I love her and how far Margarita could have gone.

At times like this I feel happy and organized. The wheel keeps turning. Alex has found a tractor demonstration at the test track at General Pacheco. There will be a press conference and a reception afterwards. It'll be interesting too, because people go to barbecues in sports clothes and sometimes loosen up. There are presents and raffles and everything is very spacious and after eating we take the left over oranges without any ado, almost as if it's a joke. We also takes packets of lunch meat, pastries, slices of pork and a place setting or so. The children gather eucalyptus leaves and wild flowers and breathe fresh air. It's like a picnic. The huge purse that Margarita always carries bursts with grapefruit.

Nevertheless we have to keep on looking. For inaugurations. Inaugurations are our special forte and attract more tarmites than anything else. Since the place is always too small, they make off with cigarettes, light bulbs, propaganda displays. They drink cognac until they've no blood left and at the end, even turn over trampled flowers, paper napkins and cigar stumps with their toes. Some, like poor Tuderi, behave very grossly; the Andradas like land surveyors; Natalio, always in desperation and Crespi, with that savoir faire of his, always pretends to have lost the lapel pin they gave him in Monaco, while Margarita, her eyes shining with fright, takes advantage of the hubbub and delicately fills her bag with ashtrays, bowls and teaspoons.

But now it's over. The wheel has stopped for a moment. We have to return the newspapers and rest. Tomorrow will be a new day and when this moment comes and I look at the sweetness in Margarita's wonderful eyes, I always imagine that, at the same time, the head of public relations with his dry throat and rouged cheeks, is gargling and commenting to his distracted wife about how successful the party was, how he chased after newspaper representatives all week long, how delicate and original the gift of a rose in each wine glass was, how they were in all the photos, how they were filmed with every group, how they'll show up in the newspapers and the movie news, how pleased the manager was and how important people will be seeking out their friendship and Margarita comes to me and we sit down on the bed. The children are asleep. Margarita unwraps the package.

We eat some of the hors d'oeuvres and without much enthusiasm, look at the tube of toothpaste we received as a gift. It's as if Margarita guessed my thoughts because the instant our eyes meet, we smile.

Now That She's Coming

by Isidoro Blaisten

All year long I'm Mr. Shit. But now that my mother-in-law is coming, I know that for a few days, I'm going to feel different because no sooner do I see her head looking out the train window and see her frightened eyes searching desperately for us, no sooner do I take her old suitcase made of reinforced cardboard tied with the same old string, no sooner does she start being attentive to my every gesture so as not to irritate me or make me nervous, no sooner does she hand me the package with the nylon shirt she gives me every year, than I stop feeling like Mr. Shit and change into an exceptional being who lives in the city, who doesn't fall off escalators, who doesn't take a siesta and who's still not sleepy at three in the morning.

My mother-in-law admires me enormously, and even when I get upset because she still saves used oil in a Nescafé jar, or because she doesn't throw out the left-over noodles from lunch, she keeps on looking at me with that admiration that only women show sometimes.

So, I don't feel like Mr. Shit anymore. Like when I go out with Louis and we order some tenderloin and a couple of glasses of wine. Maybe it's because Louis always tells the same story about when he used to travel around the provinces selling bottles of colored sedatives and made as much as twenty thousand pesos in '38, and then, when we come up with business ideas that could make us rich and weird things we could sell, then I feel like I used to.

The business that appeals to us most is wooden bricks. We'll sell wooden bricks, all identical piled up on shelves. They'll cost us thirty pesos and we'll sell them at a hundred. Clients will come, open their purses and say, "I'll take ten bricks." And that's a thousand pesos. We decide there should be just one model and just one size to avoid overextending. They don't oxidize, they don't have lids, and there can't be any complaints. It's a fabulous business. Louis and I laugh a lot, and it's at times like these that I feel the same as when my mother-in-law comes. The same thing happens when I walk along the street imagining that all the businesses are mine or when I stop to buy cigarettes and see those chocolate-covered cookies. Usually I can't make up my mind, but sometimes, after a lot of thought I ask the vendor for one and gobble it up like I used to when I wasn't Mr. Shit, like I used to when I was a child and would think: "When I'm grown up I'm going to buy all the chocolate goodies I want."

It's curious that little chocolate cookies don't matter to me now. Maybe because I don't mind being Mr. Shit anymore. It used to bother me a lot before. I could see the years falling away like my hair and I'd always figure: Chaplin is sixty-five years old, when he was my age he was already rich. Palacios was already a congressman at twenty-four, Roosevelt, paralyzed and all, was president twice.

I would look at what I had done by comparison and be overcome with a tremendous urge to weep. That's when I'd buy those cookies. And while I walked along the street eating them, as long as they lasted, I could feel faith growing inside me like an enormous, warm, green horse that went galloping through the air at the speed of a jet plane. I was taming him. He'd fly all over the world and everything was possible and I'd feel very moved and enormously fit. People would look at me cordially and ask for favors. Everything was so easy. But then, when I had finished eating them, when I made up my mind to throw away the silver wrapper (I was always pretty slow to discard it), then everything was the same as it had been before: no furniture in the house and the neighbors looking for ants with a flashlight at night. My wife and I exchanging glances with nothing to say to one another anymore.

At the beginning, when we were newly married, my wife's cousins encouraged us a lot:

"Do you remember, old girl, when we were newlyweds?" my wife's cousin would say.

"We ate bread and onions," his wife would answer.

"We really had it tough," he'd add.

And they'd continue telling stories and we'd get very excited because we knew that now they had a car and their own apartment and a clothing factory. We thought that we were going to be like them.

In those days, when my mother-in-law came, she was a little wary. She didn't say anything, but she had some misgivings when she saw the sofa bed and our clothes covered with a sheet. Then I'd tell her that we'd gone to see an ice-skating show, and what cinemascope was like and about the incinerators that houses had now and that I'd seen them filming a movie right out in the street. But what got her most excited was when I'd talk about television. Even more than when I'd tell her about the "wax museum" and the "holy shroud." I had been at the television station, seen it from inside and my mother-in-law's eyes shone with pride. She looked younger.

That was the time when I galloped the most. At the beginning, when I always used to buy cookies, when I wasn't Mr. Shit yet and the image of our cousins still encouraged me. But then that image got farther away and less clear. It was no use to me any more. And by the time we'd paid for our bedroom set, I had stopped buying chocolates.

My mother-in-law saved me. I should confess that I used to long for her to come. I remember the year she saw the shiny new furniture. She was beside herself with joy. She looked at the two of us and wept. It seemed she was envying her daughter. And then the two of them opened the wardrobe and the dresser drawers and planned how they'd put away the towels; and how the vacuum cleaner we were going to buy soon would just fit in the empty space between the wall and the wardrobe. But I kept on losing hair, the years went by and we never did buy the vacuum cleaner. I had started to become Mr. Shit. The first time I realized it was when the cousins came over to see my mother-in-law and she showed them the furniture.

"It's beautiful," one of them said, from behind me. And when I turned around, unexpectedly, I caught that look, that look he'd exchanged with his wife. Right there, and from then on I realized everything. Afterwards it seemed as if they too had realized that now I was Mr. Shit, because they never again talked about how they'd started out, but only about television programs and they always asked us if we hadn't seen the *Saturday with Mancera* show. My wife would get tired of telling them we didn't have a television set and they would always say:

"Oh, that's right…"

That was at the beginning; later they changed tactics. They'd start out this way:

— 127 —

"Did you see Mancera's show on Saturday when he had…Oh, that's right, we always forget that you don't have television." And they'd go on talking about my cousin selling trousers from the factory.

Before I was Mr. Shit, our cousins always said:

"At first, everything is hard, but later, with work…"

Later, they started talking about people who really worked, people who had talent, and about how everything is possible in this country. Whenever they mentioned some friend of theirs, they never missed saying: "That guy is really energetic," and they knew stories about all the people who had started out with nothing but the shirt on their backs and today were worth no less than fifty million.

If I mentioned that I had an idea, our cousin would have two. If my head ached a bit, our cousin's would ache more. If I said that I'd once eaten mud-baked chicken near Pacheco's, our cousin would have eaten it frequently in some illegal immigrant's patio in Ayacucho Street when he was single.

Whenever our cousin talked, his wife would constantly nod her head in agreement and my wife would be comparing me to him, looking at me with contempt.

Once, when I was out of work, my wife couldn't think of anything better to do than visit her cousin's wife.

My wife must surely have wept, because one afternoon I found out that I had an appointment with our cousin at the factory. I'd never gone there before, so just in case, I got dressed up. The cousin made me wait more than half an hour in a crummy chair in plain view of all the seamstresses who glanced up every once in a while to look at me.

Finally, the cousin called me in and gave me a lecture and a letter of introduction. I went to the service station. The job was mostly as a night watchman, from six in the afternoon until six in the morning and paid four hundred pesos a day.

When my wife found out that I hadn't taken it, she got hysterical. Everyone in the whole family learned about how stupid I was, because you can earn a lot at night with tips from people who park their cars.

From that moment on, I turned into Mr. Shit for everybody.

My wife would look at the newspaper ads every day and get mad because I didn't want to go: all sales jobs. And if there's anything that burns me up it's being a salesman. Mostly because you never sell anything and it's not like the wooden bricks that Louis and I invented.

No. It always deals with things people can't see and don't want to buy. The beauty of it is that all the relatives who recommended sales jobs to me had never sold anything in their lives. Not raffle tickets, tour tickets, or anything.

But that was a long time ago. When I had just started being Mr. Shit. Now I have a job, but nothing matters to me anymore. Not even the house.

I used to be obsessed about the house. My wife was too. Whenever she'd see a luxurious home in the movies she would complain saying the same thing: "Ha, just like mine."

I tried to change the house, I'd look in furniture store windows, consult magazines. I'd move the pictures and lamp tables around trying to copy details of rich houses. But it was useless. I don't know if it's because we never had enough money to buy anything, or because the house had a soul and also knew that I was Mr. Shit. The thing is that it always had that forlorn appearance, that faded look, like something discarded, something that doesn't work. Back then, I'd ask a neighbor for some dry branches and I'd put them in a vase the way I'd seen them in the shop windows downtown. At first I'd be real pleased, but then I'd look at our cousins' faces and I'd realize that it didn't come off. Our cousin laughed outright, told me I was crazy and, laughing harder all the while, asked why I didn't set out some weeds or a washbowl or half a kilo of dry manure.

Only my mother-in-law would be surprised and say, "Look at the kind of things they do in the city," and she'd look at me as if I were full of surprises.

I'll never forget when bouillon cubes first came out and I brought some home. The time that I brought her frozen fish she almost died. When I opened the box of dates and told her they came from Arabia, she acted upset that I would have spent so much but there was no denying the happy expression on her face. When I told Louis about it we had a good laugh.

Now she's on her way and I'm waiting for her. Me, Mr. Shit, standing at the station, bald now, leaning my elbows on the rail, waiting for the train's red light, waiting for my mother-in-law's nervous face, waiting to see her look out the window and blow me a kiss, waiting.

ALICIA STEIMBERG (1933)

As author, educator and translator, Alicia Steimberg holds degrees in education and English and has taught both at high school and university levels. A second generation Argentine, Steimberg grew up Jewish in a predominantly Catholic society and witnessed her family's ongoing difficulties in adapting to that culture's values and language. She resolved these personal conflicts with humor and wrote of them with wit and perspicacity in *Músicos y relojeros* (*Musicians and Watchmakers*, 1971). In that work she also described the conflicts between a young girl's normal adolescent curiosity and the sexual taboos of the time. Asked if her novels are autobiographic, Steimberg responds that *Músicos*, and *Su espíritu Inocente*, (*Her Innocent Spirit*, 1981), in which she describes a young woman's experiences through courtship, marriage, motherhood and divorce, are fictionalized autobiographies combining her own recollections with those of others with similar life experiences.

In *Músicos* her depictions of the political, economic and social circumstances of the Buenos Aires of the 1940s provide an omnipresent background for the protagonist's experiences. By contrast, in *La loca 101* (*Madwoman 101*), which appeared during the country's increasingly violent military repression in 1973, she provides almost no realistic description but writes in a metaphoric, almost surrealist mode as she describes a madhouse where violence is institutionalized. The "dirty war" then occasioned a seven year hiatus in Steimberg's literary production.

Not until Argentina's return to democracy did Steimberg resume the fictionalized autobiographic style of *Músicos*. Then, in her third novel, *Su espíritu inocente*, 1983, she began a period of stylistic experimentation. Her fourth novel, *El árbol del placer* (*The Tree of Pleasure*, 1986), satirizes the popularity of the psychoanalytic fad that swept the Buenos Aires middle class in the 1960s and 1970s; her fifth, *Amatista* (*Amethyst*, 1994), experiments with erotic parody. Her only collection of short stories, *Como todas las mañanas*, (*Like Most Mornings*, 1983) contains stories of a surrealistic quality like that of dreams partially remembered after waking.

Steimberg has won a number of literary awards such as the prestigious Argentine Writers Association Award, the Municipal Award of Buenos Aires, and the Planeta award. She has been a finalist for the Tusquet and Satiricón prizes.

Musicians and Watchmakers

by Alicia Steimberg

The little I know about the life of my father's family in the Jewish colonies, in Entre Ríos, was told to me by my maternal grandmother, who, without any evil intentions, may have distorted events a little.

She said that the family had lived way out in the heartlands. A ship had brought my grandparents from Russia around 1890 or earlier. The migrants had traveled crowded in like animals. Potable water was scarce and they had had to suck it through a kind of straw connected to a barrel. I don't know how they got from the ship into the heart of the country.

My grandparents met each other there, and seeing that they weren't yet grandparents, or even parents, they hurriedly got married to get that out of the way. Or maybe they had already been married in Russia; this point isn't very clear. My uncles and aunts started being born right away.

Unfortunately, Grandfather José was not a farmer. He was a teacher: he was dedicated to meditating and teaching children history and the religion of the Hebrew people. Grandmother Ana, on the other hand, became a real Jewish *gaucho*. She did all the work and bore children continuously, feeding them with noodles and milk until they were fifteen. When they grew up they left, and some, like my father, never went back; he was reunited with his family only after they moved to Buenos Aires.

From a window of his house on Saavedra Street, Papa used to watch one of his sisters came home from her English class with a friend every Tuesday and Friday at the same time. Next follows an obscure period, which includes the marriage of Mama and Papa, my intrauterine life and my birth in the maternity hospital in Rivadavia.

I am, therefore, the result of a good many comings and goings and anxieties: of transplants and uprootings, of marriages that no one knows whether they took place here or in Russia, of fights, that no one knows who started, of poor diets, readings of the Torah, and religion is the opium of the people.

None of which precluded the fact that, one summer afternoon, before I had even learned to walk, I was sitting on the Costanera, in the shade of Mama's cape and feeding the pigeons. Someone took our picture.

Everything in it has a milky color: Mama's arms, her cape, my dress, the pigeons. I'm sure that when the sun went down we left the river behind and took a streetcar that brought us home through the lights of Buenos Aires.

≫-≪

After the requisite courtship, Uncle Chico married his plump girlfriend. According to the custom of the period, he had to deflower her in a hotel room on their wedding night. As my school friends explained it to me, as soon as the newlyweds arrived at their hotel room, the bride closed herself in the bathroom where she undressed and put on a nightgown selected for the occasion. Meanwhile, the bridegroom was also getting undressed, as quickly as possible, and put on his pajamas, so that when the bride came out of the bathroom she wouldn't see him naked.

On seeing her, the groom lost all his manners and timidity and turned into a real beast: he pulled off his pajamas, tore off the bride's nightgown, threw her on the bed and fell on top of her foaming at the mouth. The victim would utter heartrending screams and there would be a great deal of blood to be removed from the bedsheets the next morning so they wouldn't look foolish to the chambermaids.

Before the wedding, no woman who had any sense at all would let her boyfriend do anything. The woman who did, my uppity aunts said, was stupid, since that way, she lost the only thing a man valued in a woman: her cork. The stupid woman who let him take it out ahead of time ended up insulted and abandoned, and had no recourse but to become a whore.

To illustrate these concepts, when I was old enough, mama put a full collection of books in my hands. They were books which had been in style in her youth, at the dawn of sexual education. One of them said:

> In the male, the exercise of sexual functions is reduced to the satisfaction of an organic necessity which reveals itself through the imperious demands of the instinct for propagation, with its atttendant sentiments, and a complex phenomenon of secretions and excretions which takes place under special conditions.
>
> In the woman, sentiment is more powerful than the reproductive instinct, love stronger than desire; the man solicits, the woman accepts [if she's stupid, the uppity ones noted], predominating in her the illusions of married life and the gratification inherent in the duties of maternity.

Dr. Francisco Otero, *General Health.*
Buenos Aires, 1919.

The uppity ones said that there were women who *liked it*. They were crazy as loons, running after men regardless of their marital status, and were a constant threat to decent homes. Among the women who "had nothing to lose," were actresses, dancers, nurses, maids, and post office employees. The decent women included teachers, pharmacists, librarians, and housewives with small children, except, naturally, for some unusual waywardness in one or two cases.

With respect to other effective premarital warnings, there were some lovely lessons, less theoretical than Dr. Otero's, written by a progressive priest. They were presented in dialogue form:

Questions: Is it permissible to kiss one's boyfriend?
Answer: It is.
Question: Is it permissible to give him a rather long kiss on the mouth?
Answer: It is. What is *not* permitted is to continue prolonging the kiss, or other caresses and embraces, because this is the prelude to something that should come later, with marriage.

Catholics like the author, scientists like Dr. Otero, traditional Jews like Papa's sisters, half fallen away Jews like the uppity ones, all agreed on one point, the cork had to be protected. In general and in particular, one shouldn't be stupid, eh?

After marriage, of course, one could do whatever one wanted, even seek pleasure, according to the instructions in a manual entitled *The Perfect Marriage*. It was understood and reiterated at every step that the practices suggested therein were to be followed only by legally united spouses: "The husband ought to massage the clitoris of his wife," etc., etc.

❧·❧

"Act dumb," Olivia used to teach me, "change the subject." So that I would understand better, she illustrated the matter by telling me about her conversation with a neighbor. It was in the month of December and there was a lot of activity because of the approaching holidays. "You have to shop early," the neighbor commented, "because it's a madhouse at the last minute." "It really is," Otilia answered, putting herself on guard. "When the family is big, one never finishes putting presents under the tree," the neighbor continued. "Hm," Otilia answered, ever more on guard. Then the neighbor came out with, "Does your family celebrate Christmas?" "No," said Otilia. "What religion are you?" "We're not religious," Otilia said, not being stupid. "But your parents, your grandparents, what religion were they?" Otilia decided to cut it off: "None. They didn't belong to any religion. Look, excuse me, but I've left something on the burner." And she left her neighbor abruptly.

This attitude did not sit well with my paternal aunts, who said that I shouldn't hide from anyone the fact that I was Jewish and that on the contrary, I should show it all the time, by wearing a star of David on a chain around my neck.

All this created a conflict within me. During an explanation about Christians and Jews, the fifth year teacher asked all the girls who were Jews to raise their hands. Several did, as meekly as when asked to raise their hands when they'd finished solving a problem. My two hands stayed on my desk. On my neck I could feel the surprised look of my Grandmother Ana, the look of the great-grandmother who had given me the jar of candies, and even of King David himself. Also, the looks of my Jewish classmates, adept at detecting origins by family names. But I also saw the satisfied look of the uppity ones. I was learning not to be stupid, by acting stupid.

Once the teacher finished looking over the faces of those who had raised their hands, she gave permission to lower them and continued with her explanation. She said that the Jews were still paying for a crime they had committed two thousand years ago: the crime of having killed Jesus. Proof of that was the number of Jews who had died in the war. ("Poor things!" she added.) The punishment would end when all the Jews were converted to Christianity and accepted Jesus, who was, she said, infinitely merciful. At that point, the bell rang and we went out for recess, but not before the teacher asked us for money for the cooperative.

After they married traditional Jews, the uppity ones began changing their way of thinking. They ended up turning into proud, confessed Jews, and as their economic status improved, they became increasingly involved in social, sports and charitable organizations of the Jewish community, competing with the other women at those institutions at having more and better clothing, jewels, home furnishings, diet doctors, and summers at the beach. "She has such a Russian face that it would turn your stomach," Otilia said about one of them. "But she's invited me to her house a heap of times so tonight I'm inviting them. You needn't be stupid," she declared. "After all, it's better to be with people from the community. When they talk about you, at least they won't say, 'That woman has such a Russian face it turns your stomach.'"

❧·❦

I want to get married in white, amidst a cloud of tulle and lemon blossoms, with Schubert's *Ave Maria* playing during the celebration. To do that I'll have to find a Catholic boyfriend and convert to Catholicism. There's no hurry for any of this, since I don't expect to get married before I'm eighteen and I'm twelve now.

To convert to Catholicism one has to believe in Jesus Christ. That's very simple. How could you not believe in someone who's just right there, hanging above the doorframe? He's bearded, smiling, he wears a white robe and a light gold cloud surrounds him. He makes a sign with his right hand: it's the *V* for victory. Jesus calls me. He touches my face. Jesus sees me. I run my hands over my body.

Baptismal water erases all, *all* our sins. PLOP. Now Frank Sinatra is exactly where Jesus was.

Strangers in the night…

But now it is neither Jesus Christ nor Frank Sinatra. Now it is Mama in the doorway. There's a horrified silence.

Hours after these apparitions, I found the following message in the pages of my student manual:

"Alicia: Today, when I came in from the street, exhausted by the terrible weight of the responsibilities I have to face in my condition as a widow with two children to support and educate, I expected to see you bending over the books that I work so hard to provide for you so that someday you will be able to provide for yourself in life. But I had the pain of finding you, lying on the bed, in a bad position, with which you can cause irreparable damage to your spinal column, and using your hands for something that I will not even dare to mention here, because I would die of desperation and shame.

Reflect, Alicia, before it is too late, on the perturbations and the incurable illnesses you might provoke with your conduct, and think whether this is the reward that someone deserves, who like me, lives and is destined to live amidst sacrifices and a continual suffering so that her children may become healthy, worthwhile adults. Don't forget that other women in my circumstances lock up their children in boarding schools instead of sacrificing their lives to raise them.

Read and memorize the parts I indicated to you in Dr. Otero's book, and then, if you want to go on killing yourself slowly, and killing me too with your conduct, go on as you are now."

Your Mother

GERMAN ROSENMACHER (1936-71)

Born in Buenos Aires and educated at the university there, Rosenmacher, a professor of Hebrew, also worked as a short story writer, dramatist, television writer and journalist. His two collections of short stories, *Cabecita Negra* (*The Black Girl's Head*, 1962) and *Los ojos del tigre* (*The Eyes of the Tiger*, 1967), established the young author as an important new voice expressing a strong socio-political consciousness. When his untimely death in an automobile accident in 1971 cut short his promising career, his third volume of short stories, *Cuentos completos* (*Complete Stories*) was published posthumously.

Although a few of Rosenmacher's stories deal with the Jewish experience in Buenos Aires ("Tristezas de la pieza de hotel"/"Hotel Room Sorrows," "El gato dorado"/"The Golden Cat," and "Blues en la noche"/"Blues in the Night"), it is the theme of social injustice with its accompanying descriptions of frustration, poverty and desperation that is more constant in his stories. His protagonists are usually solitary or marginal characters whose loneliness, despair and poverty condemn them to lives of existential misery.

In addition to these short stories, Rosenmacher also wrote four plays. *Requiem para un viernes a la noche* (*Requiem for a Friday Night*, 1964) deals with the theme of interfaith marriage and the generational conflict between tradition and assimilation. This play reflects some aspects of its author's own life, for like his protagonist, Rosenmacher's father was a cantor who had married a Catholic. *El avión negro* (*The Black Airplane*, 1970), which Rosenmacher coauthored with Roberto Cossa, Carlos Somigliana and Ricardo Talesnik satirically depicts the likely reactions of people in different social sectors to the (at that time implausibly hypothetical) return of the exiled Juan Perón. His third play, *El Lazarillo de Tormes* (1971), based on the picaresque novel of the same name, provided clever parallels to current situations in Argentine society. *Simón Brumelstein, el caballero de Indias* (*Simon Brumelstein, Knight of the Indies*), his last and most daring play–written in 1970 but not performed until 1982 because of censorship problems–dealt with the continuing problem of assimilation and the often repeated issue of whether one can be both a Jew and an Argentine.

Wild Birds

by German Rosenmacher

Slowly she raised her head among the wild, green, damp and dripping leaves. On her knees like this, her shining violet eyes and her blond, unkempt hair could scarcely be seen among the leaves of the tobacco field that were taller than she was. Straightening up, she looked backward and forward over the leaves, clutching her doll while the light rain continued falling from the gray sky, soaking her softly. She saw only Papa in the doorway of the house, Papa who was crying and strumming his guitar. And far away she could hear trucks passing, beyond the valley up there in the mountains, on the open mountain roads going north toward Bolivia.

Far off in the rain wild parrots screeched, and she stopped and was so small that the dripping leaves almost covered her. She screamed like a wild parrot and Papa kept playing his guitar.

"I'm hungry," something within her said, and then she grasped the big knife and the watermelon that Papa had stolen for her and cut off a huge slice, burying her fair little face in the watermelon that dripped over the mended wool jacket Mama had given her just before she left, even though it was summer.

"Let's go," he took her by the hand, while the invisible firm wind blew the damp leaves. Her small fair hand inside Papa's big, bony, dark, dirty, almost black hand, the two went down through the middle of the dry river bed, barely wetting their toes in the water that descended sparsely among the stones.

"I don't see them," she said, and before Papa could answer her, sensing that he wouldn't answer her because this was something you would say only once, and because he was very sad and drunk and was crying quietly, and even before she realized that Papa wouldn't answer her, she saw them and screamed and then Papa lifted her up with infinite, clumsy, trembling, tenderness; and held his child in one arm and wrapped the other around the middle of the guitar that he had stolen long before his blond daughter was born.

And she saw the enormous bloody eyes circling above them. She saw the birds, with their damp bellies scaly as lizards, their viper-like tails and wings as big as eagles', their ferocious puma-like faces and bloody eyes, their night-cold, moon-colored claws, trying to destroy them.

"Up there," she said, nestled against the dark skin of Papa's shoulder.

"Yes, I know," Papa said, though he didn't see anything. He knew that they were there, circling above them, always silent. Evil birds.

And when they reached the path, Papa sat down to wait for the truck to pass. She hugged her doll and covered her eyes so she wouldn't see them flapping around.

"I'm going," Mama had said yesterday afternoon. "I think I'm going to leave," she had said. And there was Papa lying in the middle of the river bed with water barely running among the stones, and her three little brothers in the shack with its walls of boards and burlap and flattened tins and straw roof. And then Mama had said that she was tired, she was fed up, she had been stupid because she had let herself fall in love with his eyes and his voice and the way Papa held her by the waist and she was stupid because she still loved him and because she had gone to live with him and because now she was only sixteen years old and was already an old woman who had four children and had gotten ugly from sadness and hunger and working as a washerwoman, washing other people's clothes so that her children could eat. And then Papa had shouted that it was always the same old story and had screamed that he wanted to live. And then Papa had grabbed an empty siphon bottle that he had beside him and threw it at her, but he was too drunk for it to hit Mama and the siphon bottle exploded and was carried downstream by the water, and then Papa got up and embraced Mama who pressed hard against him and wept.

And Papa said that he had struggled and brought in the harvest and they had thrown him out there, out of the valley, and then he thought they were laughing at him, the land, the owner, and all those damned wild birds that pushed and controlled and possessed him. And then the fair child had seen them too.

And he had said "Jesus, Mary and Joseph" and still kept seeing the evil birds. And Mama had said, "You are drunk, José." And she had said that she was leaving because her old man had thrown her out of the house when she went with Papa and now she was a woman and she said she needed perfumes and a ribbon for her hair and food for her children. And then her little brothers had begun to cry and she had brought them inside; so that they would go to sleep, she had imitated the croaking of the wild parrots. And trembling with cold and sadness she had fallen asleep.

And then she wasn't sure, because it happened while she was asleep, she felt that Mama was kissing her and was wanting to take her and Papa was saying that the others could go, but not her because she was so much like Mama. And then, Papa had awakend her very early, and no one else was there. And then they went down to the river and went to a farm and Papa set her down among the high weeds with her doll and she sat there, crouching and almost invisible among them and he cut the weeds with a scythe all morning and then they paid him and before leaving, he had stolen the watermelon for her.

"I want them to go away," the little blond girl said.

A big Chevrolet was coming down the road. The child jumped up and ran to the middle of the road just before it passed by them so that they had to brake in order not to run over her.

This is kilometer 1701. The road goes to Alta, the capital of the province," she said, holding out her hand. It never failed. A woman with dark glasses jumped out of the car and snapped her picture with her Leica.

"Hold still," she said. Music was coming from the car.

"Another one with no future, eh?" a man's voice said, inside the car. After they gave her ten pesos the car went on.

It stopped raining. The clouds dissolved and a heavy heat pressed down from the heavens. The colors that had faded in the rain reappeared. The summer sun beat down on the asphalt and silvered it, and melted the tar covering the potholes. The peak above the folds of the mountains was vividly green like the wet leaves of the banana trees that lined the edge of the road, heavy and dripping, heavy with rain. Now the sky was mercilessly blue. Beneath their bare feet they both felt the mud in the ditch hardening and the earth beginning to burn.

Cargo trucks passed coming and going from Bolivia. "There it comes," Papa finally said, at siesta time. And he stood up in the road and she put her little hands over her face because she knew that they were there, even though she didn't see them, flying overhead. Slowly the truck edged them aside and went on, and the laborers, looking down from above, saw the man and the child who were left behind.

Then Papa said that today there was no work in the saw mill but that it didn't matter, and that he would buy her perfumes and a ribbon for her hair and she said:

"But they're still there," and Papa said that the birds wouldn't make a fool of him and that he was strong and would kill them.

Then he grabbed the watermelon and emptied it of seeds and gathered them together in his big dark hand and grabbed the knife and then he didn't know what to do for a minute and he said:

"Damned earth," and squatted over the dirt in the ditch, and began to dig and dig. Then, when the hole was deep enough, he put seeds in and covered them. And then he dug more and more holes, and put in yet more seeds, and covered them, furious, defiant, stubborn.

"There they are," he said to the fair child. "There they are still."

And the heavens clouded over again, and a light rain fell on them. And up above, very far, only the wild parrots croaked and the trucks came and went on the mountain roads. And she looked at Papa, who was sitting in the ditch looking at her tiredly now, under the worn grey sky.

SILVIA PLAGER (1942-)

Silvia Plager's literary career began at thirty when one of the judges in a literary contest invited her to write for his publication. Shortly thereafter, encouraged by winning an award for her first book of short stories, *Boca de tormenta* (*Source of Torment*, 1984), she embarked on a literary career publishing articles in a variety of books, papers, and journals.

In Plager's stories, the protagonists are often women who reject conventional molds but have not yet managed to assert themselves as individuals. In a forceful, direct and colloquial style, she presents almost psychological analyses of her characters as they face a variety of life's large and commonplace tragedies. Her characters are varied: a widow fearing criticism for her budding relationship with a gentleman friend; a middle-aged spinster who sacrifices her youth and love to care for her widowed father; a staid college professor who changes her appearance so she can have an affair while on vacation–all characters in moments of crises or decision.

Plager has written five novels: *Amigas* (*Friends*, 1982), *Prohibido despertar* (*Waking is Forbidden*, 1983) *A las escondidas* (*On the Sly*, 1986) *Alguien está mirando* (*Someone is Watching*, 1991) and *Mujeres pudorosas* (*Modest Women*, 1933). Currently she is writing a novel to be called *Cambiar el alma* (*Change of Heart*) and another novel, *Complacer* (*Pleasing*) is awaiting publication. She also writes a literary supplement for *El Cronista* (*The Chronicler*), a daily newspaper.

In addition to writing, Plager has coordinated literary workshops, served in the Argentine Ministry of Culture, participated in book fairs in Canada and in the United States, organized and participated in literary conferences and meetings in Argentina and abroad, and judged numerous Argentine literary contests. She has won the Buenos Aires Municipal Award, the Band of Honor of the Argentine Writers Society, and has received the Outstanding Woman in Culture Award (1994) from the Argentine legislature.

Empty Shell

by Silvia Plager

The slow beauty of the blue balloon drifting away toward that other immutable blue. And Corina there, in the midst of it, in the center of what might be an average life, an average street and an average autumn day.

"I should have gone long ago, before the 'now it is impossible' repeated until it became routine, an almost hoped for 'no.' The same work, the same tiredness that envelops us, wraps around us as if we were packages that could be placed on any shelf in our office, and I with my phrase that sounds like a line from a play and that I can't avoid: 'you are killing the children within me.' And Osvaldo's silence and later the eternal repetition: 'It's impossible for now.' It seems to me that it never happened, that I dreamed that day when he came to my desk and told me: 'Here, take these keys, now we'll have a place of our own, you'll see in a couple of months I'll work out the separation, if it weren't for the children….' And later, 'It's impossible for now.' 'For now' has become today; I've been burying my todays for ten years now, there are no more credible tomorrows left for me, only the succession of todays turning into yesterdays."

Her footsteps keep time with her pounding thoughts. Across from her, where the parking lot is now, her house had stood; an empty shell, with its balcony hanging out over the plantain tree of rough leaves, and the tailor's sign on the railing and the long wire a little girl used to wrap around balls from the tree so that they would become projectiles.

A pebble skips, and lands in Corina's shoe. And she sits down on a bench in the plaza where her other patent leather shoe emptied out a little mound of sand. The moldy wall and that absurd fountain holding putrid water from the last rain are still there with that statue of a large breasted woman pouring from her eternally empty pitcher. The steps to the slide no longer lead there, but show their lusterless metal just as she does her desolation. She tries to stand up, to buy a candy cane, to recover the sweetness shaped into its hook; but her legs refuse.

The sun peeks out from behind the faded carousel giving some life to its dead horses and swans. She remembers the bar that had turned her into a graceful ballerina: holding on with one arm, the other extended; one foot set firm, the other pointed back maintaining balance, had hooked the ring, earning another ride. Why go around again? Corina asked herself.

The music of the carousel arouses a kind of dreaminess in her. She imagines herself climbing on it, leaning on the black horse. If she touched the animal's nose she thought that she would feel the warm breath and pulsing blood under its hollow shell. And she thinks that it's just the reverse, that our outer shell is warm and shelters humid cavities where we can take refuge from that skeleton that awaits us, implacable, smiling, watching how our hearts get drier and fall, defeated by him, who in turn will be defeated when his smile is merely dust.

A cloud climbs toward the light bringing changing shadows to this world that shelters her and circles round her. And she imagines that Osvaldo is there, sitting on the carousel bench, smoking. And that she is passing through the planes and cars, through the horses that move their heads in an anemic whinny, and the swans that curve their necks toward the floor, seeking a clear mirror of water in the wooden floorboards. And she comes up to him and sits looking at him, but Osvaldo's eyes are scarabs fixed on two children who go up and down, held in with seat belts. She spoke to him and he didn't hear her voice, she shouted to him and he didn't hear her shout. She threw herself on him, caressed him, shook him, kissed him until she bit him, she yanked his cigarette away so that it fell with its eye of fire, but Osvaldo flattened it with his foot, wanting no witnesses. She sat at his side, wanting to see what he was seeing; but she saw only a small boy filling a worn old pot with earth. She told herself that she and that child resembled one another; both scraping away at life's meager offerings.

The sun rested on the carousel's awning. She turned the ring on her hand again, spasmodically. The horses and swans repeated their eternal posture. On the stone bench, her wet face indifferent to what was pouring from her still eyes, she continued seeing him, his cigarette smoke ascending in spirals along with the afternoon smoke.

A woman's voice breaks into the sound of voices that fills the plaza: a heavily veined hand touches her shoulder: "My child, can I do anything for you?"

And the little boy who comes running, with a shout on the tip of his extended fingers, shakes the old woman's coat and says: "Grandmother, Grandmother, my balloon got away."

No One Will Take Her Place

by Silvia Plager

The chair leaning against the table is her mute presence. The framed photograph overlooks the empty plate, the napkin in its silver ring, the perfectly aligned place setting.

The final aria of *Tosca* inundates the rooms, escapes to the patio and enters the kitchen.

Don Genaro stands before the portrait of Mussolini and salutes it. Every day the same thing is repeated, forever the same. But there was a day when he forgot the ceremony and the record stopped. That was the time the house was filled with Rosalía's scream.

Nora knows that when he changes the record and she hears "Mama, I'm so happy," that she should enter with the soup bowl and take her place at the opposite end of the table. She is used to the turned chair calling for her dead mother. But the other chair, the one filled until yesterday by her sister Rosalía, is yet another empty chair today.

Nora eats with a lost expression. Her father notes the question in her eyes. With a push he leans Rosalía's chair against the table.

Only Nora knows how to lean the chair, place the tableware, cover the plate with the embroidered napkin, polish the glass of the picture: she does these things slowly, feeling her father's approving look. But yesterday she had to go out. She went to mass. She stopped at her godmother's house. Nora wants to be, has to be, just like that woman, resigned beneath her dark clothing, like the voice that seems to emanate from her prayers and mix with the rarified air of those rooms invaded by portraits and crucifixes.

Her desertion makes her an accomplice in her sister's strange absence. Nora had left the house. She had been away longer than usual. And when she returned, no one was there.

Her father returned at night and stayed in his room.

Nora tries to overlook her sister's absence. Not to ask.

Her father responds with another turned chair. In her room, Nora lets her hands work. Her hair is close to her head, tied in a knot. Her dress falls loosely from her shoulders, outlining her thin, firm figure. She remembers Antonio waiting for her at the workshop door, and her head covered with curlers and his kisses in the entryway and her father beside the empty chair saying: "No one will take her place."

She had explained to Antonio: "I can't leave them now. Rosalía is only twelve years old. We're young, we have to be patient. For now I have to take my mother's place."

He promised, but then there was no longer a sewing shop where he could wait for her. Sundays were divided between household chores and the renewed joy of seeing him, punctually at six in the afternoon. But the time came when she sat with her hands imprisoned in her lap waiting for him for two hours. Her father pulled her from her place of vigil saying: "I didn't want to tell you about it, Antonio has been seen with someone else."

She's thirty years old now and only knows how to look back. The future is a repetition of days that won't be strong enough to turn into the past; it will be a blot in her memory, a memory of the time when her mother was alive and she was a mountain of mornings, mornings that began dissolving slowly.

Nora places flowers before her mother's picture. One flower remains in her hand and she caresses it. She resists leaving it there, to die before that indifferent gaze. She goes out to the patio. Goes over to the flower pots. She takes the knife stuck in the dirt and digs. She places her lips against the flower and breathes. She needs to push its mouth away from her eyes. The shrill voice overriding the voices from the market. The false piety.

Nora tries to fix her attention on the red flower, but it turns into the thick lips of her neighbor: "Poor little thing, how you must feel! And your poor father, a man who, ever since your poor mother died….And Rosalía to pay you back this way! Tell me dear, didn't the police come back to your house?" And the police in my house and where is my sister and how can I ask Papa?

In the flower pot, the carnation leans its slender stalk against the knife blade.

The godmother, crossing herself, hands her a note. Nora hurries to pack her sister's suitcase. Her father might arrive at any moment.

The woman dressed in mourning kisses her goddaughter, takes the suitcase, and goes away down the corridor.

She stirs the stew with a wooden spoon; worn out, eaten away by use. The spoon that was her mother's and that is now hers.

She pulls the wrinkled paper out of her dress. Her sister is lying. It's a monstrous excuse to abandon them, to run away.

The opera music is a shower on the roof of the kitchen. Her father must be saluting Mussolini. Next he'll change the record, and she will enter the dining room with the soup bowl.

Nora puts on her night shirt. Her hair escapes its hairpins and covers the hands that free it. Her hands play with the dark weight covering them.

Her sister's empty bed lies waiting. She is surprised at the happiness she feels before that empty bed.

She remembers Antonio and prays. She remembers the submissive figure of her mother and prays. She remembers the note from her sister accusing her father of having wanted to violate her, and she prays. She remembers the chair turned around with a brusque gesture and her father saying, "No one will take her place," and she prays. Her hands, still between her legs, make a sound like a panting dog that changes into a sigh.

A sound in her father's room awakens her. The moon filters through the shutters and divides the floor. Her legs push off the sheets. The silence again turns into waiting. Again the noise penetrates her exhausted flesh and shakes her.

The patio encloses the night converting it into something of its own.

Nora's silhouette softens the shadows that dissolve as she passes. She kneels beside the flower pot and takes out the knife. The slender stalk of the carnation bends under the flower's weight. She wipes the dirt from its steel and tests its sharpness. She scrapes the wall with the blade. She watches the shavings fall to the floor and sweeps them away with her bare foot.

A tremor that starts from the knife sends her back to her room. She sits on the edge of the bed. She hears the sounds from her father's room again, and firmly grips the handle of the knife, waiting.

RICARDO FEIERSTEIN (1942-)

Feierstein, who holds degrees in architecture, letters and social sciences, is an intensely active individual who works as conference speaker, journalist, literary and film critic, television and radio personality, director of an editorial house, and co-director of various periodicals in Argentina, Colombia, Israel, Mexico, Peru, and Venezuela. An ardent advocate of Asociación Mutual Israelita de Argentina's (Mutual Israelite Argentine Association) cultural goals and programs, he is deeply committed to developing recognition of Jewish contributions to Argentine culture. As director of MILA, AMIA's editorial house, he encourages publication by Jewish Argentine writers and actively collaborates with the growing number of critics, scholars and researchers from abroad who now study the impact and contribution of Jewish immigration to Argentine cultural life and thought.

In his writing, whether mocking social foibles or depicting dreamlike fantasies, Feierstein's abiding preoccupation is with death and the loss of innocence. His stories differ widely in tone and style. Some describe the frustrations of everyday life; others, like the one which follows, hold up a mirror in which readers find their own foibles reflected, showing how by assimilating too completely, contemporary Argentine Jews are in danger of losing their heritage.

Feierstein, who sometimes published under the pseudonym "Pedernal," has written seven volumes of short stories: *Cuentos con rabia y oficina* (*Tales of Rage and Work*, 1965), *Cuentos para hombres solos* (*Stories Just for Men*, 1967), *Cuentos con un gris absurdo* (*Absurd Grey Tales*, 1970), *Lucy en el cielo con diamantes* (*Lucy in the Sky with Diamonds*, 1972), *Baílate un tango, Ricardo* (*Dance a Tango, Ricardo*, 1972), *La vida no es sueño* (*Life is Not a Dream*, 1987), and *Homicidios tímidos* (*Timid Homicides*, 1996); five novels: *El caramelo descompuesto* (*The Decomposed Caramel*, 1979), *Entre la izquierda y la pared* (*Between the Left and the Wall*, 1983), *Escala uno en cincuenta* (*On a Scale of One to Fifty*, 1984), *Sinfonía inocente* (*Innocent Symphony*, a re-edition as a trilogy of three previously published works), and *Mestizo*, 1994; one humorous work, *El pequeño Kleinmentch* (*Little Kleinmentch*, 1980);

three books of poetry: *La balada del sol* (*Ballad of the Sun*, 1969), *Inventadiario*, (*Creative Daily*, 1972), and *Letras en equilibrio*, (*Balanced Letters*, 1975) and numerous essays. He has received the Ribbon of Honor, the Municipal Prize and various Honorable Mentions. His stories have been included in numerous anthologies. Some have been translated into English, French and Hebrew.

A Plateful of Latkes[1]

by Ricardo Feierstein

$\mathcal{M}$anuel and the children arrived early, at about five. Scarcely had they had time to take off their coats and greet *Bubbe*[2] Esther— Grandfather Abraham was having a nap in the small room in the basement and they didn't dare wake him—when the children, like a noisy and disorderly troop, were already rushing up the wooden stairs which led to the playroom. Knowing her grandchildren's tastes, Esther had arranged the room especially for all seven (Esther's three, Ruth's two, and Manuel's twins) who gathered every year, around the month of September to celebrate the Jewish New Year with their relatives.

Of course they also visited at other times too, and Grandfather Abraham, with his sweet tooth would usually do something like taste a piece of cake before lighting the birthday candles, which usually earned him a gentle scolding and started a "search for the cake thief." But Rosh Hashanah was something special.

"Where's Bertita?"

"She'll come later, Mama. She had a yoga class she couldn't miss."

"Yoga…Ah Manuel, Manuel, if your father finds out that even on Rosh Hashanah… "

"Change your tune, old girl, we're not kids anymore. Don't be so old-fashioned. It doesn't become you."

They could already hear the shouts beginning to come from upstairs. Daniel had left the play room and locked it with a key from the outside. Kicks and blows resounded on the other side of the door.

[1] latkes: fried potato pancakes (Yiddish)
[2] bubbe: grandmother (Yiddish)

"Good heavens, dears, don't make so much noise or you'll wake up *zeide*.[3] What's going on, Danny, what's going on now?"

"Adriana grabbed the electronic piano and wouldn't give it to me. So I locked her up to teach her a lesson."

When grandmother Esther went upstairs to negotiate a truce, the bell rang. Ruth, her cheeks red after running all the way from the entrance of the apartment building to keep warm, entered the living room, smiling and weighed down with packages. Bernardo followed her, holding a child with each hand.

"Good afternoon...I should almost say good evening, the stars are about to come out."

"*A git iur, a git iur.*"[4]

Grandmother came running back downstairs, muttering some words mixed with blessings in Yiddish. In the excitement of all the greetings, Ruth had left the package with the pastry shells on the dining room table. Bernardo, noticing it, reached across to pick it up with both hands and held it out to his mother-in-law.

"For you, doña Esther, and to celebrate the New Year."

"You shouldn't have bothered," she said, touched.

"Your gastronomic culture is a little off, Bernardo," Manuel teased his brother-in-law. "What do you mean bringing pastries on *Roshe Shune*?[5] Why you're turning into just another assimilated Jew, there's no difference between you and a goy to tell the truth."

Bernardo only smiled. "Look, Manuel, I don't know. I've heard those stories too about how, in Poland when they accidentally mixed milk and meat in their pots, they'd bury the pots with a ceremony, rabbi included. But we're in Argentina now and these pastries are delicious, you've got to taste them with your coffee."

They talked about business and politics while they waited for dinner. Manuel, a certified public accountant, handled a half dozen businesses and avoided taxes as much as possible. Bernardo had a factory that made baby clothes. During the summer he dealt with customers from the beach areas, a practice which allowed his wife to extend her summer vacation from December to March.

---

[3] zeide: grandfather (Yiddish)
[4] git iur: "[May you have] a good year, a good year" (Yiddish)
[5] Roshe Shune: a variation or shortening of the term "Rosh Hashanah" (Hebrew)

The door bell rang again, interrupting their predictions about loans and inflation. It was Berta. After the usual greetings she retired to the kitchen with the other women. Meanwhile the small wooden blocks rolling down the stairs indicated that the gathering of twins and cousins was far from peaceful. Daniel came down shouting to announce that they were having a contest to find out who knew the most words in Yiddish, including "bad" ones; Liliana appeared behind him and said that she could speak Yiddish, but would never speak German, because the Germans seem to spit when they talk, and it's a very hard language. There was a kind of whirlwind of heads and hands and they all went back upstairs to the playroom.

Sighing, Manuel took the stairs in four giant steps to unwrap the package he'd planned to keep hidden until midnight: a video game set he'd bought for just a few hundred dollars on his last trip to Miami to delight the children with the possibility of forty different games.

"To give them something to do, I had to open the present ahead of time," Manuel announced, "but there's no other way to keep these little savages quiet."

He went back into the living room with Bernardo and poured a couple of whiskies. Ruth looked in from the kitchen:

"Is the old man still sleeping?"

"I think so, why?"

"I want to get a surprise ready for him."

At about eight Estela, Marcelo and their children arrived. This interruption, with its shouts of surprise and greetings, caused a great commotion in the game room but the video games worked as a quieting anesthetic.

"Until tomorrow afternoon," Berta commented, with a bitter tone. "After that, they'll no doubt be tired of it and we'll have to buy them another game."

The men with their tribal voices gathered in a corner of the living room while Estela went into the kitchen where promising aromas were emerging. Sunset had fallen abruptly, its passing light filtering through the embroidered curtains, and now it was necessary to turn on some lights.

Manuel, for the umpteenth time, resumed telling the details about his trip to Miami, his conversations in Spanish with the Cubans, the deaf-mute gestures he'd had to resort to, to make them understand his limited English (acquired in a "quick 500 word course" just before their vacation), adding that now he didn't remember even fifty words.

"Fortunately, Berta has a good ear and is bold, so we managed to get along. Listen to this: once we decided to go out at night to visit one of those porno shops… "

"That's in Denmark," interrupted Marcelo whose friend had traveled there last year.

"Okay, it's just an expression. One of those places where they do strip tease and the girls are all curves…"

Curiously, the few Yiddish words that the three brothers-in-law knew all referred to sexual organs and obviated the necessity of using dirty words or "strong" expressions. Except for Berta, of course, who, since she'd been undergoing psychoanalysis, had, as the family said, liberated her language and turned into a "bad mouth," who called everything by its name.

While Bernardo and Manuel lost themselves in erotic wanderings, and Marcelo, bored, was looking out the window, the women in the kitchen had divided all the work perfectly. Grandmother Esther opened the oven door every few minutes to check on the progress of the fish that was slowly browning inside; Ruth busied herself looking for various ingredients like flour, potatoes and eggs, and after finding them, pushed aside the objects occupying the marble table top with a sweep of her hand and began to work. Estela wiped the crystal glasses clean again with a towel, and Berta, leaning on the edge of a cupboard, began to talk:

"You won't believe what it was like today at noon. The restaurant where I went with Manuel and his colleague was full, they have a cook who specializes in Franco-Swiss cooking. It was a madhouse."

"Is it kosher?" Estela asked, her hand covering the smile with which she asked the question so that her mother wouldn't notice her mocking tone, even though she was still busy with the oven and wasn't paying attention.

"It's close by," Berta went on, brushing the interruption aside with a wave of her hand as if she were brushing aside a fly. "Three little old ladies sat down and it was a show. They were all three over eighty, very thin, and each was wearing a hat. Yes sir: one wore a Swiss cap with feathers, a green hat with a kind of brush on top and one a black tam with a pompon on top. A sight worth seeing. Moreover, they showed real class, holding their forks with the tips of their fingers and all that."

"What did they order?"

"Wait, you haven't heard the best part. The old girls tore into their food the way a new saw tears into wood and they drank two liters of wine! And then, when they finished, they asked for three coffees, like this: 'Waiter, bring it hot enough to burn our tongues…'"

"Are you serious?"

"They looked as if they would fall apart and collapse any minute, yet they ate and drank like starving teenage boys…without getting upset, very clear, delicate, elegant. A chauffeur had brought them and waited for them outside. The third couldn't find the exit and was complaining that her sisters had abandoned her until the chauffeur came looking for her.

"How adorable!"

"The waiter referred to them as 'my three girls,' he told us that they come in every Tuesday and Saturday to order a special that they call 'beef a la café Paris,' that they're crazy about."

"But goodness, do you really mean that you went to a *treif* [6] restaurant on Rosh Hashanah day?"

Berta gave Estela a cold look that relieved her of answering and, by way of response, went on talking to the other two women:

"The most curious thing about it is that the three old ladies spoke only French among themselves and with the maitre d'. It's a lovely language. Even though I'd studied two years at the Alliance Française I understood only an occasional word, but it's so musical, so…"

Instead of finishing the phrase she made a gesture joining both hands and then threw them up, as an expression of the sublime.

"That's what I like about the French," Estela added, "they aren't afraid of speaking their own language in front of others."

"And what about the Armenians?" Ruth added, lifting her head from the dough she had almost finished preparing. "They have national pride too: I have a close friend who never bothered to translate when a relative came into her shop and began talking to her right in front of me in her own language. There I am without

---

[6] treif: nonkosher

understanding a word and the Armenians are doing their own thing. On the other hand, we, with our Yiddish…"

"We don't even know Yiddish," Estela said, glancing sidewise at her mother who didn't seem to hear anything, and who absent-mindedly went on working with the oven.

"That's different," said Berta.

"Why is it different?"

"Please, Estela. Or are you going to tell me that when you're traveling on a bus and some old lady starts talking loudly in Yiddish to her husband, you don't die of embarrassment and start praying for her to get off at the next stop?"

"The thing is that you are so assimilated," Ruth finally said. "A lot of yoga and all that, but your children don't even know what it means to go to a Jewish school."

"What's that have to do with anything? Or, maybe you enjoy it when old ladies talk Yiddish on the bus while everyone is looking at them?"

Estela tried to get them to calm down.

"What are you making, Ruth?"

"A plate of *latkes*. It's dad's favorite dish, I'll surprise him."

"Speaking of papa," said Estela, "Isn't it about time for him to get up now? It's eight o'clock and he's still sleeping."

"Our old man almost never sleeps at night, with his nightmares about the concentration camps and all that," Berta explained with an air of self-importance. "It's logical that he make up for it with long naps, especially since he's found that little room in the basement where street noise doesn't bother him."

She looked at her mother-in-law, but seeing that she was keeping silent and keeping herself busy (now with the chickens), she concluded:

"We'll wake him up now to eat. Meanwhile, let's take some snacks in to the men. They are probably hungry."

In fact, the three brothers-in-law had finished their whiskies and gladly accepted the plates filled with goodies. Berta asked about the children, but before anyone could answer, a loud shout coming from the playroom upstairs—a number of shouts and cheers together—let them know the value of the video game in keeping the racket away from the serious conversation of the adults.

"As long as they don't break it," mused Ruth, resignedly,

Manuel patted Bernardo's now prominent abdomen.

"So you're going to eat too, eh?"

The other smiled, patting the area alluded to.

"Yes, I'm getting fatter. What do you expect when I'm sitting in the store all day?"

"That has nothing to do with it," Marcelo interrupted sourly. "I'm in the shop all day too, and I weigh 148 pounds. Exercise, my friend. Lots of exercise. Although at your age…"

Marcelo had studied law, but had decided that it would be better to go into his father's importing business.

This had given him both economic security and an expression of sadness that continually hovered about his lips. Bernardo felt enormously generous when he avoided referring to all this and replied, indirectly:

"I enjoy tennis, but I can't practice regularly. We go to the country club every weekend without fail, but there are only four courts for 150 people. Do you think it's easy to get one? And as if that weren't enough, my wife can't go there without first running around for three hours, so that we never get there until about noon…"

Ruth, who had started setting the table, turned brusquely, masking her annoyance with a smile.

"What are you saying about your wife?"

"He said that she's a perfect housekeeper," Marcelo declared, without losing his bitter tone of voice.

"What are those kids doing upstairs?" Estela asked again, trying to change the conversation.

No sounds were coming from the playroom now. She went on:

"When they're that quiet, one never knows what they're doing. Sometimes they seem strange to me, it's as if they live in a different world."

"Mine don't have any problems," Berta said, "my psychologist told me that they're normal, although not outstanding. And I'm telling you, after the ten years of psychoanalysis that I've been through, I prefer ordinary people who get along easily with others to geniuses that are crazy or disturbed."

"Psychoanalysis is a Jewish invention," intervened Marcelo. "What good can you expect from it?"

"Oh, don't be crude," said Estela, coming to her husband's defense. "He says things most people think and no one else dares to say. You said yourself, a little while ago in the kitchen that there's nothing to be proud of in carrying around the label "different" on your skin.

"But it's not the same."

"Why isn't it the same?"

Manuel got up from his armchair with an offended gesture.

"I'm not in the mood to put up with these stupid remarks in my parents' house and on such an important day. Any Jew who is ashamed of himself is a contemptible Jew."

"Since when are you so Jewish?" Marcelo asked, ironically.

"For forty years you've dedicated yourself to nothing but making money and getting business connections, and only recently did it ever occur to you to join the parents association at the Jewish school to get a bit of *cavot* [7] and standing among your equals. You call that Judaism? No, old fellow, that's hypocrisy."

"But I made two trips to Israel."

"So what? I went to South Africa last year and that doesn't mean that I'm against blacks."

The discussion threatened to escalate, but was fortunately interrupted by the entrance of Ruth, who returned from the kitchen bearing a plate full of steaming, sizzling *latkes*.

"Specialty of the house," she said. "You can eat them plain or with sugar."

"*Latkes* on Rosh Hashanah? What's this?" Manuel asked.

"It's Papa's favorite dish."

"What's that have to do with it? Today you're supposed to eat chicken and gefilte fish. *Latkes* are served only on *Pesaj*." [8]

Marcelo laughed, gritting his teeth.

"So, only on *Pesaj*? Your gastronomic formation, my dear future community leader, is really limited. *Latkes* are eaten on *Succoth*" [9]

[7] cavot: prestige, favor (Hebrew)
[8] Pesaj: Passover (Yiddish, also spelled *Pesach*)
[9] Succoth: refers to temporary dwellings used by the Israelites during the Exodus and stresses the notion of trust in God's protection. By extension, it also refers to the harvest provided by God.

"*Succoth* is that *sukkes*? Is that the harvest feast?" asked Bernardo, somewhat confused. Ruth, with the plate still in her hand, couldn't get over her surprise.

"What does it matter? Papa likes *latkes* and we're celebrating a Jewish holiday. What difference does it make whether we eat one thing or another?"

Manuel shook his head.

"It's a question of principles. *Latkes* are made with matzo flour, which serve to remind us that matzo is the manna from heaven that God gave to the Jews in the desert when they came out of Egypt," he pontificated with a professorial tone. "It's the food of *Pesaj*."

"Matzo is simply unleavened bread, a cracker that Jews made in the desert because they had nothing else to eat," said Marcelo. "What does God have to do with that?"

"I would swear," Berta said, "that when we celebrated *Succoth* at the children's school this year they served *latkes*."

"What confusion," added Marcelo, in a joking tone, as if the matter didn't mean much to him.

"The one who's confused is my brother-in-law," intervened Bernardo, who until that moment had kept a prudent silence. "I remember that, many years ago, in the Zionist party where I was a member, we celebrated a *Pesaj seder* [10] in the traditional manner, and they moistened greens and eggs in salt water and the children asked the four questions and all that. But there wasn't even a trace of *latkes*."

"All this is a like formal discussion," Ruth indicated, "and I think it's rather exaggerated. *Latkes* are a Jewish food, period. Let's not demonstrate any more ignorance. The matter in question is if they can be served today."

"This discussion may not please assimilated Jews who prefer to celebrate the Hebrew feast days with a French or Italian lunch," Manuel added. "Similarly, even though Israel is in danger, the idea of immigrating there would never cross their minds. They're busy doing other things."

This outburst seemed a little excessive and Marcelo took advantage of it to be ironic.

"Are you thinking of going to Israel? The sons of the watchmaker

[10] seder: the first two nights of Passover commemorating the Exodus.

who has the shop next to mine went there six months ago, and they've already written back saying they can't take it and want to come home. Frustrated, that's what they are, and they escape to Israel to cover it up."

"You can't generalize that way, Marcelo. In reality, the only thing you're doing is defending yourself."

"Our children are being educated in Jewish schools," Berta added, defensively.

"Let's get to the point," interrupted Ruth, who was still waving around the plate with the freshly cooked food, "all these ideological and cultural discussions are very interesting, but the *latkes* are getting cold. Shall we eat them or not?"

"Aren't they for Hanukkah," hazarded Estela, who had been pensive for a while. "The holiday with candelabras, where you light seven candles for the Maccabees? I remember that when I was a little girl we had sweet things, maybe *latkes* with sugar. *Bubbe* used to make them, don't you remember?"

"It seems irreverent to me," Manuel concluded. "A lack of respect."

The door to the kitchen opened and Grandmother Esther crossed the living room quickly, carrying a stack of plates. Some glances were exchanged, but the persistent silence of the lady of the house, who had kept quiet for so long and only seemed preoccupied with the incessant work involved in preparing a meal for so many people, made them hesitate to interrupt her. Above all, with such a stupid discussion that revealed so much confusion. When she went back into the kitchen, Berta looked back at the rest of the family.

"Why don't we ask the children?"

"Mine don't even know what we're celebrating today," said Marcelo, "only that it has to do with a big meal. I'm a modern father, I don't live in a dead past like all of you who still have your spirits anchored in eastern Europe."

Manuel exchanged knowing looks with his wife, and with a brief smile nodded his head in the direction of the upstairs floor. Berta went to the edge of the steps and called up.

"Daniel! Adriana! Come here quickly, Papa wants to ask you something!"

Noise continued from the children's room, then there was a

silence that lasted several minutes, the sound of footsteps and exclamations about the game. Nobody answered the call.

"They're concentrating on the video game and don't want to be bothered with interruptions" said Bernardo.

"Tomorrow's hope, the new Jewish generation," Marcelo laughed, joking joylessly.

"At least they won't be ignorant, like some people," Manuel replied. "They know how to sing the *"Hatikva"*[11] in Hebrew and they know all the history."

Marcelo was going to reply, but some noise came unexpectedly from the basement. Everyone was quiet for an instant, holding their breath.

"It seems like Papa is getting up," Estela suggested. They waited but didn't hear any thing else.

"Does he feel okay?" Ruth asked, somewhat concerned, as she made a face. "Maybe he's calling us."

There was another pause, but in the silence of the living room they could hear only grandmother Esther bustling about in the kitchen. Sounds of plates and pots, interspersed every now and then with a sigh.

"Well, what do we do with the *latkes*?" asked Marcelo matter-of-factly. "They must be cold by now." For an instant everyone hesitated.

"Let's take them down to the old man," Estela decided, turning to her younger sister. "And, sort of incidentally, ask him if it's a proper food for Rosh Hashanah. He ought to know for sure, without any doubt. He took his first lessons in the *heder*[12] there in Europe, he didn't pick them up piecemeal like we did."

There was a dull scraping of furniture in the basement. They all sat down, and Ruth, determined now, turned toward the door that led to the room where her father slept, followed by the eyes of all the rest.

"Go on, go on, once and for all," Bernardo encouraged her nervously.

"Papa?" Ruth asked aloud, as she started down the steps holding the plate of *latkes* high, "I want to ask you something. Papa, do you feel okay?"

The noise the children were making upstairs suddenly grew shrill, and became a whooping sound like that of Indians preparing to attack.

---

[11]"Hatikva": national anthem of Israel
[12] heder: elementary school

CECILIA ABSATZ (1943-)

Born in Buenos Aires, Absatz studied philosophy and psychology at the university there and subsequently pursued a varied career in public relations, journalism, radio, and television. She was a contributor to *Vosotras* and *Claudia*, both women's magazines, *Status*, a men's magazine, and currently writes for magazines such as *Somos*, *Playboy*, *Competencia*, *Cultura*, and the daily newspapers such as *La Nación*, *La Razón*, *Tiempo Argentino*, and *Clarín*. She also regularly writes scripts for radio and a television miniseries and coordinates literary workshops.

Absatz's first novel, *Feiguele*, was banned by the military government shortly after its appearance for its "immoral content." Narrated in the first person by its insecure adolescent Jewish protagonist growing up in Buenos Aires, the novel includes humorously realistic anecdotes about her adolescent sexual fantasies. Absatz interpreted this censorship as directed more at her publishers than at herself. Despite the resulting intimidation, she chose (unlike other authors who felt personally threatened during this period) not to leave the country. Nevertheless, she did not attempt to publish another book until military control eased some seven years later.

The dominant characters in all Absatz's writing are women. She presents events from an internal perspective, revealing their thoughts, their physical and emotional feelings, their desires, reactions, sensitivities, attractions and revulsions. Her male characters are generally drawn with a derisive, flippantly humorous sketchiness that makes them mere caricatures or catalysts for her female protagonists' actions.

In addition to *Feiguele y otras mujeres* (*Feiguele and Other Women*, 1976, which contains "Feiguele" and short stories about "other women"), Absatz has written two other novels: *Té con canela* (*Cinnamon Tea*, 1982) and *Los años pares* (*The Even Years*, 1985). A third ¿*Dónde estás, amor de mi vida, que no te puedo encontrar?* (*Where Are You, Love of My Life, Since I Can't Find You?*), is forthcoming.

Feiguele

by Cecilia Absatz

$\mathcal{M}$y name is Feiguele and I'm really fat.

I'm fourteen years old, and although you may laugh, I know a lot about suffering in this world. Like most people when they're fourteen.

I'm on my way home from school, and these funny faces you caught me making are my attempts–getting better, by the way–to learn to whistle.

My brother whistles really well. He always whistles "Whispering," so on his birthday, I gave him that record by Les Paul and Mary Ford and he likes it because they sing it and play it with seventy thousand guitars.

Nora knows how to whistle too; her father, who's in jail in Caseros, taught her. I used to think that only thieves went to jail, but I think Nora's father is a communist.

I never ask Nora anything, I act as if I know everything. I know that he's not a thief because Nora's not ashamed that her father's in jail. Almost the opposite.

When we became friends (Nora sits next to me in class) she told me that she was afraid of me because I always talked about even the most difficult things without making mistakes and because I was always arguing with my teachers. I admitted to her that actually I was pretty scared and I always talked real loud so that people wouldn't have time to laugh at me because I'm so fat. Maybe that's why she didn't laugh. She was the only one who didn't laugh when Miss Pagliamini said that to me.

But then you don't know anything about it, because I was trying to act indifferent and learn to whistle on the way home, because what I was trying to do was keep myself from crying out loud.

Because I always start crying about everything.

What did Miss Pagliamini say to me? That I was a fat shit. That's what she said. Well, the fact is that I made her nervous, because I began to pester her with those math problems about one and zero and I don't know how we ended up with objective and subjective judgments.

I'm going to try to tell it carefully—really it's not very important. But all the same it embarrassed me terribly. Now I'm getting distracted again. Miss Pagliamini is my math teacher. She's crazy. Really crazy, you know. If you saw how she dresses you'd die laughing. It struck me funny, just as it did all the girls.

But her ignorance really upsets me. The way she gets away with saying any stupid thing, you'll see that. And I always argue with her. I can't help it. I'm always arguing with everybody.

We were talking about judgments.

"Judgments, my dear girls, are divided into objective and subjective. Is that clear? Mathematics is based exclusively on objective judgments."

Now you'll realize what I was referring to before.

"If I affirm that parallel lines don't touch except in infinity, I am making an objective judgment. Do you understand me now, my child?" (This was said directly to me.) "It is necessary that you understand this clearly if you want to learn mathematics."

I was standing at the very back where I sit with Nora in the last row so that we can listen to the radio, work crossword puzzles, things like that—I wouldn't consider the matter closed. I was burning with indignation.

"And how do you…" Miss Pagliamini looked at me astonished. I was so conscious of the looks the girls gave me that I leaned against the back wall as if pressed against it by their very astonishment.

Nobody asked questions in Miss Pagliamini's class. Nobody even paid attention, not that it mattered.

That I would pay attention and would even propose to ask questions was not only unnecessary it was—as you will see—frankly inconvenient. "And how do you—" I said "determine when a judgment is no longer objective but goes on to become subjective? I mean, is there some categoric criteria that separates them?"

"Well, my child. There are things that are objective without discussion," her hat with its orange feathers (yes, you read that correctly, with orange feathers) moved in a spastic dance while she resorted to her abominable method of giving examples instead of explaining concepts. "I see you standing there and I can't say if you are a good or a bad person. That would be a subjective judgment. But there is something very objective: that you are terribly fat."

As I told you before, the only one who didn't laugh—besides myself of course—was Nora.

❧—❧

Raquel is sleeping away from home tonight. Nobody's home. Even Blanca has gone out. I decide to sleep in Raquel's room, but first I'm going to dress up. I paint my face with all the things Raquel has to make herself up with, so much better than mine.

I put on a party dress that I can't fasten, but in front it looks great on me. I look at myself a long time in the mirror.

A long time.

What a pity you're so fat, because you have a pretty face.

I'm in a nightclub in Cairo. Vice and corruption everywhere. The dark women laugh out loud and the shoulder straps of their dresses slip off. Whores all of them. I enter, and I am a whore too, but only because they abducted me. I'm the only blond. My face radiates mystery. The young Egyptian looks at me fixedly and our eyes meet. But old Abner gets there first and takes me by the arm. I cannot protest because he is the house's best client. He's old, shining bald. As soon as we enter the room he begins to laugh aloud, but his laughter is obscene. Ha, ha, ha.

"Dance for me, little whore."

He pulls my dress off with one tug (it comes off easily because after all, it's unfastened), and I'm left in my panties.

I begin to dance in my panties until I'm tired and throw myself on the bed ready for the worst and it was then that my heart froze: the window blind was totally raised, the curtain totally pulled back, the light totally on, and the seventy thousand mechanics in the shop across the street who work the damned nightshift are surely watching me from front row seats.

I creep toward the window—my heart beating hard, my head pounding—and close the blind. I peep out. There's just one. He's looking at me very seriously.

It's that dirty one. Because he's the dirtiest one of all. The one who looks at me the most and the only one who never says anything to me. He just looks at me. And now I'm going to kill him. How can I manage to kill him? So that he won't say anything. Now that he saw me, I have to kill him. But before I kill him, I'll bring him here. As if he were a dog. I'll do everything with him and then I'll kill him, so he can't say anything. I can't go out in the street anymore. He's going to tell all the mechanics about it. Fortunately, we'll soon be leaving for Mar del Plata.

→←

When it's time to go home, Momma says: "Are you coming, Feiguele?"

I'd have to be crazy to go back with them. I'd rather be seen alone than with my father and mother like an idiot.

Then just five minutes later I start back from the beach.

At home I get bored crazy too, but at least nobody bothers me.

But today when I got home people were going up and down, the elevator was in use carrying suitcases, the people on the fifth floor had arrived.

They're not the same ones who come every year. Out of the corner of my eye I notice that there's a girl my age. We both act dumb. I'm careful not to go up in the elevator with her. Her name is Coca. I know because I heard her mother say it, she never stopped talking and giving orders to everyone, especially her husband.

When I get home my mother is saying: "What could have happened to the Beremberg's this year?" (The Berembergs are the ones on the fifth floor every year.) "Are they having such a hard time that they had to rent out their apartment?" My father is drinking a beer. "Well, maybe they went to Europe…"

My father's only response is to belch and he goes to take a nap. He snores so loudly that you can hear him all over the house. My father always snores. And he makes noise when he eats. He chews with his mouth open and sucks soup real hard. He burps loudly, spits phlegm, and farts.

But really, he almost never talks. I hate him beause he's stingy and gross and never pays any attention to me. He writes down telephone

numbers on the covers of my books, tears sheets from my music
notebook to keep score in rummy, he's a disaster. Everyone says he's
a millionaire. He may be, because we live in a big house. But I also like
my father. I like it that he's so big and strong. I like it when he laughs,
when he tells stupid jokes in Yiddish. (He doesn't know how to speak
Spanish. He's been living in Argentina for forty years and he still
hasn't learned to talk.) He's Polish.

I like it when my mother says that my father used to sleep four
hours a day because he worked so hard in a factory making bronze
beds. (Isn't that fantastic, bronze beds?) Now he has a textile factory
and a huge fortune, the reward of his hard work. They say that he has
a huge fortune.

But I like him because I'm crazy, because anyone who happens
to know him would say that he's a real brute.

Ballet Dancers

by Cecilia Absatz

1

"*C*ome with me," Irene said, "let's go to my friends' place."

So I trusted myself to Irene's relatively trustworthy hands and got in the taxi.

Downtown, the Saturday night activity was churning. In the taxi, Irene continued her story about Alex in a really loud voice while the taxi driver tried to listen to the soccer game.

The story was a classic Irene type: that her romance with Alex was, how can I tell you, practical, we might say hygienic, and that the fact that he was married with three kids, though it was a bother, was no more than a bother, and that in general, everything was under control.

"Maybe Tuesday I'll be able to drag him to Martha Peluffo's opening, so you can meet him. I want you to tell me objectively what you think of him. Because sometimes, I look at him beside me and ask myself, 'Who is this guy?' I don't know if it's just my imagination, poor thing, because sometimes he's irreproachable…What a lack of men, my dear," she sighed. "If we go on like this we'll all have to become lesbians entirely. But that radio how rude," (someone had made a goal). "Sir,…" (Irene's bold red painted fingernail rang a bell on the taxi driver's shoulder) "Sir,.. "

"Eh?" the man barked, turning his head, taking advantage of the opportunity to look at Irene's knees.

"Be nice," she touched his ear lightly, "turn off that radio. I hate noise."

2

We went up to the top floor in a glass elevator. We rang a bell that sounded like chimes and a maid let us in immediately.

I sat in a white silk armchair and admired the decor: everything that wasn't a plant in this place was white or black. I wouldn't have been surprised at all if music had suddenly started playing and a chorus of ballet dancers with tulle skirts had popped out from behind the curtains, while doors and ceilings fell away.

"Is this an architect's house?" I asked Irene in a low voice. The carpets were white and plush. There was a collection of exotic vases and a Vasarely on the fireplace hanging from black wrought iron.

"Plural architects," corrected Irene, who had the advantage of absolutely harmonizing with this place where everything would go to hell if the maid turned out to be a redhead.

From behind an enormous porcelain dog (white naturally) the Handsome Architect soon appeared dressed in guess-what color.

He walked over with a marvelous smile and penetrating look, the kind that only handsome men have, the kind of look that enters a woman's eyes, sees its own reflection and goes back home.

Because the Architect really was handsome. And if this weren't enough to move me (which in any case would be open to discussion), well it was enough to move *him*.

Shortly after, the Elegant Architect entered. She was the type of woman who always dresses in beige. The type of woman who always looks impeccable, no matter how long she's been working and how many irritations she may have suffered in the last few hours. As soon as I saw her, I knew that she would eat with tiny, spaced bites, and control her sneezes.

We were promptly offered hors d'oeuvres and drinks (right then I was able to test my first hypothesis: it took her two bites to eat a canapé half an inch in diameter).

We were all absolutely charming. The conversation went along with that elegance foreseeable in persons of such an exalted social level as ourselves. The humor was subtle and involved to the delight of people who enjoy humor that is subtle and involved. Like me for example.

The doorbell sounded its chimes again and shortly thereafter two new guests entered. The Energetic Publicist and the Intelligent Psychoanalyst. The newcomers slipped into the conversation as if they were slipping into a bed with silk sheets.

The Energetic Publicist shed her perfume and spread her wings: she sat on the Handsome Architect's knees, without forgetting to caress her young husband periodically, and she even honored me with a direct compliment.

The Intelligent Psychoanalyst, on the other hand, had a beard, and a much more laconic style. If he happened to make a comment now and then, this was expressed with a certain curtness and in any case, was always an explanation about something.

I don't think it necessary to reproduce our conversation here. I'm just going to put together a brief synthesis of the themes we touched on:

1. The resplendent pregnancy of the Elegant Architect.
2. Children in general.
3. Psychoanalysis for children
4. Psychoanalysis in general
5. Sensitivity laboratories
6. Round beds in general

I have to make it clear that never for a moment was a term used as common as that in item 6. They used other terms that, in my lack of culture I was ignorant of, and that my precarious memory impedes my reproducing. On the other hand, I think the terms were in English. But one thing I'm sure of, they were talking about round beds.

The alcohol flowed and the gathering became more diverse. Irene was chatting lying on the rug with the Intelligent Psychoanalyst and the Elegant Architect. I, I'm ashamed to say, dedicated myself to irritating the Energetic Publicist, responding to her flattery at times with an infantile gesture, at times with frankly ardent looks.

The Handsome Architect played imported records, served drinks, interspersed a witty comment here and there.

We talked. Irene, drunk now, finished up a stimulating conversation with the Intelligent Psychoanalyst by saying, "What can I say: I don't like to suck a guy's dick."

This phrase, when it resonated in the sudden silence that had casually fallen among us at that moment, made us all realize that it was time to go home to bed.

The Handsome Architect offered to escort us home and we accepted, pleased.

3

"You don't talk much, do you?" he turned toward me openly for the first time only after Irene had gotten out of the car.

"No, not much usually," I answered. And we fell silent.

"Why not?" he asked after a moment.

I didn't answer right away.

"That's a surprising question."

"And that's not an answer."

"I never pretended it was."

"Why do you refuse to answer me?"

"Why are we arguing?"

"We aren't arguing!"

"No?"

Again we fell silent. The Architect stopped the car beside the sidewalk of some street and turned off the motor.

"I don't like to argue," he said. "I detest violence."

"Why?"

"That's a surprising question."

"I find it interesting."

"You're not against violence?"

"No."

"No?"

"No. How could I be against violence. It would be like being against my own nose."

"That's a sophistry."

"Or rather, what I don't understand doesn't exist."

"What?"

"Nothing."

"Are we arguing?"

"Not now."

We fell silent again.

"You really don't talk much."

I didn't answer.

"I know you don't like me. But at least I annoy you. That's something."

I smiled.

"Am I doing better?" he asked.

"You're doing okay"

"Why do I annoy you?"

"Because you're so obvious."

"What do you mean by saying I'm obvious? You hardly know me."

"Your house is very obvious too."

"My house? Don't you like it?"

"I like it as much as I like the houses of all the architects I know."

"I understand. And your house, what's it like?"

"My house is like me."

"I want to see it."

"All right."

He started the car and we continued on to my house.

We went up in silence, avoided looking at one another. Once upstairs, I opened the door and turned on the light and my house never seemed prettier.

From the door he took a look around and his only comment was:

"Can I come tomorrow?"

"Of course," I answered.

"I'll come at ten." He half turned and left.

4

At ten on the dot Sunday night, the intercom at the entrance sounded. The Handsome Architect entered the house impeccably dressed, combed, shaved, polished and perfumed. It would have been a real pleasure to see him if his smile hadn't made me feel more like a client than a hostess.

He accepted the whiskey that I offered him and sat on the sofa.

I'm talking about an enormous brown velvet sofa, one of those that when you sit on it, makes you not want to get up for at least six years. It's a sofa that has the same exact temperature as a mother's arms. The happy conjunction of back and armrest forms a hollow just like a friend's shoulder when despair spills us out in space. Its proportions are those of a generous lover and its vague odor envelopes like memories of childhood. To throw yourself on that sofa can give you the same sense of vertigo as throwing yourself into the ocean. And the Handsome Architect had sat down on it as if it were a sharp stone.

"But why don't you make yourself comfortable?" I suggested.

"But I am very comfortable."

I put on music. I offered him food, more whiskey. I felt like a mother whose child had come to visit against his will.

Finally I left him alone.

Suddenly he asked: "Have you known Irene long?"

As you can imagine, I didn't answer immediately: this question not only suited the situation perfectly but promised to initiate a very interesting conversation.

"Do you really want to know how long I've known Irene?"

"Now I understand," he commented. "A difficult woman."

"Uh-huh."

He looked around. The glass of whiskey was stuck in his hand.

"That's a nice clothes horse."

"Yes, very nice," I said.

Just when, precisely, does one begins to make love? Does anybody know?

I'm sure that it's long before making love. It starts suddenly when one is talking about something entirely different, or talking about daring topics, or not talking, but thinking intensely enough, eating, or looking at one another, or listening to music; picking a hair off the other's jacket, seeing yourselves together in front of a mirror, for example, the mirror in an elevator; each one talking about himself, I don't know, but long before anyone takes his clothes off.

The Architect, handsome though he might be, was not into lovemaking. At least not with me. He seemed very interested in the clothes horse, in the objects around the house in general, and also, why not, in the antenna that was sitting on top of the television set.

I kept on bothering him with all kinds of offers (more whiskey, marijuana, cake) when suddenly it happened: suddenly I found myself with a mouth covering my mouth.

Rapid synthesis brought me to the conclusion that this mouth could not belong to anyone other than the Handsome Architect, and then I began to tremble.

I began to tremble, I say, because I know the pattern well: 1) kiss on lips; 2) touch breast (one only) and 3) remove clothing. Whoever changes anything loses.

Rapidly I thought: what should I do?—still fully involved in step 1 and ready to begin step 2—what should I do? Stop things here?

Suddenly, just thinking about the kind of conversation we would have if I stopped things there, I had an attack of boredom.

I decided that the most practical thing was to go on: all I had to do was be still and wait: it couldn't take more than five minutes. Then he'd leave and everyone would be satisfied.

And besides, let's be honest: I still had some remote hope that the Handsome Architect would happily surprise me at the last moment.

But no. They were the five most boring minutes of the day.

After that—to give it some kind of name—austere exercise, the Handsome Architect stood up and silently retired to the bathroom. I took advantage of this to turn the record over and have some coca-cola.

After a while he returned and began to get dressed with a distracted gesture.

Once completely dressed he went up to the television set and tried to move the antenna.

He said: "With the antenna here, you don't need an outside antenna, do you?"

I thought a moment. The question required concentration.

"No," I answered, finally. "With the antenna here I don't need an outside antenna."

Bibliography

Primary Works of Authors Included in This Volume:

Absatz, Cecilia. *Los años pares*. Buenos Aires: Legasa, 1985.
―――. *Feiguele y otras mujeres*. Uruguay: Ediciones de la Flor, S.R.L., 1976.
Blaisten, Isidoro. *Al acecho*. Buenos Aires: Emecé Editores, 1995.
―――. *Anticonferencias*. Buenos Aires: Emecé Editores, 1986.
―――. *Carroza y reina*. Buenos Aires: Emecé Editores, 1986.
―――. *Cerrado por melancolía*. Buenos Aires: Editorial Belgrano, 1981, 1993.
―――. *Cuentos anteriores*. Buenos Aires: Editorial Belgrano, 1982.
Calny, Eugenia. *Las mujeres virtuosas*. Buenos Aires: Instituto de Amigos del Libro Argentina, 1967.
―――. *La tarde de los ocres dorados*. Buenos Aires: Ediciones Marymar, 1978.
Eichelbaum, Samuel. *Dos brasas. Teatro contemporáneo argentino*. Madrid: Aguilar, 1962.
―――. *El judío Aarón*. Buenos Aires: Editorial Talia, 1926.
―――. *Nadie la conoció nunca*. Buenos Aires: Carro de Tespis, 1956.
―――. *El viajero inmóvil y otros cuentos*. Buenos Aires: Letras Argentinas Paidos, 1933, 1968.
Feierstein, Ricardo. *El caramelo descompuesto*. Buenos Aires: Ediciones Nueva Presencia, 1979.
―――. *Cuentos con rabia y oficina*. Buenos Aires: Editorial Stilcograf, 1975.
―――. *Escritores judíos argentinos. Bibliografía 1900-1987*. Buenos Aires: Editorial Milá 1994.
―――. *Homicidios tímidos*. Buenos Aires: Editorial Galerna, 1996.
―――. *La vida no es sueño*. Buenos Aires: Ediciones de la Flor, 1987.
Gerchunoff, Alberto. *Cuentos de ayer*. Buenos Aires: Ediciones Selectas de America, 1919; Editorial Fraterna, 1985.
―――. *Entre Ríos, mi país*. Buenos Aires: Ediciones Nueva Presencia, Editorial Futuro, S.R.L.,1950.
―――. *Los gauchos judíos*. Buenos Aires: Editorial Aguilar, 1910, 1981.
Glusberg, Samuel. *La levita gris*. Buenos Aires: Biblioteca Argentina de Buenas Ediciones Literarias, 1924.
Kordon, Bernardo. *Alias Gardelito y otros cuentos*. Havana: Casa de las Américas, 1974.
―――. *Domingo en el Río*. Buenos Aires: Editorial Palestra, 1960.
―――. *Manía ambulatoria*. Buenos Aires: El Ateneo, 1978.
―――. *Relatos porteños*. Buenos Aires: Editorial Belgrano, 1982.
―――. *Vagabundo en Tombuctú*. Buenos Aires: Editorial Cauce, 1956.
―――. *Vencedores y vencidos*. Buenos Aires: Editorial Abril, 1985.

Plager, Silvia. *Boca de Tormenta*. Buenos Aires: Editorial Galerna, 1984.
————. *Como papas para varenikes*. Buenos Aires: Beas Ediciones, 1994.
————. *Los años pares*. Buenos Aires: Editorial Legasa, 1988.
————. *Prohibido despertar*. Buenos Aires: Galerna, 1983.
Rosenmacher, Germán. *Cuentos completos*. Buenos Aires: Centro Editor de América Latina, 1971.
Steimberg, Alicia. *Ametista*. Barcelona: Editorial Tusquets, 1989.
————. *El arbol del placer*. Buenos Aires: Emecé Editores, 1986.
————. *Como todas las mañanas*. Buenos Aires: Editorial Céltica, 1983.
————. *Cuando digo Magdalena*. Buenos Aires: Planeta, Biblioteca del Sur, 1992.
————. *Músicos y relojeros*. Buenos Aires: Centro Editor de América Latina, 1971.
Verbitsky, Bernardo. *Café de los angelitos y otros cuentos porteños*. Buenos Aires: Ediciones Siglo Veinte, 1949.
————. *Calles del tango*. Buenos Aires: Centro Editor de América Latina, 1966.
————. *A pesar de todo*. Buenos Aires: Monte Avila Editores, 1978.
————. *Hermana y sombra*. Buenos Aires: Editorial Planeta, 1977.
————. *Villa miseria también es América*. Buenos Aires: G. Kroft, 1959, Editorial Pardos, 1967.

Selected Works of Jewish Argentine History

Asociación Mutual Israelita Argentina. *Comunidad judía de Buenos Aires: 1984-1994*. Buenos Aires: Editorial Milá, 1995.
Avni, Jaim. *Argentina and the Jews*. Trans. Gila Brand. Tuscaloosa: University of Alabama Press, 1991.
Bethell, Leslie, ed. *Argentina Since Independence*. Cambridge: Cambridge University Press, 1993.
Feierstein, Ricardo. *Historia de los judíos argentinos*. Buenos Aires: Planeta, 1993.
Klein, Alberto. *Cinco siglos de historia argentina: Crónica de la vida judía y su circunstancia*. Buenos Aires: Oficina Sudamericana del Comité Judío Americano, 1976, 1980.
Mirelman, Victor A. *Jewish Buenos Aires, 1890-1930: In Search of an Identity*. Detroit: Wayne State University Press, 1990.
Moyano, María José. *Argentina's Lost Patrol: Armed Struggle, 1969-1979*. New Haven: Yale University Press, 1995.
Newton, Ronald. *The "Nazi Menace" in Argentina, 1931-1947*. Stanford: Stanford University Press, 1992.
Rock, David. *Argentina, 1516-1982: From Spanish Colonization to the Falklands War*. Berkeley: University of California Press, 1985.
————. *Authoritarian Argentina: The Nationalist Movement, Its History and Its Impact*. Berkeley: University of California Press, 1992.

Shumway, Nicolas. *The Invention of Argentina*. Berkeley: University of California Press, 1991.

Sofer, Eugene F. *From Pole to Pampa: A Social History of the Jews of Buenos Aires*. New York: Holmes and Meier, 1982.

Weisbrot, Robert. *The Jews of Argentina From the Inquisition to Perón*. Philadelphia: The Jewish Publication Society of America, 1979.

Winsberg, Morton D. *Colonia Baron Hirsh, A Jewish Agricultural Colony in Argentina*. Gainesville, Florida: University of Florida Press, Monograph 19, 1963.

Selected Works of Jewish Argentine Literature

Feierstein, Ricardo, ed. *Cien años de narrativa judeoargentina*. Buenos Aires: Editorial Milá, 1990.

———. *Pluralismo e identidad: Lo judío en la literatura latinoamericana*. Buenos Aires: Editorial Milá, 1986.

Gardiol, Rita. *Argentina's Jewish Short Story Writers*. Muncie, Indiana: Ball State University Monograph, 32, 1986.

Lindstrom, Naomi. *Jewish Issues in Argentine Literature*. Columbia: University of Missouri Press, 1989.

Lockhart, Darrell. *Jewish Writers of Latin America: A Critical Dictionary*. New York: Garland, 1997.

Senkman, Leonardo. *La identidad judía en la literatura argentina*. Buenos Aires: Pardes, S.R.L., 1983.

Sosnowski, Saul. *La orilla inminente. Escritores judíos argentinos*. Buenos Aires: Legasa, 1987.

Weinstein, Ann E. and Nasatsky, Myriam G. *Escritores judeo-argentinos: Bibliografía, 1900-1987*. Buenos Aires: Editorial Milá, 1994.

Zago, Manuel. *Pioneros de la Argentina, los inmigrantes judíos/Pioneers in Argentina, The Jewish Immigrants*. Buenos Aires: Manrique Zago Ediciones, 1982.